RETURN TO GOD'S HOUSE

Five books in THE GOD'S CYCLE

God's House:

Return to God's House
Within Without
In Winter

God's Wilderness:

Mystery Gottheim
Balder's Wilderness

Plus

Gott'im's Monster

Return to God's House

S. Dorman

~ ~

S. Dorman
P.O. Box 172
Greenwood, ME 04255
USA

(Book one of The God's Cycle)

Cover photographs by Ronald Dorman, manipulation by Nancy Jacob

Dedication

To Ron, who makes everything possible

"One thing have I desired of the Lord, that will I seek after; that I may dwell in the house of the Lord all the days of my life, to behold the beauty of the Lord, and to inquire in his temple."

— Psalms 27:4

Contents

God's Twilight

Elda stepped down from the dark kitchen doorway onto the hewn granite stoop, into predawn stillness. She stood there, almost as though to lift her nose to morning's scent, so poised was she to receive the strange day. She strained for a sight of Posey through the encroaching woods, where spindly trees grew thick and tall. Twilight filled woodland and the small clearing with nebulous shadow. It made a mist of existence, as though all things were dissolving. Elda associated twilight with Norse mythology and her grandmother's tales. It was all there in the immigrant Embla's old stories from a half-century ago, the '30s. Niflheim and Ginnunga were the source of these impressions, fathomless places of creation's inception. The cold of the abyss, of vapor and darkness, merged into a mist of sea smoke that writhed about tall teeth of ice.

In the early stages of tumbledown, tangled in budding foxgrape and woodbine, Elda's house hunkered below a fir-bound ridge. It faced south, as though its long-dead builders had been concerned to catch as much light and warmth as possible in these cold Meguntic Mountains of Western Maine. They trusted a crop of rocks to sprout through the thin soil each spring, pushed up by frost. Farming won't be easy here, said these Yankees, but the land is free. Over the run of those settlers' first century, the house was cobbled together, spreading on either side of its gray granite cellar hole foundation: compounded of hewn logs, timbers and clapboard; of casements, posts, glass panes and various kinds of shingle. Asphalt roofing crumbled on the east and west ends, causing the connected barn to cant and the roof of the attached children's house to rot.

Thirty odd years ago, Everett, Elda, and their baby Balder lived in the children's house, so-called because the newlywed children of each passing generation set up housekeeping there. The extended Simon family was immense, intertwined, spread now throughout the Meguntics like the tendrils of bindweed and virgin's-bower—creepers groping along roadsides and through cutover woodlots. The rock and conifer ridge above was called Simons Ledge after the early family and its descendants of the original proprietors. The house, in its turn, had been named for the ledge. And over them all, settlers, house, and ledge, soared Jasper Mountain.

Balder was the only human left that Elda knew intimately. Everett, Balder's father, was also gone, along with Everett's father, his mother and grandmother: All once lived in this old house. But Elda's once-crowded life as young farm mother in an extended family was seldom called to mind. In some ways her life was truly crowded still because she cared constantly for what she called "the critters." So life now seemed only full and without noise in comparison to her young adult life when people were everywhere about the house and farm.

Posey must not be in those tall encroaching thickets or she would've drifted out. Elda could not now see them with definition, but she ever sensed the trees' presence. Soon the house would be engulfed in them, but Elda was pleased by the thought. She loved the tangle that most Mainers worked to keep back. Elda had once seen the word "arboloco"—a term invented for the Civilian Conservation Corps during the Great Depression to describe the depression of young plainsman who had been transported to the Ozarks for government jobs. The exaggerated academic term made her chuckle but it fit Balder's Yankee farmer ancestors perfectly and she appreciated the respect it accorded to trees. Anyone who ever got turned around in the woods would recognize the tribute.

She kept to the path on her way to the barn, fearing the interior passages that connected the house, ell, shed and barn. She did not like to meddle with all the doors. Something might fall, the barn might tumble to timbers. Balder had inspected it since snow's passing, pronouncing it "safe'n habitable fah your crittas," but she could never trust tilted appearances. Balder had the mind of an engineer. He could believe in, admire, tune, even design machinery, but his mother was hopelessly unmechanical. Metal and mechanisms were less substantial to Elda than the inner essence of a beast.

Was it brightening? She looked toward the treetops. The bristly tips would catch light soon. Then the gods' twilight would be gone till evening. Later, in sun, Elda would go abroad, seeking animals and the impending spectacle of an eclipse. Her aging eyes could deliver that much still, surely. But first there were creatures' needs to tend.

She fingered the small plastic bottle in a pocket of her worn woolen sweater, making sure of it. Her pale veined hand reached out then, pushing a bit on the heavy barn door, sliding it aside. So slight was Elda that a crack was all she needed to slip within. The dank hay- and animal-dropping smell took hold of her. A mingled scent of skunk and bear cub permeated the cavernous place. She felt for the switch that Balder had installed: A powerful 500 watt light cut a dusty swath through the gloom, reflecting from a multitude of wild eyes.

She made the rounds, working from bins in a former tack room and from the old refrigerator where she kept meat. Working around the shored interior of the old barn, Elda fed, watered, inspected, and nursed her current menagerie, everyone in some state of recovery. Here were perched birds and furry animals caged behind fencing. There was also the reptile silent in a tank beneath a heat lamp.

Rounding the corner of one tank, Elda entered a workroom. Light was beginning in wire-screened windows silhouetting a great horned owl. Perched behind chicken wire, its huge talons were locked around a T-bar. She looked a touch too alert. The woman dug in her pocket for the plastic vial containing a dark powered root. She poured the premeasured amount of valerian and worked it into a piece of raw cube steak, rolling it up along with the bony carcass of a mouse into a sticky ball. The owl was her current dangerous case, a villainess with front-facing yellow eyes, feathered tufts jutting from its fierce brows, and a wingspan reminiscent of eagles. Even though the owl was in here out of sight, its presence made the other animals uneasy. Rabbits, a woodchuck, skunk, partridge, one racoon with kits, an orphan bear cub: All were unsettled and restive.

They should worry, thought Elda....*once its wing mends.* This mighty-legged, three- and a half-pound bird had scooped up a nine pound village dog, and punctured Asa Bartlett's head with its two-inch talons. A regular dosing from Elda's herbal pharmacy kept the edge off its ferocity, giving her a chance to check the progress of its wounded wing. Even so, Elda would wear safety glasses from Balder's shed and speak softly while treating this great female. And she would hood the owl when it was ready for her to inspect the wound.

Seeing Elda, the great horn became watchful. Then it eyed the meat, complete with a dangling mouse tail. Elda donned a gauntlet for protection and opened a small feeding gate, extending the doctored meat. The owl snatched and downed the offering.

"Back soon," murmured Elda and turned away. She turned back into the barn and began cleaning out cages.

It was still early when she went outside to look again for Posey. Silent sunlight touched the naked red-tinged twigs of the treetops. The woodland bordering the weedy dooryard was still... and apparently empty of critters. When would Posey show? Elda sighed, taking the morning in on a breath.

She would look for the deer when she climbed the ridge to seek out the eclipse.

Noon was on its way as Elda climbed Simon's Ridge. May sun shed its welcome warmth on her flannel-clad back. Taking hold of budded saplings, her joints and limbs aching, she pulled herself upward. Elda's worries bunched in her mind, clustering like flowers soon to emerge on the moose maples where she climbed.

Posey had not shown at the house and, so far, was not to be seen on the mountain. Of mornings the doe would come as on tiptoe, silently stepping, a swollen shadow in the grey half light. Was she hurt somewhere—or just sore over the owl?... Even Balder had not been home. Now that was not usual!

No one was steadier than Balder. He had a regular job and also did odd mechanical and carpentry jobs; hauling in his pickup, and even snow plowing in winter. His job at the Gottheim Chair Factory, keeping outmoded machinery running, was the kind of challenge he used to keep his skills honed. Elda tried not to worry over his absence, but that was what it was these past two days—trying. Human relationships required so much of what she seemed unable to give. When he showed again, he would probably be irritated if she gave away her concern.

Another worry was the sun—friend or foe? Could she really blame her failing sight upon the sun ... and wouldn't that be pointless? So here it comes—another lonely night in a bed of tears?—oh quit, woman quit! *Quit all this worrying!*

Just keep climbing. Almost there. Life is better when there's something on the horizon. Something like an annular eclipse to watch for. Elda had been counting on this for two weeks. It was movement in heaven—even if it didn't always live up to its billing. Maybe it was the waiting and watching that mattered, anyway. Hopeful watching itself might light and animate everything. Like an eclipse, watching could show forth an inscrutable purpose ... underscored in fire and blue air. Afterward, the remains of watching would be largely unintelligible, except in that kindling still moment before God slipped away.

The pack on her back waggled as she climbed, hand over hand, taking foothold in leaf-litter among rocks and roots. From every rotten surface slick with wet, the green life of earth was starting, tender and delicate. Frost had been coaxed out of everything, rains saturating all. Elda rejoiced in seeing pale green after so many months of winter white and brown. —But would there be gaze enough for it next year?

She lay on the hard ledge above the pond valley. She looked up through a makeshift combination of sunglasses and Balder's welding mask. Eccentric, the townsfolk would think her. Laughable. Lying out here on the edge like a stranger fallen from space—blackflies lighting but not biting. She could imagine the judgment: stop work, equip yourself, climb to the ledge ... because the moon's path crosses the sun? She was already some queer by any tale, spending her meager means on feed for wild animals, putting ads in *The Village Voter* for handouts for ailing wild animals. Animals don't need help! You can't stop animals. They come like raindrops, one after the other, a flood. A strong winter could take nine tenths of a herd's casualties in fawns, but it would just come back wombs full next May. Why all the work and expense when nature supplies her own gourdful each spring?

A nearby chickadee started its patient soft calling. Now another began further along the ledge. Elda stopped her self-involved thoughts to listen. She continued peering through the doubled glass, watching for the spectacle.

Ah. The bite was on: The sky appeared to take a piece of the sun. There would be no total eclipse because the ring of light would be too wide. From reports she knew that full annularity would be a while in coming. She could sit back, eat lunch, even doze, while waiting for the moon to center itself over the sun's disc.

Digging her lunch from the pack, Elda tried to imagine other space-fallen folks watching along the shadowline: people in northeast Asia, the Arctic, Ontario, the Baja peninsula. She felt a faint kinship with them. They too, would notice a powerful withholding. Ninety percent of all that light, for a time just taken away.

She ate under pines and slept to the soft sound of the hopeful chickadee.

The raucous call of ravens startled her awake. She donned the glasses and mask, slid to the edge of smooth rock and looked up, away from the valley of the ponds. In the sky the sun's rim was just closing the bright c, turning it into an o as the invisible moon covered it.

There. Elda beheld a complete and perfect ring of burning light. And she felt it pierce her retinas with fire. With a small cry she let the rig fall, closing her eyes. Now she saw that the sunglasses had slipped out of place after donning the rig. With haste she adjusted them, feeling tears well. Why had she attempted it with the less powerful mask—when she knew that a rating of 10 was not powerful enough protection? Because Balder had no mask with the required 14. Her reckless obsessions would wreck 'em!

Elda winked the tears away and lay very still, staring up through the mended rig at the thick ring of muted light. Quiet; stillness in the sight above seeped into her. This silent coupling of these great heavenly bodies moved her with a deep impression of silence. The sight imprinted her retinas, but the quiet embodied for her mind was more eloquent than what she was seeing. It was silence soft on her spirit. As though God had come and lain down in her.

She waited. Then she removed the rig and looked around at the natural world of her own familiar neighborhood. The light revealing this world was unnaturally toned. Here, almost, was the twilight again. A brighter twilight of the gods, but still subduing everything. She felt a slight drop in temperature and the breeze was freshening. All sights were hushed in silvery non-light: the valley, where part of Hutchins Pond and the entire village lay hidden by the hill; her house standing in trees; where pines grew dark and hardwoods twiggy and the creatures slept: Every loved thing was cast in that unsettling diffusion of dark and light. Was it an almost belittling dimness? As though the scene were no longer worth the shine of its reflection after all these years. And she felt its significance dissolving.

With care she donned the glasses and mask again, intently searching the spectacle. Now it was like an eye, watching her in turn. Suddenly. Great and heavenly, staring. She was protected from its awesome power to burn and blind, yes, but it was looking at her all the same. God had gotten up and walked away, gone, leaving this Great Eye staring at her. She willed herself calm beneath the unblinking gaze ... until it looked away, becoming a small c, opening on the opposite side of the circle. And the spectacle was undone.

She removed the mask, crawled away from the edge and stood. Elda gathered the remains of lunch, her gear, and crammed them into her backpack. From there she took the deer path up to the ridgetop, intending to hike back the long way—through the brush at the top and down to a dirt road. But she was startled to find that a cut had been made by loggers, and finished off with a bulldozer. Someone had slashed a fresh road along the spring-swollen ridge. The new road was deeply rutted, spongy with runoff and melted frost.

Developers coming! The ski resort on the north side of Jasper Mountain had opened up all sorts of speculation in the town. Outloud she exclaimed, "Someone's building ovah my head. They gont look down on me from theya porches?!"

Limping, aching, arthritic, Elda came through reddening woodland on the lane toward the crumbling house. Paunchy with fawn, Posey stepped out of bordering trees. Silently she came to Elda's side and nuzzled her hand. Relief flooded the woman.

"Why Posey! Waya you been!" She knelt and stroked the little doe's long tawny neck. Posey was an undersized, whitetail doe, befriended during a day's doctoring when the herd had taken shelter in the plowed lane. The snow was deep, so deep, then. After that, they had yarded up in the garden—not uncommon at the relatively hidden *Simon's Ledge*. The finish of hunting season sometimes brought injured deer to this house of healing.

Together they walked up the long lane. As the woman made rounds in the barn, Posey followed delicately. When it came time to check on the owl, however, she backed away and wandered outside to browse on blooming tender maples twigs.

An hour later, having released a mended partridge, Elda entered the oaken and pine paneled kitchen. There dismaying shadow fell on her, darkening the peace that Posey had given her. She felt for Posey's long ears and, reassured, flicked on the light. The doe went to the sideboard and, attempting to mount, scrabbled her small split hooves on the wooden countertop.

Chuckling, Elda snatched up the canister Posey was trying to reach, pried off the lid, and held out a handful of raw peanuts. Posey pushed her moist black nose against the heel of Elda's hand, delicately picking up the nuts with her tongue. Swallowing several, she set her hooves up again and, bending her neck, reached for the salt shaker. Elda grabbed it first and shook liberally into her hand, then held it out for the doe to lick.

The woman went to the sink, washed her hands, and filled the kettle to set on the woodstove. Suddenly she was too weary to stoke the fire. She turned off the light and crept to the couch by the stove, sank gratefully back and drew on an old patchwork quilt made by Everett's mother long ago. Posey knelt and lay atop a rag rug on the pumpkin-pine floor. Peacefully she chewed her cud. May light moved across the wall and was at last cut off by an arm of the hill. Neither creature stirred.

History in Gottheim

It was still light outside when tall blond Balder came in. Posey scrambled up to meet him, sniffing then licking the small togue dangling among those in his hand. Laughing, he laid the fish on the sideboard and reached into a paper bag. Elda stirred on the couch and sat up stretching, glad of his voice.

"Better shoo the doe away, or we'll have none fah suppah," he said, giving Posey a nibble of something from the bag. "See what I brung you?" He held the something between his thumb and forefinger. The house being so dim, she could not make it out. "What is it?" she asked, rubbing her eyes.

He frowned. "It's fiddleheads is what. I could eat the bagful." He went to the wall and flicked on the light. "You gont fix'em or am I?"

"Well, I will, you spoiled kid." Never mind that Balder was approaching his mid-thirties. She stood and went to stick her hand in the bag to feel the small plump wheels of furled fern shoots. "Look at'em all! Waya did you find 'em?" She brought out a handful for the pregnant deer and led her out the door. "Boggy Place?"

Shaking his head, Balder got out the cutting board and lay the fish on it in the sink. "Hiked into Birch River afta work. Blackflies's starting."

"So don't I know it. Not biting yet, though." Elda got out a skillet, began heating oil. "Was you down by old Mason's Mills— across fum the old granite work, hidden like?" She put on a pot containing enough water to steam the coiled fiddleheads, sprinkled in some salt to remove bitterness.

"The same." He was cutting the brown and silver fish under running water. "Wasn't it you showed me it as a kid?"

"Cuss I did. Told you about the old grist mill. They had a carding and fulling mill. Prosperous, too, said Asa Bartlett."

Balder said, "Cold in heah." He went to the stove to lay kindling and blow on the embers. The door squealed as he shut it. "Kinda like the Bearces of theya day, guess."

"Yuht. Owned all that land around theya on both sides of the stream. Maybe 100, 150 years ago. Think what things was like back then."

"Blackflies like now. And no TV. Whad they do nights— visit?"

She nodded, breading pieces of fish. "Had socials, musicals and all. Dances, school plays. They read!" She grinned. Balder was back!

The fiddleheads were steaming and the fish laid sizzling in oil. She said, "What I don't know was how they stacked that monstah granite. How'd they move stuff like that then?"

"Oxen or draft hosses, with block'n tackle. Pulleys." He stood over the fiddleheads, picking through them with a fork. "Be surprised what you can do with'em. Look what you can do with a come-along—move a truck out of a mud hole with bare hands and that."

"Whad you see down theya besides fiddleheads?"

"Skunk cabbage, wild ginger, wake-robin, bellwort." He grinned.

"Good, ain't it?" She returned a grin.

Balder nodded, lounging against the sideboard his powerful shoulders at ease. His blue gaze was still upon Elda, paying attention. "Took my break when I could see that eclipse you been talkin'bout. You notice that strange silver light when it was on? That mask work OK? Know what that ring reminded me of?" He noticed her perfunctory response to all these questions and went on: Evah read *Lord of the Rings*? Story about this hobbit—theya little people. He had a powerful ring to get rid of. You might say it was a quest in reverse. A quest to get rid of power. Anaway, by the end of the fuss book, he's seeing this ring—like an eye looking at'em—every time he closes his eyes. You ought read that book, Mutha." He stared down at the skillet where she was poking at the fish. "Under certain conditions, I can see a ring in negative if I shut my eyes. That evah happen to you? Works out it's an image of my iris."

Elda was silent, turning pieces of lightly browned togue, not even looking up. His allusion to eyes and the eclipse threatened the peace his company had brought her.

She heard him go into the front parlor and snap on television. The McNeil/Lehrer News Hour on Senate legislation drifted into the kitchen. Elda turned her thought away from distress. There was something better to think of: Something was different about Balder. Gone was his more usual solemn silence. Tonight his attitude was light. Unconsciously she had seen it, but now she was aware.

Balder was tall and as good-looking as a healthy buck in velvet. He had a cap of blond, almost white hair, but when he wore his watch cap he reminded her of a Norwegian sailor, off the stormy North Sea. He could joke and wisecrack, yet for years there had been an air of grief about him. Vietnam grief, she called it. Everyone in town had opinions on the way he had spent his time here in isolation after his tour. "In hiding," they called it. They all thought the way to deal with grief was to work like a maniac. The respectable ones said so; others thought he should drink a little harder.

But today ... today was different. Thinking about it, Elda saw that Balder was happy.

He wandered back into the kitchen, saying, "Went down to apply at the papah mill today. Ovah to G'fid."

"The papah mill." Taken by surprise, she said crossly, "Whad you do that fah!"

He frowned. "Why does anyone? Fah the money."

"God-awful place! Could get choo killed."

"Now Mutha.... " He was laughing at her!

"Theya's poison in that mill!"

Frowning, he could see that she wasn't going to lay off this saw until a tree fell somewhere. "Forget it, Mutha. Prob'ly won't get the job anaway. Getting in is like getting into Harvard. Evah man in fifty miles tries to. Didn't Fatha?" He turned, went to get the plates from the cupboard.

Elda heaped one with flaking fish and steaming fiddleheads. She forced herself quiet, said in a low voice, "What's wrong with your job at the chair factory? You make money working on cars'n pickups besides. You get odd jobs enough."

He said (mysteriously she thought), "I need more money now. Let loose of it, Mutha." Balder went back to the parlor with his plateful.

Elda followed with hers. Balder sat on a sofa, facing the TV. She sat in a woolen worn arm chair, an afghan draped across its back.

Balder said, "Fiddleheads's good."

"Not bitter at all," she agreed.

It had been years since they ate together at the table, when his father was alive, in fact. More and more, since Everett's death, the news hour has come to dominate supper. Even breakfast is now frequently eaten before the Maine morning news.

Now each sits in separate thought, eyes upon the flickering images. Balder thinks of Middle America, whose cause is before him on the screen. He has just come away from what he thinks of as a typical product of that self-involved class. The young woman is up from Massachusetts to work with her brother, an entrepreneur developing a condominium resort. Gloria thinks herself brainy and brave. They are two from a fantasy written contingent, up to tame and shape the wildlands; to make a brighter suburbia than the labyrinthine, if elegant, subdivision they vacated. He frowns. As he considers their plans for Gottheim, the frown hardens into a scowl. The plans call for the Jasper Mountain ski resort to stride practically around the base of the bald rocky giant and make a new shiny Main Street for the community.

Watching the debate on economic trickle-down, Balder grimaces and thinks of these things. Gloria Fay has a master's degree in public policy and can punch up a computer, cranking out statistically loaded reports by the bucketload—but most likely can't mop out a toilet or feed herself. Not with any consistency. He has discovered that she is an upscale restaurant dweller, as some writer-lady somewhere put it. In her mind Maine is still the District of Maine, a province of the Commonwealth of Massachusetts—as it was two hundred years before gaining statehood in 1820.

She can ski though—like she was born schussing down mountain. Must've been two weeks ago when he noticed her on Glory Trail. Jasper's trails had not been so rotten then. She was there on the lift up ahead, decked out in brightness, banishing the dreariness of mud season. When she took off down Glory, he saw her below, swift like the trail itself (and her name nearly the same, he learned later). He had to work to catch up with her, through snow the consistency of sugar up top, then through the slush below. But the next trip he was on that lift with Gloria.

Canny talker, full of fun—like sunlight glittering on the surface of the pond. A voice like honey. He was rejoicing inwardly all the way topside again. They crossed the tops of spruces, and were ready to jump the ramp together.... Just there a dreaminess entered him, coupling with a patient desire. Gloria: her smile spring-bright, and head sleek with heavy gold hair. She led them toward the near precipice that was Glory Trail. And he followed her down, this time not in curiosity but with joy.

Now, sitting in front of the television, Balder Simon considers that he needs more money. He might even go into a restaurant other than the diner—once in awhile. Love has fired a quiet form of ambition in him where nothing else could. Yet he has made up his mind not to follow in her ways. He can't. Instead, he will go after things that have always seemed good but, until now, were not greatly desired. He will buy land of his own, and a house ... or build one? Someday—daow, he's not counting on it ... though having a family is what he wants. It will depend on how wedded she is to her fantasy. Will her unconscious selfishness bruise, break his heart? It's happened before.... But, Vietnam gave him suffering in stronger form, so that Balder now knows what time is for. Time exists to squander upon the best you can find.

Lord Jesus, there it is. Happening again, after all these years.

Intent on the next News Hour segment, about possible resort development in Virginia, Elda scarcely notices the wobbling snowy reception of the TV. She's listening, staring into space, not watching. Here beneath Simons Ledge in the mid-1980s Meguntic Mountains, the only stations available are few and distorted. Thinking of the planned development on the ridge, Elda wonders. How can these people keep building these elaborate, palatial houses, such as she sees on the screen? Who has money for such places? What do they all do for a living? Not farming, not mill work or logging. Is the rest of the country so different from Maine?—she guessed. They have to come here with money earned elsewhere.

She glances at Balder who is just coming into the room with a plate of toast, cup of coffee. Work boots, jeans, flannel shirt. It's practically a uniform. She asks, "Choo see the new road up theya yet?" She gestures toward great Jasper above.

"Saw them stot logging up theya last fall. Thought they must be putting in something by the way it was cut." He remembers her after settling back on the sofa. "Waunt tea?"

She stands uncertainly, her arthritic hip giving her a jolt. "I'll get it. Maybe two dozen house sites up theya. Hope they won't be so big's those on TV."

He watches her exit: stiff tonight. A slight, kerchiefed, crooked thing.

He raises his voice. "You'll be turning middle-aged, you don't watch, Mutha."

"I am middle-age, Balda!" she calls back.

"Then what'm I coming to, deah?"

"Y'ain't middle-aged till forty!"

In the kitchen she fills her cup, dunks a bag, wanting to ask where he's been for three days. She wonders, why is it none-of-your-business if you're the one worried?

Elda comes back with her tea, eases herself into the chair. Now it feels good sitting down. She'll stay awhile, put her feet up on the straw-leaking hassock.

The last segment of the News Hour is on the annular eclipse, a public television poetic essay. There is the great eye again, looking at her, just. The eye of one of Embla's old gods. The essayist tells how a crowd of students responds almost as one, awed witnesses of the covering and rediscovering of the sun. The wholeness of the sight brings a sort of rapture to the class as they are caught up together in a joyful response.

Slowly it comes to her that she wants to tell Balder. To tell someone trusty and loved. But she knows she won't. She will only tell Posey, a whisper under her breath. Because it is Elda's way to just

... keep going. Till she can't go no more. That's what she does when things are beyond her. She will move through twilight until it's so dark she can't see. All things will dissolve in one.

In treetops, high above, late light shone on red tips and tiny blooms. Elsewhere were hints of red and green buds. In the dooryard outside Simon's old settler house, Posey stood, gulping down her fiddleheads. Came a rattle, to her pricked ears, from the duff in the woods. The little deer lifted her pointed face nervously, staring through spindly tree stems. A red squirrel leaped, scurried up the trunk. Posey relaxed a bit, drifting toward the woods. Desiring company, she began browsing her way toward higher ground. Then, climbing on quick thin legs, Posey's hooves imprinted the soft earth, still mixed with last autumn's leaves. Sometimes her split hooves gripped protruding rock, milky quartz, or glinting granite. Hearing the intermittent rush of water and wind, she followed around the shoulder of the wooded slope. There the falling sun alighted yet. Breasting a rocky crest, she found a brimming brook and smelled its clean vegetative scent. She ducked to it, taking a long cold drink. Posey jerked her head up, watching.

Now she stepped through the water and began following along the course of the brook, through emerging grasses and plants— dainty spring flowers like bluet, sessile-leaved bellwort, blue violet. The Jasper Mountain brook wound around hummocks and saplings, beneath high straight trunks of maple beech birch. The paunchy little doe found young beech with shapely limbs, alight with tightly furled buds. She stopped to tear off the tender stems and swallow before continuing on her search for companionship.

Movement off her shoulder startled her, and she looked up. There a hairy woodpecker, speckled and striped, fell fluttering from tree to tree. It inspected crevices in the bark but did not rear back to thrust for a meal. Posey went on, picking her way with nervous delicacy, lifting her pointed face to the breeze.

And still calm light lingered above as she meandered up current, but at last the shadows deepened. The brook thinned to a trickle then turned to mush with green plants sprouting. There Posey saw yet deeper shadows, standing, quiet and many-legged: three does, each filled with fawn; and one of these her mother. Touching, rubbing necks in greeting, she joined them. In dusk they stood together, chewing cud, blackflies alighting. Now the deer started back toward low ground. They sought the still waters of ponds with peepers, a mist-strewn vale, and soft bedding.

Their shelter would be darkness. Darkness had sheltered their antecedents, who settled all the mountain long long ago.

At dawn came light on the heights of Jasper Mountain. In deep shade, far beneath, six deer looked up from a sheltered cove. The bald head of the mountain was out of sight, but across the pond a fir-crowned summit floated above a wreathing mist. Distant rumbling on the highway stirred them to move. In silence the does drifted upward through hemlocks toward higher ground. The slopes of Jasper Mountain stood in ponderous mystery over the village of Gottheim.

A door opened in the ell off the kitchen of a many-angled farmhouse near the shore. Stepping out, Asa Bartlett caught sight of the many-legged shadows disappearing among dark conifers beyond the cove. His breath a vapor on the early air, Asa stepped off the doorstone and walked across the sandy weedy, but trim, yard to his freshly painted Ford pickup. He had painted it hunter green last weekend and now stood in critical appraisal of the job—as he had each morning since. The right front fender might need a touch-up. Maybe a slight but definite line with a fine brush would do it. Asa considered heading to the shed for brush and spray paint, but his stomach was growling. He wanted a cup of Decatur's coffee more than anything on earth. So he yanked the door handle, slid into the pickup.

But he stopped, cocking his head to look in the rear view at his bandaged temple. He smoothed his crewcut brick red hair, then, wincing, adjusted his horn-rimmed glasses. How can this wound be throbbing still—after two days. That owl! He ought to go into the house, get his 30-30, go up to Elda Simon's and blast its malicious head off. But, catching a glimpse of his furious face in the mirror, Asa cackled, sinking back against the seat.

Don't you just look like Buster Bearce the time we tied his pants in knots. Asa recalled the decades-old incident of the lumber baron's son who went skinny dipping by moonlight, only to emerge and find his dungarees, shirt, and socks all knotted tight and soaking wet. Asa and Wellington Bird might have run off with the clothes but that would've been theft.

Asa turned his key in the ignition, eased out onto the hot-top and headed for the diner on the highway. The camps and summer places were still vacant as he drove past. Then the road wound through the narrows among broad ponds. He thought about the folks from away who had peopled the shores for decades. Now they were being joined in the area by skiway interests. The pattern of succession, which Asa often thought about, was making new inroads of late. Mentally he ticked them off. First had lived the Indians, which he thought of as abiding here since forever—though of course he knew about the land bridge migrations. Then came proprietors, then settlers and their descendants. Next were timber speculators, then immigrants—Irish, French, Scandinavian. Now it was developers. Everybody's staking their claim in these mountains ... each new group full of dreams.

They forget, he thought grimly. We spend more time in the ground than we do walking around on top of it. "Just waya do they think they're going s'fast?" he said aloud. Maybe that was why he enjoyed tying Buster's pants in knots. Always in a hurry, those Bearces. Gobbling up the land right to left since anyone can remember. As though consolidating holdings could somehow keep them from sharing space with roots and rocks in glacial till along with everybody else.

He pulled onto the highway and drove on as the diner showed silver and maroon beneath the wooded knoll. The village of Gottheim edged a gleaming pond, sheltered beyond in shadow: the tiny houses and businesses drowsing in the dusk of Jasper's great knees. Other mountains surrounded the valley, most named for Yankee settlers who once had homesteads there. Many granite shoulders of the low ones were to this day laced with networks of moldering stone walls, covered now in standing third and fourth growth timber. Overgrown discontinued wagon roads looped through the woods. The forest floor was pocked with old cellar holes, ingrown with oak maple birch pine spruce. Moss-grown dumps of rusting tools and seamless bottles lay near more recent pits dug by prospectors—the descendants of settlers, looking for treasure: tourmaline, topaz, amethyst, beryl. There were other treasures too, buried, unseen, of which Asa knew nothing. One of these lay hidden beneath concrete in the basement of a Jasper Mountain resort condominium.

He saw Elvegy Blanchard drive out of the parking lot of the diner in her Bronco pickup, the bed loaded with manure and its powerful smell reaching out to gag anyone in sight not used to it. Asa was.

Overstreet the tower clock of the Congo Church chimed distantly, just as he entered Decatur's diner. He enjoyed the diner's smell of coffee, bubbling hot oil, and chicken soup already a'simmer. The diner's floor was uneven, covered with linoleum in dire need of fresh wax. The ceiling was peeling tin, the booths taped and tattered, but no one—even tidy Asa—seemed to notice. The regulars seemed not to see the place at all ... except in those isolated, clear moments when things were either very right or going dead wrong.

He heard the jabbering on about Elvegy as he entered the glass door just inside the glass mudroom entrance. Apparently she'd left a stench, along with that of the manure, about her brother-in-law Ithiel Whitman. Her tone was escalating of late. Fortunately for Ithiel he could brush it off with humor.

"Went too far this time," Asa heard Rensalier Simon growl. And Melvinia Sessions answer, "But Ithiel just bears it light as pie. Seems to relish it like pie, too."

Asa copied it all and greeted a few regulars and, so that he might lean back against it surveying the door, took his usual stool near the counter's elbow. He liked sipping coffee before breakfast, seeing who came in. Decatur's was the place to imbibe gossip along with breakfast. People on their way to work stopped in, retirees took up residence, and school bus drivers klatched here after dropping off the children. Recently, a resort developer had suggested that the Post Office be moved out to a proposed mini mall. God awful!—but, if so, the diner's being not that far off Front Street, on a loop to the highway, would be doubly important as communal meeting point. Asa worked second shift at the village wood-turning mill, but still he came in every morning for breakfast and a word or two before running errands or returning home to chores. The latest news was kicked around, opinions batted back and forth—from booth to booth, over the counter and back again. Every juicy subject was here. Politicians, welfare mothers, abortion, the economy, foreign affairs, plain affairs, murder.

Like what happened the year the ski resort really took off—property rates tripled as folks came from away, speculating like mad. A Connecticut landlord shot his ex and her boyfriend, then larruped round over the back roads and tried to shoot his daughter-in-law in the gut.... Over property. That was the year young people gave up thoughts of owning and just tried to adjust to increasing rents; descendants of those generations who had remained when others had fled to easier places like Ohio (Asa muses a moment upon the Ohio fever of the previous century): their ancestors still faithful on rock-bound soil. But now, on minimum wage, they are unable to afford a place. Paper corporations and other large landowners once kept everything in trees for wood products but now were beginning to sell cutover and off-aged woodlots to developers. At Decatur's diner, locals met to talk it over, complain about the machinations and perceived effrontery of flatlanders coming with threats of "a booming economy and service sector jobs." As Asa had said, "That promise of a booming economy's what scares me. Means theya's a bust some wayas down the road."

A waitress in her late fifties stood behind the counter before the order window near the coffee urn. Her gray hair fluffy and short, Melvinia Sessions' eyes glittered behind her outsized pink glasses. Her head shook with exaggerated sympathy, or perhaps suppressed laughter, so that her earings sparkled as she called out in her tinkly voice, "How's the ol'owl bite, Asa? Gut any better since yestadee? And when can we expect to see a photo in *The Voter*?"

Asa grimaced. "Daow. And it's not a bite. I ought to shoot that bud. Can you imagine Elda Simon's nursing that malevolent thing? It could come back fah the rest the town. They won't be no cats left, anahow. Someone saw it disembowel one not two weeks ago. Least they thought 'twas the same owl."

"Cuss it's the same!" returned Melvinia. "Gott'im is haunted by a demon possessed great owl. Someone ought to call Stephen King'n tell 'em about that owl."

Rensalier Simon, sitting two stools down, set his coffee mug by and, still reading the paper, said, "Things is spookier than anathin he could tell."

29

"What they doing now?" Asa craned his neck for a look at Rensalier's paper. "Haven't seen the town bellyache yet."

The big man drew back, glaring, tipping *The Village Voter* against his expanse of green work shirt.

Asa huffed, and turned back to Melvinia. "Your joints gummed up with molasses today? Waya's my coffee?"

Melvinia poured a steaming cup and set it before him, saying, "How many thousands of cups've I brung you over the years, Asa? Never said nothing bout how fast I got those cups poured."

"Don't you sound like someone's laundress."

"Me—married to you?—and have to wait on you at home too?" She shook her head. "When I get home I put my feet up."

"I sure was not asking, but so don't I—about the feet, I mean," said Asa (his Gottheim Academy schooling notwithstanding).

"Like any ol'Mainer, you keep working, frigging with something."

"You don't? What about those yuppie kids you was babysitting? Their parents went ovah to Farmington teaching nights?"

"In three weeks school ends'n then I'm taking hints fom TV newspersons—like they call 'emselves now. Always giving out these health tips, so I pick'n choose fom all the medical advice. Too much work makes you tense. That makes you unfit for work, they say."

"*Phew*—work less so you can work more? What's the point?"

"Whad'll you have, deah?" she said tartly, pencil poised in hand.

"Hev I become a different person since yestadee? Give me what I always have! And waya's the counter paper? Got to find out what's spooky in Gott'im." He didn't waste a sidelong glance on Rensalier Simon.

Smiling, Melvinia jotted something down and laid the slip on the wooden sill of the window between the kitchen and the counter. Decatur, the business owner and cook, was inside at the grill. Melvinia hollered, calling his attention to the order.

At the counter Rensalier grunted then folded *The Voter*, laying it by his empty plate. He got up, resettled his ballcap on his squat head, and went to the cash register at the break in the counter.

Asa snatched up the paper and spread it out before him, muttering. There, in front of his bespeckled gaze, was a story of the owl attack, illustrated by a photo of the great horned perched on a T-bar in Elda Simon's barn. Asa was grateful he'd had the presence of mind to slip out the back way at the Gottheim Health Clinic, following treatment of his wound. He'd probably be staring at his own picture now. There was enough to mortify in print without his bloody bandaged likeness staring off the front page. He by-godfreyed to himself as Melvinia, chuckling, came over to pour more coffee. "Too bad li'l Libby didn't get choo with her camera," she said. "Wouldn't that be pretty, just?"

"Yuht," said Asa absently. He had found the spookiness Rensalier referred to and was already knee deep in it. "Taking seen as only course," read the headline. Developers had petitioned the Bureau of Parks and Recreation to use the power of eminent domain to intervene and settle an impasse in negotiations for purchasing private property. Developers would then convey to the state the clutter of dilapidated camps, warehouses, and junk-filled lots on Hutchins Pond, yielding ground for a shoreline park to enhance the proposed mini mall nearby. Asa finished the article and looked up, saying, "History's making rounds again."

"It has a way of doing that," said a female voice nearby.

Asa looked over, surprised. Olive Lovejoy had slid into the seat vacated by Rensalier. "Well, ain't choo the stranger! They let you out, have they?"

Melvinia set a mug before Olive and she clasped it in her dimpled hand. She was a large, talking woman, not fat. The henna was wearing out of her hair and so was the curl. Olive's clothes were comfortable, practical, a blue blouse and skirt; her face full, only just beginning to show little lines. She seldom wore makeup, but when she had the chance she painted her nails so bright they made you wince. Her life was spent in brooding over a houseful of five or six developmentally disabled. Now her husband had a malignancy in his liver, and she was watching him waste and die. Asa couldn't bring himself to ask after Horace right off. He had to work up to it, so he said, "What's new among the retarded?"

"Well, I'm getting disgusted, that's new. Bout ready to give up."

Asa moved the paper to make room for the plate Melvinia set before him. "What's this!?" he barked. But he was relieved to be distracted from his duty of broaching the subject of Horace. He looked from the yellow mounds on his plate into the glee of Melvinia's slack-skinned face.

"That's your usual, in't it?"

"I nevah et scrambled eggs'n my life!" He pushed it away, scowling. His head throbbed.

Melvinia's grin grew. "You know y'look like a Bearce when you make that face."

"And you look like an ape!"

Olive said, "That looks good. Give it heah." She reached over with her brightly painted fingers and pulled the plate to her. With relish she began eating.

Melvinia shrank back, sorry, then went to the window and called to Decatur to fry a couple eggs with bacon and homefries.

Asa heard and was mollified. He turned to Olive. "How's Horace?"

"It's those people ovah to 'Gusty! All they want's papahs."

Asa was baffled. Then he saw that she spoke not of Horace Lovejoy she couldn't. Olive referred to the bureaucrats in Augusta.

She was shaking her head. "All my kids waunt is someone to take a li'l time with 'em. But 'Gusty only wants papers filled out. And numbas. X many sheets, x many towels, x many times I done this, x many times that. But all the kids waunt's attention. Stopped mopping the floor yesterday to play with Tommy. Sixteen years old'n his folks has dumped'em. He was in a pink-stink—s'lonely. 'Gusty don't care. Everything's got to be on papah." She stopped talking to take another bite of toast. Asa sat in commiserative silence. After a bit she said, "Looks like I got to give up on Billy. I've had problems with him, so Horace wants me to get rid of 'em—afterwards .... "

Asa gave a slight nod, otherwise leaving the thought alone.

"Billy's still afraid of Horace, though he's so ill. Respects 'em, might say."

"That the one uses the F-word evah other word?"

She nodded. "Billy's tough, but I give 'em time-out. Ten minutes. Like with children though—he thinks it's an hour." She turned her eyes toward the paper. "What's this history repeating itself?"

"Developers caunt get their hands on property fast enough. They waunt park land by eminent domain."

"Who evah got land that way before?"

"... Well, it's not the preferred method round here."

Her eyes smiled shut. "You wouldn't be thinking—That rumor about folks being cheated out o'theya land by mill owners— that going round again?"

Asa smiled. "That's just one example. Daow, I'm talking bout history!" He smacked the countertop for emphasis. "Go back to the beginning ... what's theya?"

"Indians. That's why Jimmy Carter signed that settlement. Ah ancestors took theya land."

"Now that settlement down east was a little different. This heah was nice'n legal. They had a grant fom the General Court afta the Indians was most subdued. All this land was reward fah theya own ancestors' part in fighting the French in Canada. But something happened even after that grant."

"Tell me." She let Melvinia pour her another cup. "I don't pay's close attention. Haven't been to society meetings lately, anaway."

She referred to the monthly meetings of the Gottheim Historical Society. Asa was the chief amateur historian and knew much of what was in the books and records. He encouraged the old folks to record their recollections. He pored over town and county documents, made trips to the state archives, and generally kept the society from moldering away. Asa urged the keeping of memoirs, compilation of photos and the donation of town related antiquities, letters.

"Oh it's all theya in the records. But I should say 'the memory of records' in this instance. Doc Kimball, writing in the last century, talked about the 'convenient fire' (what gossip of that time called it), occurring afta the founders had consolidated theya holdings. Evah notice it took thirty years to incorporate this town?"

"So?" Olive's plate was now empty except for crusts, on which she was patiently spreading jam. Intent on the story of Gottheim's founding, Melvinia leaned into the counter. Just then Decatur stuck his sweaty bald head through the order window.

"Asa's eggs is ready!"

Scarcely taking her eyes off Asa's face, Melvinia reached back for the plate. She set it before him, waiting for him to go on.

Setting an egg on a slab of homemade toast, he began eating. "Somebody had to survey that land. So the proprietors sent theya sons up from Mass'chusetts to do it. By the way, that's when the fust industry was stotted here. Boiling sap. Sugaring off was the fust industry, not milling. Even the Bartletts come up and was making maple syrup 'fore a house was evah stacked together." He mopped up some yoke with a forkful of potato.

"What was my folks doing—the Gammons? They was heah, waunt they? Woodsmen, trappers, meatmen?"

"They didn't come 'til later, not in that first cultch."

Melvina drew back at the slight.

"So, they was surveying,..." prompted Olive.

"And when they gut done," continued Asa with relish, "they says to the other grantees, 'we got to assess you fah labor'n costs. That'll be forty shillings each,' which amounted to a few months' wages."

"Waunt it only fair?" asked Olive. "That's how taxes work."

Asa shook his head. "A governing body decides taxes. There was no Town, no selectmen yet. Those that balked at the after-the-fact fee had theya lots sold at auction ... in absentia. And the sons of some proprietors bought that land for nothing. Much later, when theya was talk of litigation, come the 'convenient fire.' "

"Wait a minute," said Melvinia, seeing a righteous outcome in the Gammons' late-coming. "Your ancestors was one o'those propri'tahs! You're saying your forefathers cheated folks that stayed in Mass'n couldn't get here—cheated them out o'theya land?"

"May be. No one knows for sure who surveyed, who bought at auction'n what was bought. Look up the list of grantees fom the General Court. Lots of names you never heard of! Lots you have." He swallowed some cold coffee. "But maybe sowing and reaping's took care of all that by now—evened things out. Some families hev come up'n some have gone down. Don't yours own that goodly piece north of the mountain that developers are eyeing?"

"That's Reuel Gammons. Cousins on Mutha's side twice removed." She laughed, earings swinging. "Something like that!

Older I get, less I keep track. I mistrust I'm related to myself some way."

A huff of exasperation exhaled from the hot little kitchen. Decatur, at the window and irritated, said, "I note the family resemblance! You're late comin' to work, late getting this order out— just like your cousin Melviny!"

Melvinia said, "Don't know what you're so pleg'ed'bout today." But Decatur had withdrawn. Shaking her head, she picked up the order and emerged from behind the counter toward the far booth.

Glancing up at the neon clock, Olive said, "Looks like I got get back. Theya's no end o'things to do."

Asa nodded, saying, "Be by t'see Horace in a bit." She smiled. He watched her pay up and walk out, regretful that she could not stay to hear the cycle of Gottheim's history; regretful that Olive would experience her own small piece of succession—now that Horace was leaving Gott'im's cycle for good.

Asa was always ready to tell the story of Gottheim, but he had learned patience over the decades. Yes, they took his droppers, the repository of people's mental sheds filling up. With that and the archives, droppers enough, he thought, to keep the townsfolk in knowledge for three generations. But he had no children of his own to test this on. And, with a fresh reminder of Horace's passing, he realized that this generational spread might exclude a child born this week in the Guildford hospital. He would have to talk to someone at the elementary school about starting a program of some sort.

The door opens and in comes Robbie Robichaud to straddle the stool beside Asa. Robbie is a good-sized man wearing the worn working green of Asa's generation.

"That jeezly rig!" he said. "There ain't enough baling wire in the state to keep that piece o'junk together. Got to go down to G'fid and get parts for that pulp-loader. Ezzy's got the pickup today so I had to take Drusilla's TransAm. She waunt too happy. Spoiled kid." He drew close the mug set before him. "At least I ain't in the woods gettin'bit."

Robbie was another living piece from the puzzle of Gottheim's history, descended from French-Canadians who had come from rural Quebec at the turn of the century when Maine's paper mills were up and running. Robbie's father lost him his language in school when English was pressed into him. School children administered the prejudices of their Yankee elders in the hallways: "All frogs gut talk English—if they waunt get along. Hev to learn to wash'n wear shoes." The Robichauds would have retained their language in a community the size of Lewiston where the Franco-Americans were employed in textile mills, or in Guildford where they made paper; but Robbie's grandfather had come to Gottheim to work in a wood-turning mill when the paper mill stopped hiring. And his offspring went into the woods where it was quiet and free from the taunts of bigotry. Robbie never finished school. But now, besides sons who were in the woods, he had a daughter, Drusilla, who looked to be going to college in the fall. And Robbie was proud and glad that he was at last able to spoil someone. Drusilla's first choice had been the prestigious Bates College, in Lewiston, but she wasn't unhappy to settle for the University of Maine at Farmington with its excellent education program and in-state tuition.

Asa said, "Blackflies biting now, ah they? Waya you cutting these days, whose stumpage?"

Holding the ceramic mug between his big hands before drinking, Robbie drew the fragrance of coffee into his large nose. "Just cutting one li'l old subdivision in Copenhagen—on the east side of Mount Will. You know where Alcohol Rosy Road climbs into the woods'n stops?"

Asa chuckled. "Don't choo love cutting a subdivision?"

"Like I love searching for fleas." Robbie shakes his head. "The twins hate picking nits, too. They like to go in and mow 'em all down." He drank his coffee. "How'd that road get its name?"

"Whad y'think?"

"Ida know. Someone named Rosie sold sombreros during prohibition. Rosy who?—hed t'be a Roebuck."

"Deluded whiskey. Believe it or not—twas a Simon."

Robichaud burst a big laugh. "So they ain't all nice'n proper!" He looked pointedly at Asa's bandaged head. "Hear some of 'em even harbors killa owls."

"Someone ought harbor it in the bottom of the pond. Even ravens is better. At least they eat what's already dead'n keep the roads clean while theya about it."

Melvinia came and slid a plateful of eggs and hash under Robbie's nose. She went back to the cash register to wait on a customer. Robichaud reached for the salt and pepper. "Elda Simon's a strange bid herself. They say she's got bears, coy dogs, even a moose in her barn ... one time or another."

"I misdoubt the moose," said Asa, savoring the smell of hash. "But you never know. Her zoo's usually no worse'n Decatur's. Self and present company excepted."

Robbie grinned. "I run into Decatur coming out of Bearce's office on Front Street yestadee. He nearly run me down, never looked back. That in't like'im. Usually he's s'down right cuddly it's sickening."

"He was mad at Melviny earlier. Could be he's ill."

"Betta not be! He's cooking ah food!" He took another bite. "You hear what happened up't Jaspa Mountain yestadee? How the new snow-making got its style crimped—so to speak?" His grin was as bright as the fog lamps on his logging truck.

Asa chuckled. "Goldings got all bent out of shape, too, I guess."

"Well, Alvin's friend, Wilbur Hastings, was up theya when it happened—cutting for peanuts. You know how they pay people. Well, Wilbur was cutting a new trail, when he looks down through the trees'n sees this long shiny pipe, snaking down mountain. Heading straight fah the condominiums. Tons o'steel just sliding down mountain."

Asa had leaned back, elbows resting on the countertop, his coffee cup cradled on his stomach. He said, "Li'l spring rain, li'l thaw, some mud ... mountain makes pretzels out of good 16-inch pipe. They're lucky it didn't cream out a condo."

"Miracle no one was killed ... Piling up down theya, twisting itself round'n round. Took a couple dozen trees on its way down. What a mess."

The two men said all this with solemn faces, fooling no one. Melvinia had come over to top off their cups again, saying, "Think them Goldings believe in miracles?"

Robbie said, "They have to now no one got killed. Mountains don't put up with shit like that. But waya's OSHA when you need 'em? Someone ought've called'em to come look at that mess."

The two men sat talking, Asa starting on his fourth half-cup of coffee, Robbie finishing his hash and eggs.

In comes a stranger and sits at the stool one place away from the logging contractor. The stool squeaks as she turns a bit, squaring herself at the counter. Still leaning back in the elbow, Asa looks over at her, casual as real life. He takes in that she's wearing a blue bandanna and what looks like tourmaline—two studs—in her earlobes. Huh, haven't seen that before. Who wears more than one earing in each ear? Her speech is jagged giving Melvinia her order but she looks like any other working Mainer in her maybe mid-thirties. She asked for a cup of coffee and an English, grilled. Now Melvinia larrups around the corner into the kitchen. The stranger glances around and catches Asa looking at her. The stool squeaks as she turns toward him, leaning out from the counter. The words on her t-shirt read, "Naked-coed-diaper-changing."

"Well, Mr. Bartlett, if you look any harder you might just pierce another hole in my ear."

Asa feels himself change color, but he keeps on staring. Suddenly he knows. Chrischana Twitchell. Last of the Twitchells original to the area. Come back to Gottheim again. Seeing her conjures up so much historical remembering that it is moments before Asa can speak.

She is descended from Mahalalel Twitchell, the very first proprietor of Gottheim: the man who originally petitioned the Massachusetts powers-that-be for the Town, an inheritance for the heirs of colonial soldiers. Mahalalel Twitchell gave the town its first name—Farmingham Royal, after the two places occasioning the grant. In 1680 the town of Farmingham, Massachusetts mustered its own for the expedition to Port Royal, Acadia, to help roust the French out of the New World. The township in the wilds of Maine was their eventual reward for that effort. For a century after the town lots were first surveyed the name Twitchell so dominated the community that the index of Doctor Kimball's 19th century history contained more Twitchells than any other surname. Today, however, you can't find even one in the local phone book. Still, there are plenty of Twitchell place names.... Mountains, roads, ponds, streams, ledges bear the name Twitchell.

Now, here's Chrischana come back—who left town abruptly maybe fifteen years ago. Asa remembers: It was shortly before her father's death that summer. Hasn't been heard from since, not that he knew of, anyway. Bright as ever, she talks as though she saw him just yesterday. Still with that satin dark complexion and faintly exotic look from her mother's side; the Native American blood of the Abenaki Indian. She is broader though, maybe fifteen or twenty pounds heavier. Her features shockingly fuller. Looking at her, Asa feels the power of time. Maturity's more sedate gait is evident in her posture and walk. Her mysterious disappearance and sudden return, the effect is as lightning—instantaneous. Suddenly it's as though he *did* see her yesterday.

And a two-decades-old image, clear as yesterday, comes to his mind. She was fourteen or fifteen, chosen for the signature part of Jasper Mary, the proud Indian princess in buckskins and feathers, pony-mounted and dancing down Front Street as the parade wound through town. She was full of a tough, ready intelligence that could express itself in somewhat confident, not flashy, public performance. Yep, that pony gave her some trouble, Asa recalls. Back then, Chrischana was possessed of a notably sure spirit, with quiet dignity even in the midst of youthful joy. She was one to be depended upon. Many looked for her to leave town on a scholarship and make something of herself, returning now and again to encourage the youth of hardscrabble Gott'im. This plan she rejected, choosing to take nurse's training in Berlin, New Hampshire and be on hand to contribute to the life of the town. She worked weekends here in this diner and babysat evenings for a woman on the afternoon shift at the turning mill. All these hopes and works ceased the day she vanished without goodbyes to the people who loved her.

Daow. This can't be Chrischana. Not this early 1980s May day in Decatur's diner. According to his sequential perception, she should return to the stool in the same form in which she was last seen here—not in the broader body and matronly maturity of an aging townswoman. Slowly he shakes his head.

Chrischana smiles her same half-smile, and says something in the quiet voice he remembers: "Read in the bellyache that you were attacked by an owl. Do much damage?"

Flustered, again he shakes his head. "Might'o put out my eye, though."

She chuckles. "It's good to hear you say so. I mean ... in comparison with where I'm from ... the way people talk. In Phoenix they whimpah." She gave the word the soft elongated ending that she would have used fifteen years ago. Then, looking at the other man she says, "Hi, Mr. Robichaud. How's Alvin'n Ansel? They end up in the woods?"

"Cuss they did. Caunt expect them to work in a mill. Caunt breathe in theya, sawdust flying everywhere."

"And tuning skis isn't work, I s'pose?

Robbie snorts in disgust.

She says to Asa, "Good thing there was a Roebuck on hand to bring down that owl."

"You was always one t'think good of'em. People judge 'em hard but wouldn't you want one with you in a pinch?"

"More'n a Bearce," says Robichaud as a matter of fact. "Fust thing Lyman Bearce says to me after I sluiced my load coming down Kimball Mountain (on the phone later when I told 'em)—not choo all right, nothing broken?—but, 'Don't expect me to pay fah it!' "

Asa chuckled, nodding. Then, both to chide her and to satisfy his curiosity, he says to Chrischana, "You fom Arizona now?"

But, coming along with her grilled English, Melvinia crows, "Decatur's comin', Christy! Got all misty when I said you's out heah."

"Good! 'Cause I wanna ask 'em for my old job. He need any help just now?" She gives Melvinia an open hopeful look.

But, in the kitchen—sweating, flustered—Decatur hovers over the grill, finishing up some orders. Two omelets, ham, bacon, potatoes, and one drop egg. *Chrischana Twitchell's home! Home from godfrey Arizona!* What's it all mean? Bald-headed Decatur is thinking, How life carries on so plain and peaceful—year in, year out—little happening, as though it was no more than eggs on the griddle—? Is this Gott'im anamore? Not the ever Gott'im *I* ever knew.

Could he imagine not getting up at 3 a.m? ...Not making soup and tuna salad and Jell-O; nor potatoes chopped and parboiled for homefries, coffee brewed by 5:30 a.m.? What's life if not that? Forty years ... with Gott'im people for my relations? ...

He shovels everything onto plates, sets two kinds of toast, muffins on the side, and all on the sill for Melvinia ... not daring to glance out to the counter where little Christy sits ... her dark skin glowing and eyes so lush, no doubt the same as on that last night when she helped him close in silence (and he knew not what was wrong). If she's back—can it be so bad?

"I see you, Decatur!" calls Chrischana Twitchell through the window in her low voice. "Can't hide forever!"

But he is coming round the corner now, worried and wary; through the door, wiping his hands and taking off his glasses (just as she remembers), rubbing them nervously with the bottom corner of his apron where it's most clean. He sets the glasses on his bland face and looks at her, bald head gleaming in fluorescent light. "Chrischana, we've been missing you," he says, chiding like, and holds out his hand.

But standing she pulls on him and, drawing his pasty face to hers, plants one on his sweaty cheek. "There," she says, a stranger in his eyes. "No need to scold. Got any fishing, hunting stories, bear stories for me to hear?"

"When'd I evah have time fah fishing?" And a stricken look comes on him.

"Well, don't take it so hard. I'm here now, to help.... That's if you can use me," she adds in haste. She stops. "I'm looking for work." This is not the response Chrischana has hoped for.

Looking at him, she is surprised by tears in Decatur's eyes. And folks in nearby booths are watching, some setting down their knives or forks, one peering over his raised coffee cup.

He says, "You know, Christy, you'd have a job if theya was one. But it looks like—if what Melviny says Asa says is true—you best go to Mass fah work." Then, stopping and starting, repeating himself in a tangled way, he continues as people gape or look a question. At last Decatur gasps in frustration, saying, "God's give Gott'im back to Mass'chusetts—if it was took fom them back then." His words deepen with the thunder of his emotion. "My lease's up next month, and Bearces give me th'news: Bearces waunt this property back. The skiers gont develop it!"

Lightning has struck the tin room, galvanizing the lot of them. Two score pair of eyes look at Decatur. No one moves.

Asa says, "Gory, it's not world's end. Theya's plenty of other locations. Open that empty place used to be Virgie's restaurant.... Won't take much getting used to."

And murmurs go around the room. Some look out through smudged windows toward the parking lot and highway. There the sun glances down the road directly from the east. Drivers leaving the valley of the ponds strike down their visors.

Robbie says, "We'll go wherever you go, Decatur. We still gut t'eat." He looks around and others, chuckling, agree.

But Decatur shakes his head, reaching for a napkin to blow his nose. "All's s'dear. Caunt afford any place else. 'N they's fixings, loans, red tape, utilities, parking.... All too much!" He reiterates it all again twice, and groans. "I'm gettin' done heah on Jasper Mary Day next month. Decatur's is finished!" And, overcome, he turns back into the kitchen.

No one follows. Offers of comfort seem vain, as stunned quiet settles down over them. For a moment Chrischana stares through the order window after the man who has turned his back to go stand again over the grill. Then she sits and leans on her elbows, staring into the murky depths of coffee in her cup. Robbie mutters something to himself about ritch bahstids, says it again bitterly to Asa, who barely answers. Robbie takes his mug and moves across to a booth where his cousin Bob Bilodeau is talking to another logger.

Asa is trying to make sense of Decatur's jumbled logic. What has Asa said that made him think jobs would go to Massachusetts? Never too good at it anyway, Decatur must be too upset to think straight. *Yuht.* There is something to this idea of land being "returned" to Massachusetts. Isn't something of the sort the subject of his ruminations lately? He looks across the diner, over the warped gritty floor, brushing the peeling tin ceiling with his gaze. *Godfrey, this place this seedy.* It offends Asa's impeccable sense of neatness. His gaze rests a moment on Melvinia standing at the dirty glass door, staring out into the littered parking lot. He sees Janie and Ethel Simons sitting in their regular booth, one idly stirring her coffee, the other looking with distaste at the old linoleum. Turning, he notices Chrischana, still staring into her coffee. She looks up at the window into the kitchen, makes a tentative move, settles back.

"Maybe he could use some help," he prompts.

She glances at Asa, coloring deeply, her Native eyes somber. "I dunno. I ran out on him years ago."

His glance slides away. Silence. And then he says, "Seen Balda Simon since y'got back? Funny thing.... He nevah married." He thought, too bad you're from away now. I could tell you a story about.... Something not quite right about that business of him staying three years in his room.

She nods in response to the pointed comment about marriage. "So I'm told." Another hasty little sentence that. "He still good with machinery.... Works in the chair factory—must be a mechanical engineer by now. "

"Daow. Just a mechanic!"

She looks away. "Good person, Balder. "

Asa nods, dying for information. His curiosity palpitating yet.

Balder's Love

Chrischana pays Melvinia for coffee and an English muffin, and lays fifty cents on the counter beside her plate. Outside she inhales the breath of spring, deeply. Leaves on beeches beside her car are beginning to unfurl. Has it been fifteen years since she last saw these green and gold buds lighting the branches like tiny flames? Gratefully she thinks of the glare of Phoenix as receding into a dream. May you shrink, evaporate, be nothing but a wash, a dry spot in the sand. Be a ghost town standing in concrete.... Bet your sky will be dirty a hundred years after.

She opens the battered door of her boat of a Bonneville, slides in behind the small wheel. Chrischana wants to get back to camp, where she left the boys, but first—got to find work. She starts the cavernous car and pulls out into the highway bypass leaving the disappointed hopes of Decatur's Diner behind. She can just see the eyes, hear the tongues marking her escape down the road. Asa Bartlett will preside over the speculations and rehashing of old rumors. Fifteen year-old gossip, freshened up again. Melvinia and everybody adding their jeezly two bits worth of recollection. Even when their facts are straight—rare enough!—they get it wrong.

Her smile is tight-lipped. Wouldn't want it any other way! It wouldn't be Gott'im without beech leaves and gossip unfolding. In two weeks I'll be sick of it.... If I could see it without the squint of self-absorption—I'd have some laughs now.

In their jeezly stories there is perception sometimes, a breadth of human experience laid bare: The stories of her people she's been missing. The diner talk reaching back, back ... into the past of what the oldest gossips can remember ... and beyond. If pieced together properly, by someone like Asa, it could tell the whole Story Twitchell. In Phoenix you couldn't be known—or miss-known!—like that. In Phoenix, who cared. Even Petey, the reason she stayed, didn't care.

Hand on the wheel and passing once familiar places, Chrischana tries to remember what she can of the story. Twitchells were the principal founders of Farmingham Royal, prosperous and prominent, before slowly descending into poverty, dispersion, eclipse. They laid out the town. But, on her mother's side—the Truemans, was Nataluk, a Native who took the local doctor to an island in Mason Pond on some pretext. What he wanted was to trade cached furs for the doctor's penknife. Dr. Lapham refused to trade, but, when Nataluk threatened to keep him on the island, the doctor disarmed him by bestowing the penknife as a gift, thereby gaining his friendship.

Chrischana could not help but remember how bears had figured in the family story: There was the teenager who was wounded and treed by one on the far side of Puzzle Mountain. The bear circled below, making sporadic attempts to retrieve him, while the boy whittled a stick then dipped it in his own blood to write "KILT BY BEAR" on his handkerchief. Such tales were why Decatur once always kidded her with bear stories.

The farm of her father, Daniel Albert Twitchell, was hillside land, neglected as was a lot of that Blackwell Mountain land. He had a potato field, small orchard, a garden, wood lot, and cut over blackberry puckerbrush. He suffered lead poisoning from pesticide applications and had to give up on the orchard. That land, she knows, is all gone now in liens and back taxes.

Father either kept his blood pressure problems secret or he knew nothing of them. The treelined streets of Gottheim blur as she remembers finding him beside the spring, and struggling to lift him into her arms. "Don't drop me, Christy," he whispered. She nagged him until he promised a trip to the doctor—and then satisfied her with an easy report of an apparently fictitious visit. Pregnant, in turmoil, forgetful of him, she ran out shortly before his death. Stopping in Elko, Nevada and thinking of him, she called Olive Lovejoy for news, and learned of his death. Traveling aboard *Trailways* through the desert, she kept hearing that whisper, "Don't drop me, Christy."

Fifteen years. She's still hearing it. The words taught her to love in the midst of suffering, taught her endurance, to go on.

"I lied to Asa Bartlett!" Chrischana thumps the steering wheel emphatically: *I didn't know Balder was still single.* "Balder," she whispers. If only you knew."

They've been in the area barely twelve hours, arriving last evening as the light turned golden. They were exhausted, yet feeling the elation of a difficult journey achieved: making camp with a glad spirit, the four of them. Abenaki Notch, enclosed, protective. It was a comfort they needed. There was peace in the deep woodland beside the pool. Mountain water roared, the spring runoff, pouring greenish gold over rocks into the hole, just as she had seen it when a girl. —So cold last night, lit by great stars seen through nearly naked stems. This morning they heard songbirds, three kinds of thrush.

She left the boys fishing, something she had taught Daniel on the journey, and came into Gottheim: amazing to pass Balder's old '55 Chevy parked in the lot at Gottheim Chair. He must keep it up on blocks in winter, it looked so new. The aqua beauty Chevy, nearly chromeless compared to the '57.... It harbored their youth and shared sexuality. Daniel was conceived in the car ... right on the woods road beside the pool.

Chrischana has been circling through the village, remembering the story, wasting gas, time. The corner of Livery and Front Streets, easing the big car past the few old brick blocks, gaping at the skiers' boutiques and trendy restaurants in the old Victorian and Federalist houses. And, from back of the storefronts, gleams of Ben Hutchins Pond. The ice can't have been out too long—I guess. Rounding the corner at the common, onto School Street, past the straight white churches, and out towards the academy as the Congo Church strikes the half-hour. There is the Gottheim Academy, with its spacious central lawn encircled by well proportioned early Greek revival brick buildings. Classes will soon be over, IICE will begin summer sessions. That's Lord's Hill behind, a spur of great Jasper Mountain, and site of an old topaz mine, long defunct.

The sights and associations seep into her, a welcome distraction.... From the real problem. How can she tell him? Even how to face him? She traveled eastward from Phoenix, glibly concocting scenarios. But arriving here.... These fantasies dissolve as reality pricks at her. There is no good way to tell a man you conceived a child by him fifteen years ago and ran off in order to? ... You went to the desert, starved yourself of living green—denied him even knowledge for his rights.... For reasons—you no longer remember.

This is a bizarre plot, this tangled experience—life. He does not even know of Daniel's rich existence.... Miracles, my sons, brought out of the white hell of Phoenix.... A strange new life for her children.... Here, where they know—only one another.

She is grateful to find herself on a back street, winding her way up Crazy Knoll with its quiet old houses. Face Balder? She can't. It's as plain and smooth as one of Birch River's cobblestones. Oh, this is a devilish idea, this late coming to Gottheim!

There are other places, other woods they can camp in. Some other Maine town they can go to and live anonymously....

But Chrischana's heart is breaking. The dream of returning to her community and people is breaking apart.

In Phoenix she had taken a subscription to *The Village Voter*, under a fake name. She'd taken books out of the library by an author who encouraged her to rebuild thoughts of community. That was when Gottheim began reestablishing itself as the ideal. She sweltered in that desert city, sweating over a shirt press in the dry cleaners, and found kindly Gottheim filling her imagination. Gottheim, where people cared if you lived or died, how you lived and died. Little Gott'im, which Petey mocked and derided her sore over. Gottheim, whose people had crowned her with feathers and set her astride a pony, prancing in the midst of a parade as Jasper Mary. Gottheim made her act like a princess during those hard teenage years, when all she had to keep her in line and make her worthy was Father's pride, and that vicious pointed pitiless erring gossip. It made you want to be good—or else a stranger in some huge anonymous city. *Gott'im, I can't lose you now!*

She has reached the edge of the knoll that looks out over the railroad tracks at the end of the village. Across fields stand misty mountains. Aching within, Chrischana shuts off the engine to lean against the cool glass of the window. Above and across the street, stands the Gothic mansion of some old Gottheim family, but she takes no notice. High, inside the turret, a shadow stands still behind a window pane. But Chrischana does not look up to see. Hands now clenched in her lap, she leans over the steering well, agonizing, whispering, "Can't face him ... can't face you, can't." Filled with self-loathing, the woman whimpers.

Chrischana weeps. Long sloppy heavy weeping. Then she rests a tear streaked face against the wheel, staring out the passenger window. A wreathing mist is lifting, parting from the mountains. In the distance stands Mount Will, somewhat apart from the others. Her empty gaze rests upon its quiet summit. A collar of white mist adorns it, quietly ... and now that quiet is seeping into her. Slowly she absorbs it, like greening moss in rain or dew. It is as though the vapor is crossing invisible barriers between the known and unknown worlds ... only to impart this quiet to her.

And now, as she looks out on Mount Will, a thought occurs, a story. Sitting in that unbearable trailer in searing Phoenix, she read in *The Voter* of changes in Gottheim, along with the more familiar neighborly disputes, school questions, Water District problems; a ski resort was growing and impacting the character of the town. Resort family members trying a night landing at the unlighted Edwin Brown Field. Someone was waiting at the other end of the dark strip, headlights on to light the way. But the plane never showed, for Mount Will stood in the way. Only the young daughter, or somebody, of the resort owner survived the crash among the trees on that dark summit. Concussed and bruised, the child made her way down mountain. Somehow she made it to a little house beside a dirt road and was taken in. The man there guessed she'd been in an accident, but had no way of knowing it was in flight on the mountain above. The girl managed to call her sister, and a sisterly response loosened her recollection. She said a dark Angel had taken her from the plane and brought her down toward the light. When she looked around, the woman was gone.

Chrischana sits upright, musing, looking out on mysterious Mount Will. *A guide met her and carried her down.* The quiet continues in this resting woman. Reluctantly she turns the key, starting the big rough engine again.

The daughter of Mahalalel Twitchell, nine generations removed, sits looking up at the array of wide Bavarian gables on the Jasper

Mountain Hotel. Behind the hotel and new lodges strands of lift-cables ascend, lit by the morning sun. The little rope-tow skiway, cut long ago in the dark expanse of pointed firs ... where is it now? That lone trail of her youth—gone under this pile of concrete, half-timbering, glitter and glitz. Where once was a ritualistic part of her heritage, images of fiberglass ski-toting hordes with their shiny-faced children, new cars and two homes now filled the slopes of her imagination. She remembers the yellow bonfires, the old gasoline powered rope tow, her heavy secondhand wooden skis bought with savings earned in Morrill's potato harvests. The slopes are covered in money now—No, plastic. Isn't that how people buy things like this?

Maybe skiers just needed something to keep them out of trouble. No, she wouldn't trade her rough-textured life for ten smooth ones. There's no earth in them. All I need is enough. Won't hurt myself with envy or hostility. She wanted to be alive. The boys gave her substance and purity in caring for them. Without Benaiah, Nathan, Daniel—she'd be dead inside.

Have to get the boys out of that tent before winter. She might do it in three months, in time for the start of school in August. They could enroll tomorrow until the end of this term—with only a P.O. box number. They'd have enough money for gas and food to last till week's end. They could stretch to two if the fishing was good. Hope the game warden doesn't show. No money for a license or fines.

Chrischana removed her bandanna, loosened her braid and brushed her hair smooth. Applying lipstick, she glanced at herself in the rearview. No longer having that withdrawn sightless look, her eyes had calmed since the prayer of Mount Will. ...Since leaving Petey.

She grabbed her knapsack and purse, reached in the back and took down the hanger with her good blouse and skirt. She would have to change in the women's room. *Naked-coed-diaper-changing* won't make a good impression in personnel. Chrischana glanced solemnly into the mirror. She sighed and thrust open the door.

Stepping out of the tiny condominium unit into the carpeted hallway Gloria Fay gives the Morgans a bright smile. Simply and sweetly she thanks them for letting her show them the time-share units. Walking toward the lobby together, their comments are light, appreciative. In the absence of his assistant, brother Jimmy has Gloria mopping up this morning, showing prospective buyers some of the facilities of the Jasper Mountain resort complex. She has just given the young couple—he, an investment counselor, she a junior partner in a family law firm in Massachusetts—a tour, including jacuzzi-pools-sauna-fitness center-day care-restaurant-conference rooms-ballroom *et al*. Upon reaching the commons, which overlooks the Great Room with large mineral stone fireplace, Gloria offers a business card and shiny brochure. "Please feel free to call us if you have more questions on this plan." Again the smile. "Thanks so for considering us."

The Morgans make an encouraging reply and saunter off, murmuring to one another over the brochure.

Gloria glances at her dainty wristwatch cum bracelet and makes her way into the spacious reception center just off the commons. She picks up her little purse from the desk then stops to look out the wide windows up the faintly greening flanks of Jasper Mountain. She has a lunch date down in Gottheim, but there is still plenty of time. Gloria walks over and stands looking at the still somber slopes, streaked with spotty trails patches of snow, outcroppings and mud—a haze of delicate green now forming like a cloud to transform all.

Sometimes her feelings for Jasper Mountain approach reverence. Here upon its flanks she's too near to see the central rounded batholithic head, which gives the mountain its mighty appearance, yet she addresses it in her thought. *You are one of the old stone gods, and I am so happy to be here.* Looking fondly up these flanks, she can scarcely believe that she is actually here—at last living full-time on the mountain.

Here is where she has wanted to live since that first winter vacation as a twelve year-old tomboy. Jasper's pull on her is mystical, as though its great gravity and her small gravity tug upon one another. Jasper is the thing she has ever been faithful in feeling to, having lost interest in Christianity ages ago. Of course she loves mom and dad, her brothers and sisters, but they will always be background love that she counts on. Mom has instilled right thinking, confidence, the ability to dream, a sense of the possibilities, ambition to succeed on her own. Daddy encouraged ambition solely with funding, and this happy daughter will reap its rich harvest. Jimmy, too. This is how life is meant to proceed.

Gloria's thought scarcely touches these themes, for living in Maine is what absorbs her. The place invigorates, whereas study failed to support her in the low times. *So* glad to be finished with the rigor of academic deadlines. Staring up Jasper, she gives herself a grin. Getting through grad school is the hard part because studies are only a means to an end. Without that gold-lettered piece of paper there is no work with appeal to be had. That baccalaureate degree might as well be a high-school diploma. Like many of her friends, though weary, she went back to school once she saw the abominable rewards for kids with liberal arts degrees. The '80s are not the picnic Republicans like Jimmy, with business degrees, think it is. Kids who can't swing the money for grad school settle for the nightlife and minimum-wage jobs. And kid themselves that it's only temporary.

Jasper Mountain! Rugged face streaming with trails. Here, in the privacy of my mind, you are the mythic symbol of both intimate friendship and aloof majesty—my best friend. In my childhood winters I grew up with you, watched your industry grow. The resort thrives, but no one here sees you as I do. They can't know what you mean to me. And now I'm going to earn my own little piece of you. *Earn.* I'll never be childish, dependent, again.

Gloria smiles, her reflection faint in the glass. She turns, starts for the door, then pauses a moment looking back with a child's imagination and spirit. "And thank you for showing me Balder." Gloria will not be ungrateful.

Her small purse slung from a spaghetti strap on her shoulder, her little heels clicking over the slate floor of the lobby, Gloria is a burnished blond, tanned the year round, immaculate and classy. She pushes her way through the glass doors of the lobby just as a brown woman in bandanna and backpack, with garments slung over her arm, approaches. Gloria reads the T-shirt she's wearing, holding the door for her, laughing. "Hey! That's the way! Make those boys own up to their actions!"

The woman returns a faint smile. "Which way to the restroom?"

"Through the arch opposite the stuffed buck and turn right. Can't miss it!" Still holding the door, Gloria watches her cross the lobby. Turning toward the parking lot she finds herself thinking about the locals. A bit darker for a Yankee, that one. But the dress is all Maine. The girls are basically stylish, but the women wear practical clothes, and that's it. All on their way to becoming "old Mainers," dowdy and neat with the style all washed out of them.... But so full of character! Especially when they talk. Not possible that I should ever get acquainted with one—but then comes Balder. And he's well on his way to being an old Mainer, but he's awesome, absolute! A wedge-shaped hunk—the kind to send shivers down your legs.

She trots down the sidewalk, smiling deliciously. Gloria will not kid herself on this: She would never be attracted to just any Mainer unless he was as good-looking and witty as Balder. She admires them all in a quasi-romantic way. They're hardy, smart (but some are illiterate!), and far tougher than she will ever be. *I'm way spoiled while they have to work hard for low wages.* And she wonders if they feel exploited. They make a living—Is that enough? She should ask Balder, get an angle on attitudes to augment her study. Anecdotes will liven it.

Spying her little red Caprice against a row of dark conifer, she smiles. Gloria loves seeing her new car against a backdrop of forest green. That touch of red perks up the somber scene. Just a spot of it can give a painting that little extra appeal. Like an El Greco. A Monet. Everything has significance if you look for it. She unlocks the door and slides in, laying her purse on the passenger seat. Gloria starts the puring engine of the little sports car and pulls out into the lane.

Significance, that's it. Winding her way down toward the highway, she decides to stop at the library in search of some. The library! Way too tiny. Cramped, stacked with ancient falling apart editions. Some of those things haven't been checked out in forty years. Dark in there, too, the only light some glaring bulbs. Their hours are abysmal. She's used to strolling into a library whenever. It's frustrating to arrive at 4:00 p.m. on a Wednesday or eleven a.m. on Monday and find the door locked.

She could go down to Guildford, but she is meeting Balder for lunch and can't be late. Being a blue-collar worker, he has to punch in and out. Gottheim Chair would probably go under if he wasn't there to keep the junk machinery going.

Once in the library she rummages to find what she's after, then seats herself where light falls in at the window seat. H.A. Guerber's *Myths Of the Norseman* would have it. May light comes through the panes onto the old pages. The glass does not quite mute the singing of a dusky little bird on a budding branch outside. Gloria turns the pages, glancing curiously from title to title. "The coming of Brunhild," the "History of Frey." "Balder." Yes! She has teased him about that name almost from the beginning.

She laughed about it while picking fiddleheads yesterday. "What kind of mother names her son Balder?"

He grinned that great grin at her question. "One who caunt think about children's names. Comes up with some beauts fah animals, though. Gram give me this name. That branch of the family were Norwegians who believed in Jesus Christ but told stories of faeries and gods. Balda was pot o'Norse mythology."

"Like with the Vikings?"

"The same. "

"I hear lots of strange names here in the Meguntics. A lot of Bible names. Viking names don't seem appropriate."

But he grinned. "This is Viking soil. Nevah heard 'o Vineland, Markland? Theya south of all the other lands: Finland, Iceland, Greenland, Helluland. And, more recent, Scandinavians came here along with other immigrants." He plopped a handful of fiddleheads into the sack, and said with a touch of mockery, "Thought you knew so much about this place fom your big master's study."

His grin was provoking and she felt her face flush. "Well, I have been doing that study! Balder Simon, I know more about the statistical dynamics of this area than you do—demographics— population trends, composition of labour force, income distribution, housing costs, seasonal variations—! I know projections in manufacturing, transportation, retail, location quotients...."

He let her trail off, then said, "And it's all in your computer, waiting for you to touch a couple buttons. You wouldn't be able to think if you had no fingas!"

"I might say the same about you! What can you do without those tools of yours?"

"Got me!" Light shone through the tree stems, gleaming off of his white-blond hair as he shouted his laughter.

Gloria read on page 197. "... Balder, the beautiful, was worshiped as a pure and radiant god of innocence and light ... which gladdened the hearts of gods and men .... " The young woman sits in the mote-shot light of the window in the musty library, poring over the first part of Balder's story.

> The god of light was well versed in the science of runes, which were carved on his tongue; he knew the various virtues of simples, one of which...was called 'Balder's brow,' because its flower was as...pure as his forehead.

Thoughtfully she lifts her gaze, staring without seeing at the bird on the budding branch. Mmmm. It's rich. This must be the Romance my linguistic analysis professor poked fun at. I must be ignorant: I like it! She smiles a secret subversive smile.

"The only thing hidden from Balder's radiant eye was the perception of his ultimate fate."

Gloria Fay closes the book, looks about the cramped stacks behind her, and the precarious piles heaped on the floor. Someone should do something for this place. *Maybe I should.* Clasping the book, she moves lightly over the bare floor to check it out at the desk.

She flies down the highway toward what she thinks of as the grubby chair factory. A very interesting place, though. Like something out of a children's book: dark corners, wires and pipes, conveyors, strange passages, mezzanines, sloping floors, old open elevators and weird dilapidated machinery. Fresh wood shavings, old sawdust piles everywhere. What fun—talking to Balder at all hours while he worked like a fiend on some dangerous-looking contraption. (He might spend hours on one, get it running, and have to work on it all over again three nights later.) All the while he cracked jokes about the way Ms. Prescott ran the place. Gloria's impression is that the owner is eccentric. Apparently she forgoes buying decent machinery, or paying her suppliers of wood for production, in favor of spending many thousands on an elaborate generating system. "Just what we need," cracked Balder, over this system which is outsized in proportion to the company's needs: "Gott'im Chair, manufacturers of fine waste vapors."

Evidence of the jest appears as Gloria rounds Mount Morrill. The factory, spewing excess steam, comes into view. The precarious hodgepodge of disheveled buildings looks as though it will fall over. How has the weight of winter's snow spared it? Volumes of steam pile up before the dark somber face of Mount Morrill: enough steam to heat forty houses at ten below—or so Balder claims. Gloria has heard talk to support the supposition that Gottheim Chair is the derision of all the mill owners, those whose mills dot the surrounding towns in these mountains.

The little mills are scattered all over the Meguntics, providing low wages for those who can't get into the paper mill—where some can earn as much as fifteen dollars an hour. Even Balder says he will apply for work in Adirondack Paper down in Guildford. Gloria thinks it a bad idea. "Place stinks! When the wind's wrong you could smell it all the way up here. Think of its always being in your clothes."

He retorted that the wind is never wrong. "You caunt say that a weatha system spanning a quarter of the globe's a mistake."

"Why not apply as a Sno-Cat mechanic at Jasper Mountain?"

"The idea's t'earn a living."

She slows the little red car, turning off the highway onto the puddled sand and gravel lot, allowing it to roll down toward the open rear door of the mill. Gloria waves gaily as he steps out to meet her. Balder leans into the window, kissing her quick. He is as happy as a territorial loon.

Gloria's here! "Now we can swim!" he says.

She pulls back. "Like hell, fella! Snow's still on the mountain. Patches of it, anyway. This ain't no swimmin' weatha." Her blond pageboy swinging, she shakes her head.

But Balder hurries around and jumps in the car. "Turn this fuss bucket round'n head down the highway, that way. There's a turn off down theya, leads back into Abenaki Notch. Evah been t'Deep Hole?"

"Sounds cold and *is* too cold for swimming."

"Not too cold fah a ritual. Snowmelt's the thing t'get winter out'o your joints." He looks over at her striking profile, the fringed eye, the chin that juts a little too much. The chin, he decides, is the imperfection that heightens her beauty. Lord! He's lucky.

She protests. "But skiing keeps me limber, shaped up all winter long,"

"I'd say!" He grins. "But Deep Hole's fah more bracing. We need t'get the wimpiness out. If you're gont live heah now we got toughen you up."

She glances at him. "Will it make me a real Mainah?"

"Nothin'd do that." He grins. "You'll nevah be nothing but a summer complaint turned inside out. Skiers ah winter complaints—Wuss'n summer people. Least we got them trained to have a li'l humility. Only took about three-quarters of a century to whip 'em into shape."

Her eyes still on the road, she flings out an arm, belting him across the ribs. "I'll have you know that diner woman calls me *dear*. If I'm not becoming a Mainer then what's that?"

Balder can only shout. "It's no space above flatlander!" He touches her arm. "Theya's the turnoff."

Daniel Twitchell's stringer of three small brown trout is tied to a twig of the yellow birch leaning out over Bear River. The fishing pole now stands idle among the thin birch stems. Watching his little brother, he sits on a rock, blackflies clouding his solemn face. Nathan hops from rock to rock above the icy stream. Daniel is thinking for the umpteenth time that he has to make sure Nathan doesn't tumble in and get chilled. At least they are far enough away from that fall over there into what Mother calls Deep Hole.

The middle brother, Benaiah, is alternately hopping around with Nathan or wandering off down the muddy old logging road. Never spotting Mother, he always comes back after a few minutes. Daniel can sense his unhappiness. When will Mother come back? Gone looking for work in the village called Gottheim, she has left him in charge of the boys and their camp. Daniel shifts on the rock, looks around at emerging buds, into the tall thin stems of the endless thicket; up into the swollen tips, and up up to the blue northern sky.

Never has he seen sky so blue. Missing the concrete of Phoenix, his glance falls back down to Nathan.

"When's Mother coming?" Nathan calls. Waving his skinny arms, the boy narrowly avoids a tumble.

"Get back here, Nathan," Daniel yells above the rush of the water. "Now!" Those rocks are way too slippery.

"Don't haf'ta!" But he hops back to Daniel, saying, "What does Dad look like again?" It has been maybe two weeks since they've seen their dad, Peter Prince. And every day Nathan asks Daniel this question. Yesterday the older boy answered, "Like a man working on his motorcycle." Now he says, "Like Benaiah with his green eyes, only bigger."

Nathan's fresh features form the word, "Oh." Then, pointing out the metamorphic swirl in a nearby rock, he asks, "How come the rocks are all curly like that? Did we have curly rocks in Phoenix?"

Daniel looks down at the stone spread by the little pool where his trout flash and float. The wet surfaces gleam with transformed mica. He says, "It's what happens when rocks sits in water too long. Like when it wrinkles the tips of your fingers after washing a big pile of dishes."

"Oh." Leaning on Daniel's knees with his thin hands, Nathan begins jigging himself up and down, up and down. Sometimes he alternates, kicking back with his feet. "When's Mother coming?"

Daniel addresses the deep fierce sky. "She'll be back when the leaves are all the way out." He drops his gaze, searching through stems for Benaiah. There he is, a gangling form in T-shirts and holey jeans, coming this way. Light shines through the woods except where dark clumps of evergreen seem to absorb it. There is a close feeling about this place. Closed in. Daniel feels the walls of the Abenaki Notch encroaching, though here they are cloaked in great thickets of endless brush. Puckerbrush she calls it.

Nathan shakes his head. "I don't think so," he says about the leaves coming out. "I'm hungry."

"So'm I," says Benaiah, approaching on the track. "Let's cook the fish. "

Unmoving, Daniel sits slumped on the rock.

"C'mon, Daniel," wheedles Benaiah. His tangled brown hair frames his wide fair face.

"You want to fillet 'em?" says Daniel at last. His own face is somewhat square and dark, a drab almost greenish color in comparison to mother's more glowing brown. His brow is wide, eyes seldom smiling. He hears an engine, quiet and too smooth to be the Bonneville's. Looking off toward a bend in the track, he tenses until bright red flashes through the stems. The game warden wouldn't have a red car. Mother was unsure if Daniel was over age for fishing without a license.

Together the three boys watch as the little car pulls up among the opening may apple near their campsite opposite. A tall man and pretty woman get out laughing, talking. She's as bright as the sun, classy, stylish. Her suit seems to shine. The man dresses like Dad, the way highway or construction workers, mechanics, dress. But he is bigger than Dad, has a quiet power. This man moves with confidence. Daniel sees these things, makes these comparisons as they come toward him.

The man smiles a little, asks, "That your camp?" seeing the fish, his smile widens. "Nice brookies you got theya. "

Daniel only nods.

"My brother caught'em," says Nathan. Reaching thin arms up to a budding branch, he begins pulling it up and down up and down, up and down.

"Don't the blackflies bother you, camping?" The woman asks this, fanning them away with her pearly manicured hand.

"Sometimes," answers Daniel, wondering what they're doing here. No fishing pole, and the woman doesn't look ready to fish—not in high heels, slinging a little purse.

"They won't bite till they're already t'lay eggs," the man says to her. He flashes a smile at Daniel and moves her off onto the soggy path through trees, toward Deep Hole. As the boys watch, she steps gingerly over some protruding roots. The murmur of their voices is soon lost to the sound of rushing water.

Nathan starts to run after them and, after hesitating, Benaiah goes too. Daniel looks away, restive but resigned. Now I'll have to go, to make sure Nathan isn't hurt. Benaiah might get into trouble too. Daniel wonders what he'd do if either one fell in. He's not much of a swimmer himself, there being no place much for them to learn in Phoenix. He wants to call his brothers away, but the strangers make him shy of it. The boys will probably just ignore him and then he'll feel like a fool. No doubt the man can swim, but what good will that do if Nathan hits his head going down? You can't tell what it's like under that water except that it's rocks rocks rocks, nothing but rocks. Why doesn't mother come back? He worries it all, taking the path.

Over rocks in the rushing water he approaches toward the fall, seeing that the man is already down to his jockey shorts, about to drop. Yelling, he's gone. Standing back, Nathan and Benaiah are at the brink, looking down from rocks into the roaring swirling waters. As Daniel nears, the roar of the river is like that of a bear roaring without surcease. He stands above with the boys now, looking down, shivering. The man's head is visible in the white water. He calls to the woman who is undoing her clothes on the bank.

Daniel motions to Benaiah and takes Nathan by the arm. Why did mother bring them here? Placing his feet just so on the rocks, he leads his brothers, keeping to the rough and avoiding the smooth and slick surfaces, watching the others as they step. At last they are on shore in the budding bushes, looking back.

The woman has stripped to her shining white slip and is stepping into the stream above the greenish narrow fall. She throws up her arms. She is gone. The boys hurry down the sloping path to see her bobbing in the shimmering pool of Deep Hole. At a little distance they see her water-dark hair molded to her head. Amid the roar and foam she is shouting for joy.

Daniel cannot be sure.... It sounds like she is crying, "I'm alive! I'm alive!"

Doing Business in the House Of God

Tidy and small, bespectacled and blond, James Fay hurried out of the men's room, nearly colliding with a woman in bandanna and T-shirt with idiotic logo. Already late for his lunch date with the boss, he brushed past, leaving her to sidestep any way she could. Mr. Fay scurried past the mounted white-tailed buck and across the lobby toward the Gemstone Restaurant. This sales dynamo was suddenly preoccupied with a new pitch: *Harry, the housekeeping staff should be wearing uniforms.*

The hostess, Karon, stood smiling a welcome by the velvet rope just inside the panelled room. She too was a member of the Jasper Mountain brat pack, people who had grown up together, winters, on the mountain. Karon was luscious in deep blue, her dark hair pinned back with matching barrettes.

Jocular, beaming, James Fay came up to her. "How'd you like to wear a uniform?"

Her smile dropped. A scowl puckered her white brow. "I'd hate it, you?"

"But you'd look good in a uniform!"

"I mean how would you like to wear one?" His smile was so maddeningly fatuous.

"Some people have no sense of humor. I am wearing a uniform. Three-piece, with a silver textured tie—for that touch of elegance." He turned smartly, still with the joke, indicating the tie with a flourish. "Don't worry, you're safe. Hostesses must look elegant too. But you know, Karon, you should have gone back to school instead of opting for ski bum." He grinned at her raised eyebrows and said, "Maybe it's not too late."

Then, craning his neck and looking past, he missed her glare. "Is Harry here yet? Never mind." He grabbed one of her menus and hurried away.

"Sure," she hissed, looking darts at his retreating backside.

—

Harry Golding, formally of a suburb outside Boston Massachusetts, is descended from Palmer Golding, one of the original proprietors of Farmingham Royal. He will take a break in a few years, his head-of-steam dissipating, loss and personal sorrow breaking in. He will settle back, feeling the emptiness of empire drying him out. In dryness he will turn his hand to less acquisitive activity, genealogy among other things, and stumble into the fact of his predecessor Palmer Golding and his initial proprietary claim in the wild district north of Boston. He will sit at his desk, looking out on a mountain far distant from Jasper, an absent smile in his gaze, remembering Gottheim as he first saw it ... a quiet New England village sheltered by a great round-headed mountain with a small neighboring skiway on its back slope.

At the moment, sitting here in the Gemstone Restaurant waiting on Fay, he is unaware of this salty fact. He came to Gottheim more than a decade ago as a young entrepreneur, buying little Jasper Mountain skiway from developers who went belly up in a bad economy. And his brother Julius later joined him. Although his touch is generally sure, Harry Golding is always amazed at the fates of finance. For instance, four years ago, when the mountain had half the trails, condominiums newly built in the area went bankrupt. "Condos of cards," went the joke around here, but the fortunes of three good people were destroyed. It happened in the wake of a real estate boom that had seen property values rise three hundred percent in a single year. There were others who lost that year. Cory, Graham.... He begins ticking off investors who lost everything during that period. They sank dollars and dreams into Gottheim area construction and properties, bought land from the old-timers—all on the basis of what he is doing here. But their timing was ever so slightly off. Interest and development in the mountain itself had not fully ripened, and in consequence everything went down under the hammer, sold for twenty cents on the dollar. Last year, even two years ago—That was the time to begin. The auctioned properties now prosper but the original dreamers are gone. He sees the timing clearly now, and is sure the losers do too.

"Did I keep you waiting, Harry?" James Fay pulls out a chair across from him.

"Not at all, Fay." He looks for Evan, the waitperson.

"Uniforms, Harry! I just bumped into one of the vulgar T-shirts—"

"Let's order, shall we?" Evan has appeared, pad in hand.

Briefly Fay scrutinizes her neat dark shirtwaist before ordering.

When she is gone Golding says preemptively, "This is your only chance to talk to me before I'm off to Quebec for a week."

Open for further confidence, Fay raises an eyebrow but knows better than to ask about Canada. He also knows he does not want to waste what time he has on uniforms. He clears his throat. "You heard me use the term 'aggregate' in connection with this idea?"

Golding nods. "I've read of the concept. A hamlet, of some sort, surrounded by no more than a score of second home single-family dwellings—the nucleus of a rural 'neighborhood.' Perhaps complemented by a working farm or other rural enterprise."

"Exactly. A more lively development concept." James Fay is beaming again, excited. "Harry, it's as though family culture is finally coming first—showing a wise, moral way to proceed in the practical business of development."

Golding smiles. A very slight smile. He picks up his martini as Fay continues.

"After decades of trial and error—From ticky-tacky crammed together over vast tracts to spacious-gracious five acre lots—we've come back, Harry, to the sense of—of what's best for people!" Fay emphasizes the words by tapping the side of his hand on the table top. "Ever since Levittown we've been trying to kiss away the very thing that's best for people. How, finally, do people want to live? They want to live in a caring community, one where they can be sure their kids will be safely nurtured." Again he taps the tabletop with the side of his hand.

Light hazel eyes gleaming, Golding aims his slight smile at Fay. With forearms propped on the table, his chin lightly resting on the laced fingers of his manicured hands, he stares at his tablemate. Harry Golding wears a brown cardigan shot with amber threads. His open shirt collar reveals a tanned throat. He has a definite and undisturbed fondness for the young man across from him, for his naivete and enthusiasm.

And tidy James Fay pitches ahead with enthusiasm. "We put at most twenty percent of the land in development—infrastructure, houses, telemark trails, even a millpond, and leave the rest markedly wild. As with condos, there'll be an owners association for maintenance—but the aggregate will have far more aesthetic appeal." (Tap tap tap tap.) "And a healthy ambience...."

Golding lets him continue until Evan returns with their salads—Golding's tabooli, Fay's crabmeat. And then, as Fay pauses to eat, Golding asks, "How much land, where?"

"Fifty plus acres. On the wild Birch River, secluded at the base of Mason Mountain. There'll be cross-country till the cows come, due to a network of logging trails on adjacent paper lands. The centerpiece will be an old mill race. Have to rebuild the dam out of the hewn granite lying around. In summer it'll be idyllic, in winter elegant, austere. Oh, and it abuts one of the unincorporated towns. Wild, Harry wild."

Losing its ironic tinge, Harry's smile slips toward admiration. "What's the problem in Copenhagen?" He asks suddenly.

James Fay stops, signals Evan for more coffee. *Why does he do this?* Lately, Golding seems to enjoy throwing him off. Just as Fay is finding his rhythm, relaxed and finely concentrated.... And, true to form, Harry hasn't even shown any immediate interest in the figures.

"Nothing to worry about, Harry. It's just that little piece on the outlet of the fifth pond along the valley. For Dad and Mom. Not enough setback from the pond due to the road. Since it's less than an acre it's undersized for regs for construction. But the board has said they will hear the appeal." He wants to say, it's personal, Harry, but that would sour the conversation ... if not the relationship. "They need a variance, that's all. "

"So, why was it splattered across *The Voter* last week?"

Fay fiddles with his napkin, taking his time. He hates being checked this way. It's demeaning, as though he were Golding's son, not his associate and the man is only thirteen years his senior.

Casually he says, "Because the appeal was delayed. Look Harry, you must've read the thing. The deadline passed before they received my request."

But Golding is not in a merciful mood. "The envelope was postmarked ten days after the date of your letter inside, Jimmy. You tried to cover with an excuse about harassed assistants and constraints on your time. Don't you realize what an ass that makes you look?" His chin resting lightly upon his laced fingers, Golding closes his eyes. "I'm not sure I want you handling the village negotiations. The news of the proposed 'taking' has just hit the stands and already there's talk of circulating a petition. It's not really necessary for me to remind you that the contingency for your removal has been provided for in our agreement?"

Fay quieted, clearing his face of earnestness. He looks down, resisting the urge to scan nearby tables for eavesdroppers. This is as much as he can stand. He says quietly, "Is that what you want?"

His eyes gleaming once more, slowly Golding smiles. He withdraws his gaze, leans back, looks across the room. "What I want is for you to handle yourself better."

Fay looks quickly at him. But already the man is far away—in Quebec. Relieved, the younger man expels his breath. "I can do that, Harry. "It is a soft reply.

"Good." Golding looks at Fay, smiles.

—

The clock in the gleaming chrome desk set said 12:45. Jimmy pulled out the chair, sat down. He had not told Harry of his plan for several aggregates around the base of Mason Mountain, thinking it best to sell him on the concept first. He drummed his fingers before reaching for the phone, dialing his father at the Hancock Building in Boston.

"Dad! How's it going? How's the back?... Glad to hear it. What'd you do last weekend?... How was it out there? Your first time to the Vineyard this year wasn't it? How's Mom liking it?" James laughed. "Well she loves to give you a hard time."

He drummed his fingers on the blotter, glanced aside at the monitor. He swiveled around and leaned back, looking up at somber Jasper Mountain, saying, "It's still got that drab muddy look, but there's a haze of red higher, and green nearer the base.... OK, I guess, but she's been hanging out with a mill mechanic.... All right, but don't expect her to listen. *You* can't do anything with her, neither can I.... Yes, if it does I'll let you know. Better not say anything to Mom. Right now she's so embarrassed she doesn't even want me to meet him—won't admit it, though.... No, don't worry; the waiver should go through. Get out your plans!" Fay's voice gentled: "OK. Tell mom I love her, will you?"

Fay hung up, turned and pressed enter on the keyboard. The screen lit up, green and ready for spreadsheets. But he turned back to the mountain, absently. Smiling faintly, he ran a thoughtful finger across the faint cleft in his chin. A quiet gladness came into him. He had managed to refrain from bragging to his father about his deals. But, as quickly as it had come the peace was gone, supplanted by anticipatory glee over Mason Millrace. Or, maybe it should be Millrun. Which was the more euphonic?

The single original building of the Gottheim Chair factory was built by the Town in 1890 for ninety-five hundred dollars. Initially, Amos T. Prescott leased the property and building, formed the company and began manufacturing some of the finest chairs in the country, employing sixty townspeople. Over ensuing decades the original neat structure and property were purchased from the town and haphazardly amended on all sides, as expansion warranted. Increasingly, its outer appearance mirrored the shambling business practices of Amos Prescott's descendants.

Tidying her desk his granddaughter, Theodora Prescott, glances out the window in time to see Balder Simon get out of a little red Caprice and round the corner on his way to the rear entrance. She sighs, and gives him time to enter the maintenance shop, then steps into the hall, herself heading toward the parking lot. Exiting the building, she is careful to shake out her skirt in case of clinging sawdust. On her way to the car a shadow crosses the lot, momentarily shading it. Theodora looks up.

Oh, that awful steam! She watches as the breeze passes, leaving the cloud to shoot upward again. Such an embarrassment. She wants to hide herself in a hole whenever she sees it. That generating system is why she stopped showing herself at community functions. In the mill she won't come out of her office for fear of workers being reminded of how Jerold had used her. Once that

65

system was installed he dropped her like a load of lumber. Theodora is weary of her continuing charade of admiration over the technological upgrading of the company. Vernon must get her a contract with the power company while the window is still open. That was Jerold's selling point. Bearces and the others have managed to get the bugs out of their systems. They've been selling to the utility for something like thirteen cents a kilowatt hour!—even though Central Maine Power is selling on the grid to Massachusetts for one cent. They are bound by law to buy from co-generators at the higher rate. She wanted to check with Vernon on his progress this morning, but he is in Lewiston on some errand for Aunt Aggie. When will he stop that infernal dubbing around on errands for her? This is a business for godsakes!

Theodora rummages in her marshmallow blue leather bag for the keys. As she opens the door of her custom painted powder blue Saab 900, Balder roars past in his '55 Chevy. Her jaw works. The mechanic is gone in a spray of gravel. *Come back!* She wants to scream. *You can't leave in the middle of the day!* Involuntarily she has raised her arm, trying to wave him back. But sudden awareness of her action embarrasses Theodora. She fumbles with the key, unlocks the door of the Saab.

Out on the highway and after some moments the woman feels calmer. The car's sleek interior soothes her. The mathematical precision of Bach's harpsichord fugues in the cassette player imparts order to her beleaguered psyche. Then, eyeing the clock, she sees need to hurry. The pre-season session is due to begin in a few minutes and reception for tardiness can be frosty. Once she was actually excluded for it. And she needs these labs! You never know what will happen: depending on the chemistry of program and people, you could be bored numb or thrilled to desperation. Sometimes you can't even remember, afterward, what exactly has taken place. It must be an effect of hypnosis. And a very relaxing one. She once joked with Brandel about getting her money back: "How do I know there even was a session?" Theodora spends thousands on IICE courses and sessions, and has donated thousands, too.

How did I survive before IICE came into my life? The dynamics of organizational development and personal growth is transforming existence for everyone. By it things are improving all over the world. Theodora herself has now an almost constant glow of anticipation about life and its possibilities—thanks to IICE. She acknowledges to herself that her affiliation with them is her prestige in this town. No one here takes her as seriously as they do. And now she is looking forward to working with Eveledore on formulating a program tailored for personnel at Gottheim Chair.

This, finally, is something she can sink her teeth into without fear of falling into an area she knows nothing about. It will redeem all her previous blunders at the chair factory. Theodora has been interested in interpersonal communication all her adult life. It gives her content, structure to her thoughts, enabling her to feel vitally connected to the world. *IICE has given me participation in the global community.* Think of it! A timid local graduate of Gottheim Academy, lacking courage even to finish a semester at Vassar— always shooting about in search of a meaningful response to life—and they were right under her nose all the time! Once boring to her, a little absurd—IICE! That oddball community that came to town every summer to study.

Theodora giggles, remembering the first time she laid eyes on Brandel. Sitting in Felicity's having coffee and conversation with Eveledore and this supposedly suave stranger, Theodora was too timid even to look him in the eye. And suddenly she was looking him in the eye! Eyes wearing shadow, liner, mascara! A face full of makeup! What a laugh she had with Eveledore over it just the other day. Eveledore.... Even her name is significant, felicitous (like the restaurant!): It is a veritable echo of Theodora. She smiles a secret smile: Of thiscourse, the other's name doesn't contain the word God like mine does. At IICE they appreciate my sensitivity to significance.

Unconsciously a frown troubles her brow. Trying to remember.... Rounding beneath the far curve of Mount Morrill she passes the state roadside park without seeing it. She sees little along the highway most days. The landscape rarely changes, a new building might pop up.... Harry Golding's resort is doing so well.... But today the burnt-out structure of that unfortunate Ithiel Whitman grabs her gaze. Passing, she looks at the charred cross-timber sticking above a blackened roof.... Like a giant crucifix. Poor man. An old classmate of hers, very popular. He has certainly endured a lot! His wife vanished, a sister-in-law that won't leave him alone....

But suddenly Theodora gives a little quiver, remembering at last. That awful rumor heard in the post office this morning! Is—can IICE really be thinking of leaving?! Upon first hearing it, laughing, she could scarcely give it credence. Her frown deepens. Can it be true? IICE actually thinking of breaking their affiliation with Gott'im?! Can't be true. *Can't.* "Let it have no real substance," she murmurs, repeating it several times.

But IICE is a far-reaching entity, she knows, and looking to reach further. Its natural they'd want affiliations in other places abroad—countries with any potential for growth in interpersonal communications. Why that's nearly the whole of the Third World! Nations on earth are in transition, and IICE is exactly the kind of organization to help them stabilize. According to Dr. Anami's lecture, every new institution would benefit from the social and psychological programs of the institute. Of course IICE must expand, but they needn't leave Gottheim to do it! Wouldn't that demean us?

Well, that can't be their intention. If they need bigger facilities, more of a world-class center.... The Golding's! That's it! The Jasper Mountain Hotel .... More seminar and conference space is planned. Oh, IICE'll see. It's just a rumor anyway. *Only a rumor....* Theodora hurries toward Gottheim for a session at the International Institute of Coordinated Experiments.

But, later that night—Theodora might have been seen racing wildly along back roads, her headlights crossing bare branches, branches that thrash on the breeze. She would be crying, wildly weeping, tears flowing ceaselessly. Hiccups engulfing her, anguish roaring in her heart.

"*How*! *How* am I unacceptable to you?!"

Remembering the horrible session at IICE, Theodora's hands will clench and unclenched on the beveled wheel. "Why oh why don't you accept me as I am? It was you who told me initially: 'Don't be ashamed of who you are. Never be ashamed,' you said. Why? Why are you people trying to change me?"

Theodora will tremble with anguish, wail. Heave and sigh. Whimper. "Why are you trying to change my personality?..."

She will whisper it to the wind, to the grinding wheels. "Why, why, why?"

Sipping coffee from one of Decatur's mugs, grubby old Ceylon Segar sat on a squeaky swivel stool in the diner. Smelling like old tires and ripe underwear, he enjoyed twisting on the stool just a little bit, producing this squeak. Those coming in avoided the stools on either side of him. Sitting beside Ceylon Segar was no picnic. He was big in the used tire collection business. Not that he went around picking up tires.

Lyman Bearce, the lumber man, had vacated his usual stool to get away from Segar. He would not be associated with that abuser of property even by physical proximity. Besides, the smell was enough to gag a man and drive him into one of Decatur's booths. If those goddam tires of his ever caught fire they could kiss the surrounding woodland goodbye. The fire would burn down into the ground, run along the roots in the acreage roundabout and there'd be no putting it out till after the grandkids started having kids of their own. If then. It set Bearce's blood on fire to think of it.

He was a powerful, vastly bearded man who brooked nothing against his purposes. First, foremost, always he was a businessman, deliberate. Yet Lyman Bearce, with his dark hair and white beard that hid the acne scars of his youth, looked like a logger who had just come out of the woods. His forebears had been in the woods since history, setting up mills on any stream large enough to float a log. Yankee Maine had a history of illegal lumbering dating back to the King's broad arrow, a seal set on every tree deemed the King's. Houses with punkin pine floors attest to the "thievery": Uniform planks shaved to under twenty-four inches can still be found in colonial houses. That diameter was reserved for masts in His Royal Highness's Navy.

The family Bearce were relative newcomers to the Town of Gottheim, arriving only after the turn of this century. By the mid '20s they were a sprawling fixture; Beatitude Bearce, having obtained a fair parcel of forestland, was well on his way to amassing the large tracts they now owned. Lyman, one of his five sons, was a formidable and conscientious forester, promoting healthy timber through sound harvesting practices. In balancing the mills' requirements with what the woods might safely provide, his rule was, leave the best, cut the rest. His forests were almost uniformly beautiful, healthy; possessed of a quality to revive the bruised soul of almost anyone who walked them. Only once in his thirty-seven years as forester had he allowed clearcutting, preferring to achieve stands with canopies to provide support in case of high winds and storm. Erosion of his land was practically nil, the stable stands slowing runoff, reducing siltation of brooks and preventing dessication of the floor. However, last spring under pressure of the changing community, he decided to try his hand at mountain development, selling stumpage on five hundred acres to Adirondack paper for the possible subdivision of the land. Bearces could be counted on to try just about anything not unwise and not—at this date—publicly unseemly for profit.

Lyman Bearce frequented Decatur's Diner, as had Beatitude before him decades ago when it was operated by Jeffy Decatur's father. The business, that is. The site and diner itself, of course, belonged to Bearce. Sitting here in the booth by himself, Lyman thought of this. He had begun the process of exercising his option to develop this site, local icon or not.

He smoothed his great white beard with a calloused hand, one sporting his Gottheim Academy class ring. He still wore the ring after forty years. What people failed to recognize in him was his sentimentality. (He would certainly never acknowledge it himself.) If anyone had suggested this fact to Town historian Asa Bartlett he would have hooted: "That diner disposer—sentimental?" But, sipping his coffee, Bearce thought, *Not one of these people ever realized the near sacredness of this place till today.* Without betraying it by even a gleam in his eye, Lyman Bearce smiled to himself. He was glad to be the one to teach 'em! He looked around at its fixtures—the garish neon lit clock, sagging booths, chipped tabletops. He had no idea what he would do with this ugly bucket of crud. He was half-tempted to have Howe tow it into the woods someplace, just let it sit till he could think of something.

Flatfooted, Melvinia Sessions came up and nearly slammed a cheeseburger plate in front of him on the linoleum tabletop. She sent her nose toward the ceiling and sailed away.

Lyman Bearce almost smiled. He ought to demolish this place but he couldn't quite bring himself to it. Keep this thing? Lyman Bearce was good for a surprise now and then. Like four years ago when he up and ran for selectman. Folks weren't surprised that he was elected. The surprise was his candidacy. There'd never been a Bearce in Town government. Never. Bearces had always been content to influence politics through the mere expression of opinion. That was all it took.

But Asa Bartlett thought he had pieced it together, and what he came up with was Jasper Mountain. Lyman Bearce was not about to let outsiders Harry and Julius Golding walk off with policy in this town. He had to keep things favorable to his mills. He had sat back and watched the little skiway expand bit by bit and recognized that it was going to snowball into the biggest resort in Maine. The dynamics of Gottheim were bound to change and Lyman Bearce was going to be the one to affect them. Asa Bartlett was sure of it. It helped that his wife Rhetta was on the Planning Board.

A Bearce mill manager named Elmer Robbins came in, hurried past Ceylon Segar, and sat down opposite Bearce. Robbins was a generation younger than Lyman. His was a sandy complexion replete with freckles. He had reddish hair and a falsely serious mien, meant to ward off remarks and familiarities occasioned by his slight appearance. He signaled Melvinia for coffee, then began complaining about the quality of logs he had turned away that morning.

"It's a good thing Bearces made the switch," he said, referring to recent upgrading of the panels and bentwood mill. Rising world demand for hardwood sawlogs had depleted supplies to the point where quality was getting harder to come by, though the softwood mills continued to prosper thanks to Bearces' woods management and high standards. In recent years they had acquired a furniture components mill with a hunger for hardwood and the strange touch of technology. After much study, Lyman had decided upon bending the wood with the powerful tool of electricity. First developed in northern Europe, radiofrequency produced a value-added product using less wood. Robbins stirred his coffee, saying, "Now that we've got that contract with Alabama Furniture fah those bow-backs, we'll hev t'increase our suppliers."

Bearce grunted. "Already been talkin't'some. Should hev it nailed down by the fust next week." Lyman took another bite of his burger.

Melvinia set a Jell-O salad in front of Elmer Robbins. He watched her walk away, saying, "She's in a Christless pink stink. It's all over the town about this place. The old timers is boiling."

"Give 'em something t'be opinionated about, 's all. Ought keep'em happy awhile."

"Got that right," said Robbins, which phrase was habitual with him. "Heard the latest in snow-making, boss?"

"You mean freeze-dried piss?"

Robbins restrained a smile. "Only Harry Golding would brave the publicity o'that." He couldn't help grinning then, revealing a slight gap between his front teeth: "Next he'll hev 'em schussing through frozen shit. Has about the same appeal, don't it?"

But Bearce did not laugh. "It is an efficient way to dispense with two big resort problems: snow-making and sewage disposal. When snow guns spray sewage under high pressure, rapid freezing kills bacteria." He speared two fries with his fork.

Elmer was incredulous. "Theya's got to be a downside. They just haven't come across it yet."

"Phosphorus in the runoff. It'll run down'n pollute the Arossagunticook."

Elmer swallowed his coffee wrong and choked back a mouthful. Like it wasn't a dead river now.

Bearce looked disgusted and slid his plate closer to his bearded chest. To him the great river was no laughing matter. They had all grown up with the open sewer that the bountiful river had become since Andrew MacDonald built his paper mill and Magic City near the great falls. Three more paper mills were built after that, all since changing hands. They had been going at the dumping of toxic chemicals for nearly twice the span of Bearce's life. The federal Clean Water Act of the decade past had put a stop to fumes strong enough to peel paint off riverside houses, but along with many others Lyman could not get used to the off color and foam, the odor; and dioxin that made it advisable for pregnant women to eat no fish caught in its waters. Despite the Act, the river looked bad, it stank; and he could not accept that it spawned mutants and had been carelessly commandeered by corporations who ignored the rights of their neighbors. Now, in the latter half of the twentieth century, they were absentee stewards, headquartered elsewhere. No stewards at all.

To Bearce the effect was that they found the river useful but hated it. But Bearce had informed his representatives in Augusta. Yes, they would spend a substantial amount of time and money wrangling over this bill. The battle would be fierce, but Bearce had thought it all through. The river should not be for the papermakers only, even if it meant joining forces with the fluff-headed environmentalists. The Arossagunticook belonged to Maine.

Yes, Lyman Bearce cared about such things, but, as everyone knew, he did not care for individuals. He cared more for Decatur's Diner, as a piece of Americana and even for its function in the community, than he would ever care for Decatur or Melvinia. He liked to see Melvinia stomp around or Decatur scratching his bald head and wondering what to do next.

Robbins was asking how the meeting went last night. "They gont avoid that eminent domain thing?"

"You read about it. We're gont request a delay on deciding that. The twerp says they look t'finish papah work on land swaps by the end of the month." (The "twerp" referred to James Fay, who was handling negotiations for resort interests.) "A selectman'll represent the Town in 'Gusty once everything's secure. But far's I can see, it's all worked out. What a haggle. Fay's crowding t'get building—like the outsider he is. A shoreline park is a good idea, though. Wouldn't want this place turning into another North Conway."

"Got that right. Had t'go theya last week. Nothing but strip malls'n outlets. Traffic wuss'n Freeport."

Bearce nodded. He doubted North Conway looked much different than the rest of America. He'd read somewhere that anyplace now looked like every place. They'd written right. It had no business happening to Gottheim.

This was the secret of Lyman Bearce and his father before him. But Beatitude never had to deal with outside forces. Not like this. The old man was retired now. Maybe he didn't know it, but he was. Forced into it by decrepitude, and his son was so much like him: Beatitude could no longer keep his dogs on the way Gottheim grew, and Lyman made sure his own orders were not superseded by the old man's.

In the time allotted him, Lyman Bearce planned to make sure it never happened to him. His influence would be sure. And Gottheim would be kept looking and feeling like Gottheim.

Asa Bartlett would've hooted, but this imperfect stewardship was but one of the secrets of Lyman Bearce.

Family Secrets, Secret Family

Catching movement off his right shoulder, Daniel looks up from the swimmers in Deep Hole to see the dull gold of the Bonneville coming through the buds above them. "She's here!" calls Benaiah, the river rushing over the falls drowning his cry. Followed by his brothers, Nathan runs up the muddy path. Mother pulls off the puddled road into their campsite well away from the Caprice and gets out wearing her good skirt and blouse. She glances at the mud spattered red car just down the track. The two youngest rush her, but Daniel trails over to the stream for his fish.

"Mother! Mother! You shoulda seen it!" Nathan tugs on her arm and she embraces him briefly. "They went o'er the falls into the hole!"

"Told you people swim here," she says. "When I was li'l older than Daniel, we cooled off here summers. There was a runoff ritual—if you were older and brave enough. I'll teach you all t'swim, come July."

She watches dark Daniel crossing the track with his stringer. "Nice catch, Daniel. Everything all right?" She looks carefully into his face. "What's wrong?"

"Aw, we're okay. The man called these brookies." He holds up the stringer. The fish are patterned and speckled, but small.

"Good eating," says Chrischana. "I'm proud of you for feeding us. We're going to need more.... I didn't get my job yet."

Daniel looks away. So hard .... Hafta ask her to find some other place than Deep Hole, or Nathan will drive me nuts.

"Eat now, eat!" cries Nathan, pulling on the budding twigs nearby. He lets loose a fistful, swatting Benaiah across the chest. He runs off, Benaiah after him yelling.

"Don't hurt your brother!" shouts Mother. The rushing of Bear River drowns her out.

"Can we go with you this afternoon?" asks Daniel as they near the campfire. "I can watch Nathan better in the car. The river's too dangerous, Mother. He's gonna fall in. Or, maybe there's a park or playground somewhere?"

"He did like you said about staying off the river, didn't he?" She lays the fish on an old mossy stump beside her secondhand Coleman stove. Here are utensils for cooking, an old fry pan, fillet knife, battered dinner plates. She sets a brooky on a plate and slits it.

What do you think? "Pretty much, but he's too itchy. Doesn't really want to stay away."

Chrischana hears a murmur of voices above the water and looks up to see a man and woman coming out of the bushes toward the track. They are laughing, animated, invigorated by their plunge. Distracting her, Nathan and Benaiah zip back through camp, Nathan hollering. Each laying blame, they tear about yelling at one another. But, upon seeing the couple approach the little red car, the boys stop to stare. The young woman goes around to the driver's side, but the man stands a moment looking from the old Bonneville to the camp where the little family stands watching. Chrischana recognizes Balder. Feeling hot in the face, she turns her head away—but too late. He comes toward them. There is no evading it. He strides past the Bonneville and stands sternly regarding her.

"Chrischana Twitchell?"

"Yes, it's me, Balder. "

A frown creases his brow. "Waya'd y'go?"

"To the desert. Nevada first, then Phoenix."

They look at one another. The young woman comes up behind Balder, saying brightly to Chrischana, "You changed out of your T-shirt."

The older woman recognizes the striking girl from the Jasper Mountain hotel. Her hair is still plastered to her head, her clothing damp and disheveled.

"Had to, I was applying for work. Chrischana Twitchell." She steps forward, holding out her hand.

"Gloria Fay. Nice meet you." She shakes the proffered hand. "Balder's friend?"

Chrischana nods. "From high school. I was away." She steps back to her place beside the boys. "These are my sons." She sets a hand on each, naming them. The youngest is spinning the slit brooky around on the oily plate with his forefinger. Benaiah stands by Daniel, staring at the pair.

Taking his stern gaze off Chrischana, Balder now sets it on Daniel. He looks from Benaiah to Nathan, then back to Daniel. At last he looks again at Chrischana. And silence has taken possession of them all. His glance on her is pensive, as seeing into her. Gathering an impression of someone changed in body and soul. A person he knew once, held intimately in his thought.

Now, slowly again, he puts his gaze upon Daniel. Beside him Gloria says something, too brightly, but no one attends.

Feeling the intensity of the man's gaze, Daniel looks down. He picks up the stringer with the remaining two fish and begins removing them, gently lifting a hook from each mouth. He wishes the man would go away now, the woman.

Gloria shifts nervously, lightly brushing the tips of Balder's fingers with her own. She looks at her watch, says lightly and sweetly, "Lunch's about over. Got to get back."

"Nice meeting you," says the dark skinned woman.

Her shoes in hand, Gloria turns and walks toward the car. It is then that Chrischana notices her bare feet, the wet slip wrapped around her wrist and clutched against her palm.

Staying, Balder looks from Daniel to Chrischana once more; and, frightened now, she returns his gaze. The look she sees is very quiet in him. Dark, crestfallen. He stands a moment, looking so at her. He turns and walks away.

Several nights later, Daniel stepped from Hannah Sessions' filthy kitchen into fresh night. Stifling the urge to vomit, he'd got out of there just in time. The stench and squalor in the sagging clapboard Cape were almost unbelievable. Now, in the swatch of yellow light from its window, he checked to make sure he still had his notebook and pencil, as well as the tape recorder belonging to Mrs. Melville. He needn't have worried, for the condition of that house had precluded any idea of setting something down. He had clutched everything fiercely while inside. Did he really see Cindabilla's Uncle Ferddy slurp his spilled beer off the table scattered with chicken shit and crumbs from supper?

The stench of the pigpen in the backyard now assaulted his nostrils as he passed. He went picking his way through the littered yard, hoping his eyes would soon adjust to the dark. He found a path Cindabilla had told him of, cutting narrowly through piles of junk. Distantly, he heard spring peepers chirping. Trailing past clumps of sodden feed sacks, pieces of rusted metal, old tools and parts, a path led him by the looming hulk of an ancient pickup and on into neglected pasture at last.

Daniel was on his way to meet Cindabilla's great aunt Nellie, who lived in a camp alongside a track in the woods beyond the field. Last year's grasses were dried and stark, and shot with emerging brambles in need of spring burning to encourage fresh growth. Now he went up the pasture path toward the woods with confidence. In those woods beyond he soon saw a glow, very faint. Was it a light from Aunt Nellie's window?

Daniel looked up at stars, May stars, Mother would say— Hercules and Arcturus heading toward the zenith. Rarely, they had gone out on the desert to escape Dad, or more often gone with him, to leave the heat of Phoenix. Even with the light and pollution of the city beyond, you could see stars. Mother seemed to be learning the stars right along with them, teaching them out of an old book. Leaving the Metropolitan desert was necessary, but ....

The memory of his euphoria after she had confided the planned departure remained, but being in Maine was not what he had foreseen. It was a more impoverished, sorry experience. And tough kids at the new school hounded him almost moment by moment, sometimes punching, kicking or tripping him. He hated the bigotry of their view of his skin. The sound of their speech grated on him. In Phoenix they pronounced their r's, and the view of his skin was accepted erroneously as being Hispanic. Daniel knew he was part Native, like mother, though the fact had never excited his curiosity.

But the move had to be the right thing, despite it all. Mother was doing better.

The glow in the dark woods flickered now with his movement through the trees, even as it increased. The light in there would be soft, he knew, because Aunt Nellie had no electricity in her camp. A good thing Mrs. Melville's tape recorder had batteries. Cindabilla's aunt had a wood stove for heat, kerosene for light, and a refrigerator that ran on propane. If Mother really wanted to live cheap, maybe they could rent a camp somewhere.

He was relieved that they were no longer camped at Deep Hole. Mother thought they should find a safer place, and Daniel had the idea that her joy in Abenaki Notch was gone. The cove at Twitchell Pond, where they were now, was much safer and secluded, but Mother said another move would be necessary when July brought swimmers.

Daniel was lucky to find Cindabilla a friend among his classmates, but would she go on to Hazel Newell High School next year? She knew how to read, which she said was more than a few in her family could do. " 'N they all try t'hide the fact they caunt," she had said. Cindabilla reminded him of Huckleberry Finn—wild and free. But, where Huck's Pap had been a drunk, it was Cindabilla's mother who abused drugs and alcohol. Hannah Sessions' was Cindabilla's struggling grandmother; and the old woman's daughter, Etta, was Cinda's mother. Why, Daniel wondered, do they say people abuse drugs? It always seemed to him the other way around.

Blackflies and mosquitoes were swarming him. He could feel the collar and crown of thorns the latter made feasting on him. The blackflies were biting now too, but he would not feel their bites until later when he tried to sleep.

Clutching his notebook and recorder, he hurried up to the camp and pounded on the door. "I'm here, Miz Sessions! Daniel Twitchell—for the interview."

"Just come in," came a high voice from within. He lifted the latch, pushed on the weathered door, entered and shut it quickly behind him. His back to the room, juggling his notebook and recorder, he heard her say, "Blackflies's is surely bitin', in't they?"

"Yuht." He heard himself say it the way they do in Gottheim. The pronunciations had begun slipping into his talk whether he wanted or not. Before long he'd be flattening his r's and adding extra syllables to words like "here" and "there."

Turning, he saw the frizzle-headed and bespeckled Nellie Sessions, sitting at the table. Her hands were at rest among bits of what look like rock. One of her wrists was splinted and wraped in elastic. Looking about, Daniel saw shelves with white labels, their contents in shadow.

"Sit down heah—Daniel, is it?—n' tell me the purpose of this visit.... See if I undastand Cindabilla right."

Daniel set his things on the scrubbed wooden table. He pulled out the worn ladderback chair and sat down, seeing that what he had taken for bits of rock were arrowheads—bits of quartz and flint. A magnifying glass lay among them beside her long hands, their nails clipped short and clean. Looking about, he saw that this house of Nellie Sessions was like those hands—clean and orderly and calm. What a relief to be away from the wretched house where Cindabilla grew. Why couldn't she live here with Aunt Nellie? But it was small, only a camp. There was a cot with quilt, a sideboard with pump and sink, the shelves, a refrigerator, a table and three chairs. The flame of her lamp gleamed back reflected at him from the windowpanes.

"Miz Melville, our English teacher, told us to do oral history tapes so we have something t'write about. That we learn other things besides writing that way. Cindabilla doesn't wanna do it, so she said I could have y—I mean, talk t'you about arrowheads."

"That so? 'N I say it t'th' recorder?" Nellie looked at the machine significantly. "Will I get t'read what you write?—afta?"

"Yuht ... if I get a good grade. Won't waste y'time if not." He checked the cassette to see if it was in right.

She grinned, saying it sounded fair to her. "You're a Twitchell, in't choo? Heven't had one round in a long time. Twitchells was fom the first."

Daniel wondered what she meant. Did she expect a response? "This is ready," he said. "We test it?"

"You're the boss."

"I'll play back what we said'n see if it works." He pressed stop, then rewind and play.

"Twitchells was fom the first," came her thin voice from the recorder. Across from him, she grinned.

Now He opened his notebook and said, a bit nervously, "Got questions written down."

"I'm ready." Her hair was a frazzled mixture of light and dark around her head, like a nimbus of shadow and silver in the glow of her lamp. Her glasses shone, the eyes behind a penetrating black.

He began with biographical questions, asking when and where she was born, grew up, went to school, and worked. When asked what she did on her job at the glue pin factory, she said, "I fed dowel rods to the machine. That's all. Just stand theya all day ovah that clackity-clack pin machine. It rumbles'n whirls round'n round making that sound. Evah time it goes round, it clips a course into pins, 'n they fall into a basket while the dowels get shorter'n shorter. I watch fah empty sockets'n drop in another rod. Thirty-six sockets I keep filled. Sometimes I work nights. They turn off the heat when office workers go home. Don't try that job in winter! We work in coats, mittens, hats'n stamp ah feet a lot."

Daniel said, "How'd you become interested in arrowheads?"

"These ponds round heah, and the lakes t'the west in't same as they once was. For instance, the dam by the mill down theya controls water levels. When the Indians's heah the water was a lot lower. My Daddy wanted nothing to do with the mills. So he was a caretaker."

"Caretaker?"

"Yuht. He watched ovah people's camps. He was in the woods, cutting, too. When I was li'l I go around with him, and checking on the camps. In the fall, water'd be low and I'd scout the flats fah arrowheads. That started when I was climbing round Littlehale Lake once'n saw this funny crescent shaped rock. It was about fifteen inches long, three inches wide and thick. Slightly ridged. Being just li'l, I couldn't imagine how it got that way. Lugged that thing from camp to camp with my daddy. In one camp was a botanist and he said, 'That looks like mid-archaic.' 'Mid what?' I asked. 'Archaic,' he said. 'Was likely made by an Indian three or four thousand years ago. It's an adze.' Well, my daddy got all excited bout that. Some pleased. I had my regard of him by that."

Nellie Sessions grinned, sweeping wide her arms to take the room in, with its shelves ceiling to floor. "All this, of that regard.

Thanks to that botanist, scientists hev seen my collection fom early days. I've took 'em to places, showed 'em things. Theya's collections in Harvard'n other places on account of that funny old stone. Fom Paleos down to Ceramic Indians: I picked up what Mother Nature washed out fah me'n let the archaeologists do theya digging and sifting. Look't this."

She held out a five-inch piece of worked over rock, slightly raised in the middle. "That's chert formed into a clovis point. Tip's broken off. Paleo-Indians shaped 'em with a hammer stone, just hitting it from side to side—like this." She demonstrated, using a round white stone, but without actually striking.

She looked hard at him, her eyes growing sharper. "Picture this. Round bark-covered huts, or may be covered in hides. Hunks of dried fish hanging in the sun. A man in breechcloth poised to thrust a spear with clovis point into water. Dogs barking. Folks chippin' fom a log in order to hollow out a boat. Some sitting flutin' clovis points. That's how people got theya livin'. *You* could make a living like that!" She poked his dark hand where it lay by the recorder.

Daniel had been watching her, entranced. Now, startled, he stopped the machine. "Better check it," he mumbled. Fumbling, he rewound a bit, played the last words, and stopped.

"Wait a minute," she commanded, laying hold of his wrist with her uninjured hand. "You're Chrischana Twitchell's boy, ain't choo?"

Uneasy, he nodded. She was beginning to spook him. The multiple flames of wicked kerosene reflected in the divided lights of the window panes, and from her glasses, casting a spell. The blackfly bites were beginning to torment him. He wanted to rake his neck with his fingers. He wanted to speak, to hurry on with the interview—or just get out. But Daniel waited, forcing himself to stay with the assignment.

"Chrischana Twitchell's son," she said. "Theya y'go! You're pot Indian! Indians was fom the first."

Nellie curled her good hand around his wrist. "Don't push that button!" She commanded. "I'm gont tell you something, Daniel Twitchell'n I don't want it on tape!" Then she let go his wrist and sat back in her hard chair.

"Now theya is no proof o'this. If they was, I'd let the tape run. But I know for fact. Y'see, my daddy's people is millers. They all made money'n their kids is mill owners today. But my daddy had no pot of milling. We stayed poor, but did all right. Look at all this." She nodded her head, indicating the contents of her shelves.

But though agreeing somewhat, Daniel could only think how some kids in his class would say, "All what?"

"You seen these mills in these mountains, Daniel. Every year these owners meet and confirm to keep wages low, to a certain rate. They fixed it so workers who quit the mill would be blackballed— meaning not hired in another mill till six months, at least, passed. Every year, at that meeting, they agree on it. It went on five decades.... Maybe still does."

She said all this and stopped—significantly—her eyes glowing like coals, flames reflecting.

Daniel looked down. What did she want? What's this got to do with anything? He was only fourteen years old!

"All right," He heard her say. "You can go on now." She nodded toward the recorder. "When we get done taping, I'll show you my fust adze."

On his way back down the path, he looked through trees toward the distant lights of Cindabilla's farmhouse. He found himself recalling what Nellie Sessions had said about finally receiving a dime's raise last month. After twenty-five years of making glue pins, she now earned ten cents over minimum wage. He thought again how her wrist was braced against stress and pain, and wondered what it was like to stand for more than two decades in the same spot. Eight hours a day, dropping dowel rods into a pin machine. How many rods did she throw in over the years? Did she get dizzy watching them all spin around?

Sheltering from abnormal spring heat, Chrischana sits huddled against hewn granite. She is drenched in repellent, keeping blackflies at bay. The sound of Birch River, flowing through a channel between the hewn rocks behind her, sounds a note of coolness. But even the shiny leaves of beech and maple shading her give no relief from the heat. The fiddleheads left over after Balder's harvest a few weeks ago have opened into ferns at Chrischana's feet. The sound of water pouring past huge remnants of last century's industry soothes from the heat and exertion of her hike in. Chrischana's not used to walking, and her limbs are leaden, also, with defeat. Lying back, she lolls against the cool old stones of Mason's Mills. Still, she finds no thought to guide in her troubles.

And what about the problem of survival.... AFDC is promised, she has food stamps and a rent voucher. But welfare is not what Chrischana wants. Going down to Guildford, sitting in that office ... being questioned by that woman.... The awful admission of domestic degradation. The grief of it. Yet Chrischana has used nothing given her except a few food stamps. She can accept none of this. How can she? It's the failure of everything, and, yet, even this wouldn't be so bad ... if only the ache will depart.

....She keeps seeing that light intimate touch of his new young love ... upon his hand. That intimate brushing of Balder's fingers....

How could she have allowed herself to hope? Worse, how could she have hoped ... all the way across the country ... without knowing it? Across mountains and plains, going through great Midwestern cities, on rolling farmland and into the woodland of Pennsylvania and New England.... Through all their current trials and the free familial joys of their travels. Through it she tried to keep after herself: The Balder she knew no longer lived. He had changed into a heavy, slow family man of responsibilities. His mind, like her own should be, would now be, a world away from the moony-nights-through-trees of their joint youth. At one point in her life she had forgotten him altogether—for years! In the early years of Peter's love, with childbirth and partying and the endless gabbing with other young mothers—she had been happy. It had become a fact that the Balder she knew had receded into memory, not to be known in any other way again.

....That intimate brushing of his fingers.... Chrischana feels the heat of her shame and failure rising in her, rising and recurring as it has again and again since she saw that touch.

Seeing his car at Gott'im Chair—the exact car in which Daniel was conceived!—and hearing from Asa Bartlett that he was unmarried still. These things had encouraged the false hidden hope. Seeing the intimacy of Balder and Gloria exposed it.

Oh! She is bright, that Gloria Fay.

Balder's own features have matured; his body with more muscle, heft, power. But how can it be that he seems barely aged? He is still vital, young, happy. It must be from a lack of responsibility, that true heritage of adulthood. No one can walk and laugh—as he did with Gloria, who is occupied or burdened with real life. He lives without a care!

She opens her eyes, staring up at the configuration of fresh leaves against the spaces of colorless sky.

He has a problem now.

.... That fallen look. The darkness of his expression.... With compassion, with shame, water rises in her eyes. He suspects a son. A stranger, but his living offspring. Of whom he was bereaved.

There is a path into woodland where mill foundation stones stand silent in their moldering vigil. The stones are massive, dark, split here and there by living roots; crumbling from frost and lichen, bitten by organisms too small to see. The spirit of human industry is idle here, industry once powered by water brought from above. Here boards were sawn, shingles cut; wool combed then carded, cloth dressed; and grist was ground for the ovens and stomachs of townsfolk round about. In this now secret and abandoned site, the human and material needs of the community were with constancy met. Here labor provided sustenance, fitness, aim: the feel of rough boards in hefting hands, of lanolin soft in the shorn fibers of sheep; sound—for the listening ear—of water pouring and the creaking, turning of cylinders. Here, at Mason's Mills.

All the quiet ghosts about this place are invisible, unavailable to the troubled woman who sits idle against the stone. Chrischana is here, thinking again of leaving town, finding nowhere in Gottheim, in God's House, to earn her living and that of her sons.

But now she stops her ruinous thoughts to listen. Is this someone coming down the path? Someone is singing—or chanting? She can't make out the words for the ceaseless flow of the stream. Gradually, the murmur of human speech increases, as the walker comes on:

Bear, bear keep away....

Chrischana peers through the leaves hiding her face from view. The sayer approaches, but it is moments before Chrischana understands this odd sight. Surely she knows the strangely burdened person? Yes, and another soul hardly changed in fifteen years. *Maybe a glance at her shy face will tell me of her aging ... and the stoop and stiffness of gait.*

Yes, this is the only difference in the pattern Elda Simon's ever made against stems and foliage of the woodland. She wore a red or pink bandanna, a T-shirt, and dungarees rolled up at the ankle ever since Chrischana can remember. But, what's the great thing on her arm?... a bird is it?... with a cloth over its head?

Yes. Mrs. Simon shuffles along, balancing a great living burden on her arm. It's the weirdness of the woman. Always she was weird. You could remember upon the eternal strangeness of Elda Simon like you could the gossip of Asa Bartlett. Most people in Chrischana's place, seeing this woman, would be stifling laughter. But she has always respected the older woman's ways with animals. There's something maybe spiritual in her handling and care of things found insignificant by others.

The woman stops on the path among woodland shadows, looking around. Chrischana's discomfort watching in secret grows. Yet, she does not want to startle Mrs. Simon at work. Can't tell what a wild creature might do.... She's looking for something.... A perch. She kneels at a hunk of deadfall, shifting the great bird onto it. The bird feels with its horned and feathered talons then moves off onto the branch.

Mrs. Simon sinks back on her butt, weary from her exertions; seeming to fold upon herself as though the impulse of life has evaporated. She *has* aged. Chrischana restrains a kindly urge to aid her. Better let her see the task through without distraction.

—Asa's owl is it?—stands quietly, locked to the branch. After several moments, the woman straightens up, begins loosening the bird's hood. Watching, Chrischana tenses.

A hooked beak emerges, followed by fierce frontal eyes and ear tufts. The great horned owl shakes itself off the branch, as Elda backs away. Hissing and beating, the bird tilts off. Looking fiercely back at the woman, again and again the owl moves its wings, as if mightily to fly. Failing, the bird yet manages to put several yards between itself and its benefactress.

Chrischana rises, rustling foliage as she emerges. "Mrs. Simon!"

Startled, Elda whirls. "Who's that!"

Chrischana steps out from the leaves, saying, "It's only me, Mrs. Simon. Chrischana Twitchell." Crossing through new bracken, she takes the path.

"Chrischana ... Twitchell?" But a moment passes. Chrischana wonders if she will remember—if she will even know who she is. But the other says, "Oh. The li'l Indian maid—Jasper Mary—waunt you?"

The woman must've forgotten she was once Balder's girlfriend—if she ever knew. Balder was not one to talk much about things personal. And Mrs. Simon always seemed a bit remote, ever immersed in wildlife and more absent than not when among people. Now she turns back to the bird, saying, "Caunt talk just at the moment."

Chrischana comes up behind her to watch the owl's struggle. The bird is well into the bracken and moose maple, but its thrashing has stopped. Elda says, "She's resting a bit, I s'pose.

Now, as they watch, it beats again but with more power and control. Beating, the owl flies into the branches of a middle distance maple.

Elda relaxes. "She'll be all right now." She turns toward the younger woman. "People guess I should've let the Roebuck boy finish her out of her misery, but I just caunt do that to an owl, could you?"

Chrischana couldn't help but think that anyone but Mrs. Simon would have made some statement designed to get her explaining herself in some way, maybe to talk about where she's been.

"Why not help an owl?" Christy answers, looking into her shy eyes. "Look at the good they do keeping the rodent population down." She smiles her slight smile. "Rats don't stand a chance."

Elda Simon looks away. "If I hadn't been to the grocer's that night to see it happen...." The sentence trails off.

"This is a long way from Simons Ledge," says Chrischana; flushing, aware that her internal criticism of townspeople might extend to herself.

But Elda smiles her shy smile, answering, "Had t'come a good way t'help 'em get stotted away from people. Elsewhere they might not give'em a chance."

They start down the path together, Elda with a last look over her shoulder. The owl is still resting in the maple.

Chrischana says, "There a bear around here somewhere?"

Elda nudges her. "See that track? Fresh."

Looking in the mire among sparse grass, Chrischana sees what might pass for the print of a fat barefoot child.

"Uh-oh." Startling a mother with cubs would be a project. "I always wonder what they find to eat this time of year. Flowers haven't ripened to berries yet."

"Oh, they'll eat just about anathin. Slugs ants honey rodents carrion everything. Root round like an ol'pig. They ah pigs!" She has been looking this way and that, admiring what she sees. Now she says, "Just look at all that's growing heah. Starflower, gaywings, lousewort, baneberry. Look! Jack'n-the-pulpit!" She ticks off flowers, families of flowers, as they go along; looking carefully, taking great pleasure in seeing. "But I guess you know what's good to eat and steep—being pot Indian."

But Chrischana flushes saying, "People think Natives should know that stuff, but I'm not native enough. I was raised like anyone else around here.... Like Balder was. Used to trap.... That's about it. I did some fishing, berrying of course."

Elda grimaces at mention of trapping, but she says only, "Balder knows what to eat, what not. We learned that stuff from field books, whatnot."

Chrischana feels rebuffed, whether Mrs. Simon intends it or not—which the younger woman doubts. She thinks now how far she has moved from Balder. Or, no, how little she ever really knew him. Again she sees Gloria's caressing fingers ... that gentle cutting gesture. And here is Mrs. Simon, likely unaware that Chrischana is a stranger here now. Does Mrs. Simon even know I've been away?

The older woman is saying, "Anaone can learn this stuff. A good guide would be *Grove's Basic Herbal*. All the uses ah in theya:

culinary, medicinal, cosmetic. Lore's in theya too. The book's in Gott'im Library."

Not you, too.... Everybody's got something you're doing wrong. Chrischana murmurs something to signify a response. Actually, she has thought of searching out this kind of knowledge, but someday, not today. There are decisions, and challenges enough ahead. Daniel, Nathan, Benaiah.... Her boys need a community, safe, sure. *They need a home.*

The two women walk on, more words about plants and animals spoken along the way. The trail winds back around Mason Mountain, comes to the gravel shoulder where Chrischana's faded old Bonneville is parked. She offers Mrs. Simon a ride, and, after hesitating, the woman accepts.

And last they reached the shaded lane to the old Simon house, Elda saying, "Just let me out heah. Posey might be about'n she's due to fawn. I'm afraid we might disturb her."

Chrischana watches her hobble the lane, watching this way and that. Now she seems to loosen up and walk with some grace. Just as the woman becomes lost in shadow at the far end, it strikes Chrischana. She turns her gaze away, up the gravel road toward the heat-hazed mountain.

There goes Daniel's grandmother.

Elda Simon walks past hummingbirds sipping in the honeysuckle tangled thickets about the house. At last she thinks she understands.

Her coming took away his Vietnam eyes. Her rejection brought them on again. Why did she come back—if not to be with him?

God. Worried about Balder again. He's been in his room, issuing only at night to look up something in a book. Or go look at the stars. Not this! Not when he got done with that awful war in Southeast Asia ... in his room three years. Why can't all that melancholy seclusion stay back where he left it? She sighs. Was it two weeks ago he was happy?... It's like a fall from heaven.

To her Balder Simon is a secret, hidden. She has never been able to fathom him. Yet, she, more than anyone, knows Balder. She ponders him in her heart.

Thinking God's Thoughts

By day, and outside the window, he sees green buds emerge, leaf, filing along lit branches. But at night Balder turns from surveying the jungle to see his best buddy's guts, blossoming, a curtain of blood: blood, tumult, blood, shattered bodies and friendships, blood; his mind populated with it. He might lift the sash to hear pine boughs intoning up on Simons Ledge, acknowledging the booming, hoping to displace the roar of the war, of choppers beating and B-52 bombers howling to heaven. But the wind-freshened moonlight, washing faint whiteness into the woodland, cannot take it away. If he went down to stand in the yard (and sometimes he does), and looked up to see stars in the branches, even there the war would pursue.

These thoughts the window of Balder's room reveals, as it has always revealed, since all those years ago when, as a riven veteran, he returned to Gottheim. One reprieve from the anguish of that time came during his stopover in New York. Was it Pennsylvania Station or Grand Central? There was the vision ... was it a vision?.... It was a profound sense of *Love*. God, loving the bounty of humanity Balder saw walking—like sheaves of wheat walking in God's great eye. Only travelers, commuters, panhandlers—walking, crisscrossing multitudes ... all deeply, profoundly respected and loved.

When will he be able to spit out the cud of self recrimination? If only he could forget (no not forget, but something ...) that Dana Mills is dead, that Tim has—. No. Tim Bean was a casualty of Nam as surely as if he were killed in a chopper crash on the Cambodian border or earmarked for death in Cai Lay as an enemy of the Viet

Cong. Except Tim drowned off the coast of Maine while sea kayaking in a storm. Like Balder, he was never able to leave the pictures and defeats to their place in that strange, but never distant, land.

A Roccomeeco native, one of eight hundred Maine Indians to see combat, Tim Man Bean maniacally set himself on self-destruction. Not once or twice, but three times he took his tour, never fulfilled, never satisfied, ever seeking the great intensity of life. After the second tour, Balder understood that Tim's road would be both deeper in punishment and shorter in duration than his own. Tim's name will never be engraved on the Wall, being but one of that number which would double or treble the list—suicides every one. Balder looks at the stars in the dark branches, musing. If Tim had held on a bit longer.... Maybe maturity and involvement would've exorcised the torment of Tim. Eventually. Maybe. But it's too late now. Tim Bean died right before Gloria came.

Balder is one of eighteen thousand Mainers to receive the bloody baptism that crippled a generation. War. It turned the dominant preceding generation into heroes, and its offshoot into "draft evading cowards" or "emotional cripples." What's the good, the purpose, of this psychological pain? Why does he find himself in this room again—pondering pain?

Beyond his personal experience he sees the mistake of that older generation—self-deceived, impinging almost unforgivably on its children. They conceived and developed an ideal of valor based on World War II, and then, being so impressed by their mighty experience, used it ever after as a template on those to follow. That template promoted industry and profit, greasing its increase with young man in Cold War surrogate "skirmishes." What was that bumper sticker he saw yesterday? "El Salvador is Spanish for Vietnam." Each great power embroiling its young, as, today, the better-red-than-dead of the current Soviet generation is juice in a fruitless war in Afghanistan. He understands that the older generation will continue, until its passing, to exacerbate the pain, and to divide the Nam vets from the non vets with painful regret, recriminations. Balder wants none of the division. He sees his generation as a whole—wounded whole. Yeah, he has forgiven, is no longer bitter. The older generation is mistaken, that's all.

Tim has died. Balder, on the other hand, is alive. Seeing the stars. And now, even though he's back in this room, so much is mitigated. The emotion bringing him back this spring is—other. Like budding leaves on beeches maples popples, he will emerge, open and leaf in this new spring. What was cut off, taken from him in the fiery war, is not being restored to Balder (youth peace wholeness cannot come again this side of heaven, blessed be the name of God)—but something new is given. A son.

Family. People. Intimate, connected.

(One thing greatly interested him to look up: the biological pathways of conception; intricacies of how people are formed.) Sitting before a window (sending in the scent of spring), he sees these people ...like the stars up there in the dark boughs. In muscle and bone, in genetic material, they are in it together with him. He knows how Abraham felt, Abram.

That's who I was, but now Abraham. And Daniel is my Isaac. Generations could come of this. Generations—begot in a single night in my '55 Chevy.

Sitting here in the old Morris chair, looking up through the branches, he smiles.

Can I stand being told that Daniel isn't my son? My son. Seeing them there like that.... At Deep Hole! Daniel must have been conceived there. Apart from Abenaki Notch, Balder has no memory of her body (of Chrischana's high brown breasts, long dark tangle of hair hanging down). Because of her, Deep Hole is the most intimate place on earth. Isn't that the real reason for bringing Gloria there?

Gloria. Gloria Chrischana Daniel. And mother. These are the people. They are the reason Balder can live. Without them he might zigzag, flounder. Mechanical ability has given life structure, but now there are people to be responsible to. This is what the baptism in blood brought him (and almost cut him off from): the knowledge that life's meaning indwells human flesh. His brothers of the battlefield showed him this in bloody dying, some in his arms. Relatedness: deep, indelible, painful. In this becoming a father— beyond being only a son—he finds a pattern revealed: a tricornered pattern, inscribed with human faces. Father, Mother, Child.

Again comes the sight of Chrischana standing there in the budding with her three sons ... Chrischana. Older, fuller, unhappy, *mature*. She steps out of the remembered form: the tawniness; shapely, limbly, the earthy exciting smell of her. Surprising how well he remembers the quiet proud girl on a prancing pony, feathered like a bird. An icon changed. She stands now between children, fruit of her sexuality, generosity, verve.... And that look on her face.... Unhappiness yes, and something else. Fear. Somehow he frightened her, but not intentionally. He recognized his sternness toward her only afterward.

She must have been wary of seeing him ... having abandoned him abruptly fifteen years ago. Leaving without a word. Because of Daniel?

He has been in this room more than a week, an indulgence. But now his soul is steadied; it's time to leave this place. Can't leave them out there like that, homeless, camping at Abenaki Notch. It's rained twice already. Each time he fought the impulse to jump into the truck, bring them back to *Simons Ledge*. He can't just force himself on them, impose his own order on their lives.

Where's the other man, the father of the other two? For all Balder knows the man is with them now....

Gloria. Balder Simon loves Gloria and plans to divert his life into her. Into her, not into her "life-style." Their plans are so opposed it's funny. Cosmically funny. Though he is nothing but traditional— fiercely so—this match can't possibly travel a traditional road. But he will not cease to love, though Gloria will go her way—zigzagging, sure—and he will go the way he must. No matter how she tugs.

Now that Daniel has come he feels sure about building his own house. May it be like a great tree, housing many birds. Gloria and Daniel will be in the roots of its foundation. Bride and son? ...

Balder frowns, his gaze sliding down the weathered window frame. Could do with scraping and painting, inside and out. So much work this old house needs. The breeze slides under its slightly raised sash, falling cool on his lax hands. A frown deepens. He loves two women. Chrischana was the wife of his brief youth. But Gloria is his bride. When he first came into this room again, he did not know what to do with them. Still doesn't. But his feelings are sorted. He finds order in the way things have fallen: Chrischana has been faithful in raising their child. Though his being left out was wounding, he is not angry or bitter on consideration. (*What is that haunting Chrischana's eyes?*) Soon he will thank her for bearing and raising Daniel.)

He shakes his head. The boy is something. Balder feels luckier than he can express. Finding Daniel is like finding gem quality beryl in the belly of a fresh-caught trout. *Don't let her tell me he's not my son.* The fervor of this hope surprises him. Sitting between the old wallpapered walls, he feels it again and again. Daniel was watching his brothers. He has a sense of responsibility. Daniel caught dinner. He understands and acts on the realities of life. Only fourteen years old, right? After it all ... how can a gift like this be delivered whole? (But he should not have subjected Daniel to such scrutiny as he did upon seeing him. The bald look will make it harder to gain his trust.)

Life! What a mystery. How can Gloria come here and fall for him, like the sun dropping into his lap? He was all set, resigned, to being only an aging mother's keeper, a tinkerer and fishing fool ... after the fires of Vietnam. It was to be a plodding existence in Gottheim. That was a month ago (and the grief of Tim's death still fresh).

Balder rubs a thoughtful thumb along the whiskers of his newly bearded jawline. The breeze brings a distant sounding of the village clock up the mountainside to him. Even after a lifetime it surprises how well the sound travels. Early morning, 3:30 a.m..

Stretching, the man stands. Time to go fishing.

—

Gloria pulls up to the sidewalk beside white washed half-barrels overflowing with flowers. She looks at her watch. Almost lunchtime. The day is breezy but beginning to heat up. *Might put the top down on my little red baby after lunch.* She picks up Guerber's *Norseman* from the seat beside her, thoughtfully fingering the old and lose binding. She opens once more to the place marked.

"Gradually the light died out of his eyes, a careworn look came into his face, and his step grew heavy and slow." The words signified the god Balder's want of spirit in the wake of foreshadowing dreams. The son of Odin and Frigga, whom nothing else might conquer nor weapon destroy, would be slain by the lowly mistletoe, a parasite of the oak.

What a charming story, not at all the kind I'm used to.
Brooding and romantic, sad. Before this I read only contemporary realism. Idiosyncratic and subjective, it was how she got her realism—not from actual life. But the sagas are not sentimental. She feels in them the blood and steel of thirsty swords, a dark violence of molten fires, the monstrous cold and ice of the European north.

Gloria looks up at the brick building where the Gottheim Library is housed, dim stacks visible behind the divided lights of its twin bay windows. She looks at the word Gottheim over the granite lintel of the entrance. The roots of the word must be related to words in Guerber also ending in *heim*, Teutonic or German for *home*.

She turns to another marked page. "To give light to the world ... the gods studded the heavenly vault with sparks secured from Muspells-heim, points of light which shone steadily through the gloom like brilliant stars." *Muspells-heim*, she muses. Home of fire. Nifl-heim, home of mist. She shivers with delight, smiles. Gloria is liking this mythic way of seeing things. It's like the way she feels about Jasper Mountain. Mythic imagery seems appropriate to the life she finds in Maine. Couldn't life all over the planet be expressed mythologically? Thoughts like this didn't occur to her until Guerber.

Closing the book, she opens the car door into the wind. Nearing the library door, she is disappointed to notice the sign, *closed*. Oh well, use the slot beside the door. Now she will have to come back for it instead of renewing. She drops the book and turns, staring absently off across the Common toward one of the churches.

Gloria is eager for her lunch date with Balder at the crappy diner. More than two weeks have gone by since the snowmelt ritual at Deep Hole. His long absence must have something to do with the woman they saw at Abenaki Notch. There was a quality of hardness in his continued silence in the car afterward. Gloria feels the need of reassurance. The strange separation and silence have shaken her confidence in the relationship. If not for his blunt avowal on the phone early this morning, she might believe it was over. He never spoke of love till now. It's the gift this time apart has given. But she has promised herself to be honest. I'm not capable of undying love. I know that much about myself. I know from past experience. Even so, Gloria is sure that she will go on loving Balder a very long time. Maybe she'll be loving him still at thirty, even. Five years is a practical scope for fidelity. If you can't manage it with someone like Balder ... well, there's something wrong with you! She smiles to herself on the windy sidewalk.

Gloria slides back into the sports car. On the satisfying purr of its engine, she glides round the corner and past the storefronts lining the shores of Hutchins Pond. How can Balder stand that crappy place, that greasy food! Oh well—it will be gone soon. It's in *The Village Voter*. Letters to the editor are shriveling up the page. Doesn't matter: Balder will die an old Mainer, felled by grease, not mistletoe.

Near the elbow in the counter, Balder sits at the end booth of Decatur's Diner, idly stirring his coffee. The colorful, greasy old neon clock above the order window gives him a small block of time till Gloria shows. Maybe there's time to go to the chair factory and apologize to Vernon for his unexcused unexplained absence. He owes them that. While he was out, there was only Gilbert Gage to keep things running, but he's capable. Then, after dinner here with Gloria, he'll go to the Abenaki Notch to see Chrischana. Daniel's probably in school now.

But, instead of rushing, he sips the light coffee; frowning, thinking of that walk around the mill in Guildford this morning. It took more than an hour to compass the paper maker. He had come out of the employment office and caught sight of its steam billowing on the wind. The stacks and gray monolithic structures stood just beyond the town's red-brick blocks.

The woman in the employment office was encouraged by his qualifications, saying the mill would be taking applications owing to scheduled retirements in maintenance. The state employment service was to screen all applicants. The crisp and angular woman put Balder's file in the Adirondack Paper stack. "Just between you and me," she said with a resigned air, "It's a plus that you live outside the immediate area. The company's new office of Human Resources avoids the hiring of town applicants if it can."

"Why's that?"

She hesitated. "I think the reasoning goes ... that people here think they're entitled. I'm not sure I blame them—The G'fid people, I mean. Look what we put up with. I don't need to tell you about the river. Or the smell in our buildings and houses that can never be eradicated. It accumulates, turns stale, gets staler. 'It's the smell of money,' they say. So more people ought to share in it. Look at this town. It's picturesque; views that don't include the mill are beautiful. I know—'Without the mill there'd be no town.' But they take all the sludge and spread it on woodland along the townline. No one knows what the result of that is on wildlife. Fortunately, the taxes they pay keep education on a par with that of Southern Maine. We're grateful for that. Many of us are. Schools to the east are faculty poor, technology poor, extracurricularly poor in comparison."

She stood then, looking a bit chagrined, probably for revealing so much. "We'll be in touch if you make the first cut."

It was afterward that he decided to take that walk. Balder had been coming to Guildford all his life on errands. Adirondack Paper was the single impressive fact about the would-be gracious New England town, with its spires and rooftops clustering among the foliage. Although it had changed hands twice in the last few decades, the mill was a singular legend in the county during the late 1800's. The town and mill were founded by Andrew MacDonald. Unbeknownst to Balder, he did this by quietly buying up land north of the tiny farming community of Guildford Center, and securing riverfront property around Roccomeeco Falls. A holdout against the proffered seven dollars an acre, one shrewd farmer demanded top dollar from MacDonald's agents who reported back to their boss with scorn: "Crazy fool wants fifty an acre for the rocky old headland!" MacDonald got a glint in his eye (not unlike the glint James Fay often noted in Harry Golding's eye). "Pay the crazy fool his fifty dollars for each of those rocky acres!"

For all its bold monolithic stance in the community, Balder had rarely considered the mill when he was driving around town on errands. He would have noticed only if it turned up missing. Now he thought why not take a look at the place he'd been taking for granted. If things went as he hoped, Balder would be spending his work-life to help keep the place going. So he tramped on a dirt lane beside the railroad track leading toward the company railyard.

Dust devils spun on the lane ahead of him. Enlarging as he neared, the mill spread out before him like a city; end to end in conveyors, concrete and steel. Heavy with great insulators, the girders and gridwork of substations complicated the view. Smokestacks towered, pouring forth a white mixture of smoke and steam. Electric towers strung with miles of cable and conduit were dwarfed by the monstrous buildings above. Inside, he knew, forests were debarked and chipped, wood pulp was chemically digested; as slurry it traveled a wire mesh toward dryers, presses, calendars and winders, mysteriously transformed as paper.

Now, as he walked, Balder was assaulted by a brutal, even tactile, stench—both chemical and organic. A corruption-of-vegetable stench, piercing to the back of his nares and prickling through his lower face as though he had swallowed hot mustard. Stung, he looked down into the mill yard. Rumbling clinking roaring and screeching, the yard moved with trucks, cranes, conveyors and tiny hard-hatted workers. Over all swam shadows of vapor, swift and dark upon the swarming mill yard. Walking on, he rounded a bend beside the crusted sludge-delivery building, stopping to watch dried residue of papermaking crap itself into the filthy bins. Crusty trucks were lined up to receive and cart sludge off to the edge of town.

Continuing on, Balder passed a lake of sewage, hidden behind a half-hearted screen of popples in spring leaves already flecked in dried spume. Looking at them, he recalled that when paper was first made in the Meguntic Mountains popple were considered premier papermaking trees. Today spruce was supreme and popple only filler. When they saw it quivering in the woods people said with scorn that, like weeds in a garden, it should be eradicated. Ever sensitive to the faintest breeze, the popple screening the sewage before him shivered mightily in the dry wind. At first he thought little of their dry hustling sounds. But as he peered down through the spume-coated leaves on the scummy colorless pools, the hustlings turned sorrowful and frenzied in his ears. He watched the wind whip up the filthy foam, bubbling and spitting in scuzzy glee.

Glee? He thought it then. And he thinks it now, sitting in Decatur's diner. What made him think of glee?

Later, rounding the sewage plant, he came out above the pulpwood yard where mountainous piles, from clearcuts all over the northern woodland, towered. Beyond these ranges of pulpwood, were great ridges of wood chips. He walked on, watching chips spewn out of the wood room from nozzles with necks like those of praying mantises. Truck dumps upended the beds of semis, puking out chips from distant shipping operations and wood mills; bulldozers busily worked them up into the great piles. Pulpwood had come, in one form or another, from all over Maine, Vermont, New Hampshire, even parts of Quebec. Gazing on the monstrous piles, Balder thought suddenly what a fixture it all was. Week in, week out, every week of his life, he had seen this place full of junked trees—trees cut to junks and piled to a height of seven or eight stories. He stood watching until he could absorb no more. Then he turned and walked back to his decades old Chevy.

He holds up his mug, signaling Melvinia to pour him another. In comes Huldah Littlefield with her boy, setting the toddler to stand on the booth behind Balder. He turns to look thoughtfully at little Simeon. The boy's great eyes and soft expression impress the man with innocence. Transfixed, he feels a slow smile coming.

"Hi, Balda," says Huldah. "Didn't I see y'cah in G'fid earlier?"

"Yuht. Down applying t'work in the mill. You work in theya, don't choo?"

Her fringe of hair bobs as, nodding, she settles Simeon. "Might put me on a papah machine, but fah now I'm doing custodial work. I was down't the basement last night, hosing out stock. Waste's unbelievable! Theya making way too much prep fah the storage chests t'hold."

"Whad they do then with all the extra?"

She shrugs. "Goes to the sewage plant. Turns out sludge, I s'pose."

"So they cut down trees, truck'em t'the mill, chip'em, slop'em, hose'em out, then turn it all into sludge t'spread on the woods?"

Huldah giggles. "Sometimes seems like it."

"I'd be taking the woods apart every day with a wrench'n pair of pliers. Don't it make you mad?"

"Not if I'm getting paid. Y'get use to it. You wouldn't believe the waste goes on—evah department. Wait'll you get in. If you got mad all the time, you wouldn't work theya."

She spies her sister, Polly Proctor, waving from the other end of Decatur's. Grabbing up the boy, she hurries off toward Polly.

Balder watches after big-eyed Simeon as she carries him, bouncing, away.

Outside, in Decatur's parking lot, a dust cloud blew past Chrischana's Bonneville. She studied the windows of the maroon and silver diner through her pocked windshield. Balder's aqua Chevy was sandwiched between a Ford pickup and Bronco. She had not counted on this, wanting only to see Decatur and find out what his plans were when the diner got done. Chrischana's gaze stopped at the far window where Balder sat in the end booth, motioning to her. Too late to pretend she didn't see him. She felt tears coming and widened her eyes to stop them.

He was still waving her toward him as she came through the glass door of the diner. "Sit down, Chrischana?" he asked as she approached.

She sat down across from him and clasped her hands on the tabletop, pretending to study a missing chip in its linoleum covering.

This is silly, she thought, and looked up.

With surprise she saw that he needed a shave. Or, was he growing a beard? But hunting season was months away. There were plenty who got started during buck season and never bothered to shave again.

He was saying he had planned to drive out to the Notch to find her. "Sorry I waited s'long. Could we meet at *Simons Ledge* or someplace t'talk?"

Avoiding his eyes, she looked again at his darkened jawline. It was expectant, taut. Glancing around, seeing that they were alone at this end, she said, "Well ... I can just tell you .... Yes, Daniel is your son."

She saw him swallow, relax. She'd forgotten the way he tensed up over something important to him. And how his jaw relaxed suddenly when he was eased. She looked into his intense northern blue eyes then, not wanting to lose his gaze during this confirmation.

Balder was the one to look away now. "... Knew it!" He murmured, and turned to face her again. "I'm glad, Chrischana. Very, very glad. We made him together. "

She nodded, lightening. Feeling a smile slowly rising in her. They looked at one another across the table, smiling. "Damn!" He smacked the old linoleum with the palm of his hand. It stung, but he grinned.

Melvinia came over, grinning behind her outsized glasses, saying, "Don't choo two look happy's clams." She turned toward the door, tittering. "Look out! Heah comes Libby with that camera."

Little Libby Greenleaf came swinging down the aisle, clutching her camera. "Miz Sessions," she said, "How about a picture o'you and Mr. Decatur fah *The Voter*. We are doing a story on the history o'this place!" She walked back toward the order window, calling for Decatur to come out.

And so it happened that a photo would appear in next week's edition—a symmetrical grouping of Melvinia and Decatur flanking a grinning pair in an old booth in Gott'im's local diner. Chrischana would clip it out and give it to Daniel along with the strange and unsettling news that the man at Deep Hole was his father.

When Libby was gone and Decatur had retreated to his kitchen, Melvinia took their orders. Balder prevailed in buying Chrischana lunch, and now they sat back, each wondering where to go from here. At last he said, "I waunt t'help."

She looked at him with her Native eyes, slowly shaking her head. "We're a unit, the boys'n I. Together we're going t'make it."

She was letting him know that the other man was out of the picture and that she would not split up the boys. He smiled a bit, saying with regret, "You lost the Maine way o'speaking." He was dreaming some, remembering the girl he knew.

She nodded but hurried on. "All I need's a job. Picked up a few house-keeping jobs—spot work only—last week, but we need something permanent. I was going to ask Decatur about his plans."

He grinned. "You can have my job. I in't been t'work since I saw Daniel. Chair factory must be hurting by now."

She smiled and slowed down some, taking time to remember—seeing him bent over the engine of a Chevy. "If only I paid attention when you tried to show me how engines work."

He was looking at her, taking in her blue kerchief, the long dark braid hanging down along her breast. Her black T-shirt with a winged Harley-Davidson emblem on the pocket. He looked away, out the window at the faded gold Bonneville. "That rustworks bring you all the way fom Phoenix? Must'o cost a fortune in gas."

She nodded, murmuring *a fortune,* waiting for him to continue. He ran his fingers absently over the blister scars on his arms. The sleeves of Balder's flannel shirt were rolled up. Chrischana looked carefully then at his forearms and drew back. "What's this?" And instantly she regretted the exclamation, regretted prying.

"Those are my A.O. tattoos." He rolled his sleeves down over them, saying, "From Vietnam. It was hard to avoid that stuff over theya."

"Agent Orange!? You were *in it*?!"

"Went theya afta you left. Got scared when MIT tried t'draft me. 'Twas the only way I could think of to escape."

But his humor could not bring back the ease of a moment ago. So hard to see him now, to try talking as if nothing had happened. Dimly she understood that a period of adjustment was needed, a sense of where they stood today. But it eluded her. The moon had moved off from the earth, the sun had reversed its course over the mountains. A child had been conceived, shot off toward manhood. Two hearts had been broken and horribly scarred on the mend. She felt her father in her arms, falling. She wanted to fly again, leave the ordered burger, *the world,* behind. But Balder's voice checked her.

"Look Chrischana, it was what I chose to do, fight Communism, get out of Gott'im, see the world." He wanted to take her hand, but stopped. The gentle touch might complicate the fragile new relation. "We've got Daniel. And I'm not gonna leave y'blowing in the breeze. We've both got something t'do in caring fah him. Is this right?" With relief, he saw her nod, eyes once more on the chipped linoleum. He wanted to open his wallet immediately but understood that this would only embarrass them both. "We'll go to some court and have'em work out support payments. I'd pay t'them, they pay you, OK?"

She looked out the smudged window, bemused and sad. A little red car pulled into the parking lot. Chrischana gazed absently at it until the blond driver got out into the wind, buffeted by a dust devil. Chrischana looked toward the kitchen and saw Melvinia lifting plates from the window onto her tray.

"That'll be fine, Balder," she said, snatching a pen from his breast pocket and hastily scrawling her post office box number on a napkin. "Sorry t'rush." She pushed it toward him and stood. "And thanks for the burger. I'll eat at the counter." She walked away.

Surprised, he turned to look but saw Gloria coming up behind him. The light of her smile filled him; her great eyes, glossy swinging pageboy; her crisp classiness rejoicing him. She leaned over to kiss him, a brushing kiss, soft as the petals of a wild rose. She pulled back, startled by the scratch of his whiskers. He caught a whiff of her perfume, smooth and light, as she slid into the seat across from him.

She resolved on no mention of the one who had just vacated the booth. Nor would she be the first to bring up the separation immediately past. She would not say what she thought of the *facial hair*. "Ah." She chuckled, eyeing the food Melvinia set before him. "Having our grease in the form of the hamburger plate today!" She lifted a shapely eyebrow, smiling. "Somehow, I don't think I'll miss this place as much as you will."

"Well," he returned, "I may not have t'miss it! Nevah know what can happen. Decatur's could go down and spring up over theya." He gestured across the road with a wave of his fork. "God is spooky that way. Can't deprive a small town of its grease'n not have repercussions."

She made a wry face, said, "And who's going to see to it? The Goldings? The condominium owners on Roberts Pond? How about that new bed'n breakfast on Livery Street?"

"Maybe all! You fail to take into account the whimsey of God. Evah think theya may be some cause fah his name to be in Gott'im?"

She pounced on this. "How *did* Gott'im get its name?"

"Ask Asa Bartlett—over to the historical society. Now back to my point. Ever hear of God playing practical jokes?"

"Never." Again an arch of the eyebrow. "Why should She want to?"

"How about that time God had Noah spend a hundred years building a big boat—his neighbors jeering at 'em evah day? How about that forty day rain'n flood?"

She pulled back, indignant. "That deluge *killed* everybody. If it happened." The last was said in a mutter.

"Evahbuddy but Noah'n his family. But take now. S'pose he was t'make some small adjustment, say in the earth's rotation to wipe out the westerlies and make the prevailing winds come from the east? Evah mill owner on the west side o'town—all over the country— would have to breathe the stink o'the mills they built."

She shook her head. "They'd all just move to the east side. —No, they'd move to some place like this—and telecommute!"

"Yuht, but then property values'd plummet on the west side'n regular folks could afford t'live in the nice houses left behind. It could happen like that in Gott'im. Some minor adjustment—say in greenhouse gases raising the temperature a notch or two. *Phut!* Ol' Harry'n Julius'd have to go north fah theya snow. And Decatur'd be back in business."

Dimpling, she said, "You're desperate, y'know."

He grinned.

"Besides," she said, "Would the cause be God or man?"

"May be God'n Satan."

"What's *that* supposed to mean?"

"Didn't you say you was a college person—then think on it. Y'don't want an ignorant mechanic thinking your thoughts fah you."

Melvinia set coffee before Gloria, got out a pad to take the order. Balder looked up at Melvinia, seeing the wheels work as she wrote, knowing what the conversation would be in here after they left. Lunchtime, and the place would be full of tongues.

Melvinia paused pointedly, then picked up Chrischana's cup. She carried it to the counter and set it by her elbow. But, as Balder watched, Chrischana stood and went into the kitchen.

Gloria watched Balder. Kissing him earlier, she had seen him fold the napkin—marked in ballpoint pen—and stuff it into his pocket. Now her imagination busily occupied itself creating scenarios. She looked out the window, idly stirring her coffee, waiting for him speak. First the separation, now this. What's going on?

His voice came low. He took her fingers and began rubbing the top of her thumb gently with his own. It was an exciting, yet thoroughly tender, gesture. She turned from the window and looked in the face that was delineated in whiskers, suddenly deciding that it was sexy. The whiskers could stay, but she fervently hoped he was not growing a beard. She couldn't bear a bushy growth on that sexy face.

He said softly, "Forgive me the silence of these last days?" She nodded, squeezing his hand.

"I got some odd news'n it unsettled me." Thoughtfully...he stopped talking, still gently stroking her thumb. The place was now filling for lunch. A noisy foursome came in to occupy the next booth. He leaned over the table, and she edged forward to meet him. Again he spoke low, thrilling her with the sweetness of this attention.

"Glory, have you ever considered kids? Having kids?"

Loosing his hand, Gloria fell back against the seat, astonished. But she recovered herself, leaned forward again and took up his hand. Gently. She smiled. It was one of his wonderful jokes. He went on seriously, intimately, his voice soft and low. "I know it's maybe kind'o odd, asking you like this ... ovah a dinah table'n all..." (here he did grin a little) ..."But it's—well, I got something on my mind." He was finished now, awaiting her response.

But she was unable to frame one. She sat there, feeling his gentle touch. Quietly, she began stroking his thumb in return. Is he wooing me? Is this what we mean by pitching woo? No one had ever bothered with anything remotely like this. Plenty of heavy breathing, groping and clutching—but never *never* anything like this. She and Balder had not yet consummated their intimacy, were still mostly sexually innocent of one another. Now, slowly, thoroughly, as his thumb wrought, he was filling her with desire. As though filling a glass with sweet wine from the bottom up. Filling her with arousal, where she sat—here! In Decatur's Diner!

His face, close to hers, was expectant. She felt his breath on her hand as he waited for her to speak. She leaned close, very close, saying, "You know I want you." Whispering, she felt meager and appealing ... the best she could be. Yet she felt it strangely small and unworthy. He had invoked deep desire, but her answering seemed uneven in comparison. Did this sort of thing take practice? She thought her sexual experience would have qualified her, but somehow, inexplicably, she was disappointed in her own response.

He said, still low, "And I want you. But do you want children?"

Puzzled, she pulled back. What is this? Is he actually asking if she wants to have children? Give birth? *Take care of kids?*

Balder was watching, gauging the emotions passing through Gloria's features, and suddenly as she looked at him it was as if she looked in a mirror ... seeing that disappointment in his face. He had seen her setback, that she was shocked: indignant and unable to cover this disenchantment.

She said it flatly, withdrawing her hand. "I'm still a child myself, Balder. The child in me needs nurturing. I need all the fulfillment that I can responsibly muster." She hurried on, her voice now a mixture of anger and pleading. "The possibilities for me are boundless, exhilarating. Do you have any idea what children would do to that? Balder," She finished raggedly, "Balder, it would not be good for them, either."

His jaw tightened. He looked away. Outside the window he saw Chrischana getting into her rusty Bonneville. He heard its deep-throated rumbling as she started it up.

God.

He turned back to Gloria, for in another moment he would've seen her drive off. He felt his breast pocket where her napkin lay.

Gloria saw this movement and looked away.

"Gloria," he said with finality. "I'm a fatha now. I found out fah sure this morning. When Chrischana left here fifteen years ago, she was pregnant with my son Daniel."

Her eyes widened. She looked out the window, seeing the dust cloud from the big car settle in its wake as it went.

Balder was saying, "I waunt t'be with you, but you got t'understand. I'm a fatha now. I want to be one. To be a fatha to Daniel ... and his brothers if they need one. Can you share me? We'll build us a big ol'house...."

But, looking at the fish sandwich Melvinia had just set in front of her, she had stopped listening.

"Heah y'go, deah!" said Melvinia.

Gloria stared at the greasy thumbprint on top of the bun, the revolting glossy tartar sauce in its little paper cup. Dully she looked around, the whole place revolting her. Clasping her purse, she stood. "I'll have to think about this," she said, eyes on the door. "Gimme time. I'll get back t'ya."

She was gone ... out to her little red car. Balder grinned unhappily up at Melvinia. "Some people in't cut out fah eating in dinahs. The food makes'em lose theya appetites."

Melvinia snorted, her dangly earrings shaking in disgust.

Gloria Fay is holed up in her bedroom, looking out at the grey flanks of Jasper, laced in green. The view here isn't like that of the reception center where she sometimes works; but no matter, for, leaning her wet face against the screen, she doesn't see it today. For the summer she is sharing her parents' townhouse condominium with her brother Jimmy. She can remember the day the resort broke ground to build these units. How she jigged up and down, excited, jabbering to her siblings, to Daddy and Mom. On a subsequent visit she ran through the white stud works, exploring the connecting units of the townhouses. She is part of this place, of Jasper Mountain. She belongs here as much as anyone, as much as Melvinia and Decatur and Balder and that crappy diner. She'll show them. She'll convince Balder of her fidelity to it! No one is going to exclude her from this place. It is dear, dear, dear! Gloria wipes at the tears with her fingertips.

How will she show him? It takes more than selling time shares.... Or, why should she care what he thinks? Why not just let it happen? Be what you are, forthrightly ambitious and hard-working. Find what you can do to be of use in Gottheim. To Gottheim. Just hold on to the mountain, and to those dreams of owning your own place. And schuss straight to your goal, no switchbacking.

But the tears start again, her face already sticky with mascara and tears.... When there comes a soft rapping at the door.

"Open the door, Gloria. Talk to me." It is her brother, James. "Don't stay so long in there, Gloria.... Please? It's not good for you. Talk to me. Gloria? Please?"

God Takes Care of God's Creatures

In a corner of her office panelled in dark oaken squares, Theodora Prescott sat turned away from the antique rolltop desk. Behind her sat a stack of printed forms. In a posture of assumed relaxation, she tried to lounge against the desk in this tiny office from which her great-grandfather had first run the then flourishing business of the Gottheim Chair Company. Opposite sat Balder. The room was a solid piece of craftsmanship, illumined by two tall mullioned windows. It could have been a study in an elegant nineteenth century industrialist's mansion. The offices of the company were the only sound components of the now ramshackle array. The connected buildings were at odd angles, crazily leaning either toward or away from one another, variously sided in wood, asphalt, metal or block. From behind the closed oaken door came the muted racket of the furniture mill. The smell of sawdust, shavings, resin and glue penetrated here.

      Theodora was just finishing up on her subject of turning the mill into a cannery. She had been reading Maine history and was intrigued by the fact that the state once had a reputation in canning. And she was uplifted in discovering that Gottheim's first industry was the processing of maple syrup. Ms. Prescott thought that Gottheim Chair could stand updating: In view of this trend, in which tourism was edging out the woodsmills as the town's leading industry, she had decided on finding an historical niche and exploiting it. Thankfully, Gottheim was practically a full-fledged four seasons area. The new mountain biking craze, foliage tours, and skiing are all here to round out the future of God's House.

"Balder," she said, wrapping up her little talk, "I'm seriously considering a merger into our historical industry, complete with old fashioned canning jars and quaint labels. It would be a sweet appropriate endeavor here under our roof, and we could have a viewers' gallery for tourists to watch the process. Now what do you think of that?" She smiled, hoping the gesture would be construed as conciliatory, though she continued to be annoyed by his recent actions ... and those whiskers.

But the smile struck Balder Simon as coy, though he credited her with genuine ignorance of this. By unspoken mutual consent they had left off the topic of his prolonged unexcused absence—for which she had attacked him and his utter lack of consideration for the business. He had apologized, offering to work the current week without pay, which she promptly noted at her desk. But the apology itself went unnoticed, a habit of hers that he recalled from childhood when they were neighbors at camp. As children they had exchanged insults across the cove of Kimball Pond, where their extended families spent part of the summer. Now that they were grown, each occupied a defining role in community life, she as a business-person philanthropist, he as irksome wisecracking mechanic. His deference today was genuine and proper, but Theodora's sometimes blind frantic personality precluded notice. It seemed a necessity for her to express the last drop of indignation over neglect. The process could be lengthy.

Now Balder thought, *The Gott'im Can Company.*

He was tempted to respond to her question about the proposed syrup cannery with a blunt agreement: We could shut down for the ten months following sugaring off. However, he did not feel like cranking up the feud again. Instead he nodded. "Will we can blueberries, apples, and other fruits in season?" He said it idly, absently. Balder was still seeing Gloria's horrified expression against the grimy backdrop of Decatur's diner.

The question checked Theodora. How could she have forgotten that huge chunk of time between sapping seasons? She felt embarrassment burning through her features and rushed to cover the error by concurring with his suggestion, then hurrying on. Her arm resting on the stack of paper on her old desk, she leaned confidentially toward him.

She was immaculately coiffed and demurely dressed in a powder blue suit, smelling of perfume. Balder restrained the urge to lean away. She had displayed coquetry before, and he found it embarrassing.

But her eyes gleamed instead with ambition. She said, "We are about to embark on something new here at Gottheim Chair, something innovative. People don't expect this sort of thing here in this industrial backwater (where Western Maine is unfortunately tangled in the shallows)."

Now she was reaching for poetry. Balder dropped his gaze. He was used to suppressing his humor around her. Sometimes he felt pity, even tenderness toward her, but her lapses into self-deceived arrogance annoyed him.

She drifted shell-pink fingertips down the stack of papers, saying, "As you know, I've become increasingly associated with the International Institute of Coordinated Experiments." Her look was eager and bright; she used its full name to remind him of its scientific cachet. "Gottheim Chair is going to benefit from that association. I've contracted for our employees to join in testing, and seminars, specially designed to help make for a smoother running, more friendly operation here. Help will be in the form of consensus building, psychological profiles, and what I would call respect and respite sessions—where people can relax and say what's on their minds. These measures are designed to evoke a more positive attitude in the mill. Can you agree we need that here, Balder?"

As she talked, a frown gathered between his brows which she failed to notice. He hated anything like what she was proposing. Had she not displayed such bright hopefulness, he might almost have verbally savaged her on the spot. Instead, he fell back on the ploy he sometimes adopted when he felt contempt for one of her ideas. Balder leaned back and averted his eyes, frowning. "I don't know, Ms. Prescott. I'm just a mechanic heah."

Theodora sat upright, heaving her small boson, lifting her chin. He'd done it to her again; just as she was feeling at ease in the emotional reliance he must know she craved. He was so reasonable just now over my pain and trouble during his absence.... That miserable machinery could *not* be kept in repair with only the hands of Gilbert Gage to coax it. He *knows* how much I depend on him.

Balder knew she had always loved and respected him! Together they had taken all those college preparatory classes at Gottheim Academy when it served both town kids and the preppies from away, for even though he had gone on to Vietnam—volunteered when others were burning their draft cards!—he was an intelligent man. Not like Six-pack Sam who went into the woods or turned furniture legs for a living. He had always claimed some kind of kinship to those people by his associations (and now with that awful facial hair!) but she knew he was no mere mechanic. He just used that as a copout whenever he came up against anything he thought would threaten the precious dumbness of this wretched little community!

But she had a respect for Balder bordering on fear. She couldn't bring herself to go verbal with him on this because he might shred her with his wit. She now tried to cover her initial heave of the bosom with a contrite look. And recalling his skill in ridicule, Theodora *did* feel contrition.

She sighed, venturing timidly, "Well ... I was trying to lift my employees up with this program from IICE ... but it's fine with me if you don't want to talk about it.... Incidently, Vernon thinks it's an excellent idea." She could not resist this last thrust, but she stood quickly, holding out a dainty hand.

"Thanks for coming in." At least she had learned something at IICE. You must employ courtesy and develop a habit of respect if you're to build toward compromise and consensus.

Aside from his greeting, apology, and leave taking, Balder had scarcely spoken three sentences during the interview. Going down the worn wooden stairs toward the shop, thinking of the plans for her employees, Balder Simon grimaced.

Lift those employees right up there. Up where you can hang 'em out to dry!

The long June twilight had lingered, dark was just about down. Beyond the fretful borders of the sagging Cape, Cindabilla stood near the lane awaiting Daniel. She climbed onto the great low branch of a huge maple not far from the broken gate, and looked up.

A tufted owl in the higher branches somewhere up there. Thing was on the far side, in the leaves, spitting out another mouse. Heavy old thing—swooping down on rodents all evening, killing and spitting them out; not even bothering to eat. It gave her the creeps but she was fascinated anyway. Owls don't usually do that, do they?

She had crept out her window and scurried away from the fetid and furious house. A long wait, but Daniel would be here. One thing she could count on was Daniel. Feeling the impress of jagged bark on her palms and even through her jeans, Cindabilla swung her bare feet back and forth.

A crash came from the Cape style house. She looked over her shoulder at the yellow rectangles of light that broke the dark surface of her home. Shadows crossed the blinds, and in one shadeless window she saw Uncle Ferdinand lurch out of view; heard his drunken cursing drift out. He was taking aim at his girlfriend again. Babette sometimes looked 45, but Cindabilla knew she wasn't more than 33, or 34—ancient but not that ancient. Daniel had said she went to school with his mother in the '60s.

The soft rush of quiet wings went past. The owl was at it again. "Cruel bastid," she said in her high thin voice. She looked away from the house toward the lane. Why don't Babette just leave? Why take that abuse ovah and ovah and ovah?

She leaned out, looking up the road. Is that a shadow moving toward the lane? Yep, here he comes. She slid to the ground and moved toward the lane, running like a pale stripling through the dark of grass. So cool and sweet out here tonight.

Daniel came up to her, his quiet face with its slightly Indian contours visible in the June evening. He had high cheek bones and a broad brow. She had never seen him smile.

"How's the school play t'night?" he asked.

"Cruel bastid's beating on her again—like last week. Wish she'd leave."

"Can't your grandmother do anything?" He was thinking of how there'd been no family in Phoenix for him to call on when Petey went ballistic.

"Call the cops's all. It's something t'do, but ain't much use t'Babette. She nevah presses chodges, so Gram gets discouraged." Her eyes brightened in the night. "Waunt see something?" She pulled him toward the maple.

In the shadow on the ground beneath lay an odd little mess. What's this? Then a dead mouse fell on top. Daniel started back.

Cindabilla said, "Cruel bastid's up theya."

Daniel glanced up into the foliage and saw a gleam of something. He looked on the pile at his feet, recognizing tiny bodies, legs and tails.

"Cruel, stupid horned owl," said Cindabilla. "Been heah all evening, swooping down, spitting 'em out. Someone ought shoot it!" Staring at the heap of little bodies, she said, "We ought." She looked back at Daniel.

Cindabilla's face was ghostly and there was moonlight enough to see her cloud of freckles, the pale lashes around her eyes. Her long ponytail glimmered in the night as together they moved out from under the tree. Her arms were thin and white, her chest just developing under her T-shirt. Other girls in class were stylish in comparison, wearing bras, makeup, earrings, and blouses to top their imitation designer jeans. Their shoes were petite, feminine, but Cindabilla would go barefoot as much as possible this summer. Her sneakers, bought by Gram last fall, were now smelly and shot.

Daniel's look was doubtful. "Whose gun'd we use?"

"One o'Uncle Ferddy's."

But Daniel looked off toward the woods beyond the Sessions' pasture behind the house. He fancied he could see the glow of Aunt Nellie's camp. He pictured her looking at the arrowheads through her magnifying glass. But the thought of Cindabilla's great aunt at peace was suddenly shattered by the cries of Babette Roebuck.

Daniel seethed some words between his teeth, inarticulately wondering what they could do. Should he go in there and throw himself on Ferddy—a stranger? He had thrown himself on Dad— Petey—not long ago, in Phoenix. Ferddy is bigger than Dad, but it might distract him long enough for Babette to get away.

"Let's go look in the window," said Cindabilla, turning toward the house. "If it's bad we could decoy'em. Beat on the house, break a window, something."

Through weeds and bits of trash they crept up to the weathered windowsill. The rank smell of Hannah Sessions' kitchen came out at them, along with the glare of a naked bulb above the table. There were cans and clutter, plates and pots everywhere. Chairs were askew or knocked over. A cigarette lay on the floor, burning a hole in the linoleum. A cat lapped at something under the table. Over in a corner beside the refrigerator hunkered Ferddy over Babette, yelling like a maniac. He was a demon hollering himself hoarse, right into her ear where she sat scrunched against the appliance. She didn't seem injured, but her head was down, covered with arms clasped in an attitude of protection. Hannah was nowhere to be seen.

Wide-eyed and tense, the children watched as long as they could, but Cindabilla soon pulled Daniel back. "She's all right. Let's go get the owl. We'll climb in Uncle Ferddy's window'n get one o'his guns. One of 'em's bound to be loaded. He's like that. Surprised he never threatened Babs with one." She shivered, thinking of an ever present dread. Maybe she'd come home some night to a scene of blood.

Threading through junk, weeds, and swatches of streaming light, they moved toward the dark end of the high-gabled cape. Cindabilla clambered over the sill and in through a tear in the screen. She landed on a pile of dirty clothes, popping up to whisper, "Wait heah. I'll hand out the gun."

Daniel stood peering in as she moved around. Light from the kitchen at the far end of the house slashed into the open doorway. He saw the shade of Cindabilla crossing and recrossing the bright line made by the open door. At last she handed out the gun and climbed after.

"Just what we want," she hissed. "His bid gun—loaded'n ready t'shoot."

Going down the lane, she asked, "Your aim ana good? We'll shoot that owl, run back'n dump the gun on the clothes pile. Tomorrow he'll probably know 'twas me done it—if he even 'membas it then."

"I never shot a gun," said Daniel, a bit breathless. "In Phoenix only gangstas had guns."

"When we get done, hightail it t'the woods'n you can tell me bout Phoenix more." She nudged him. "There 'tis, on the other side in the branches," she whispered. "Gimme."

She crept beneath the overshadowing boughs with the bird gun, lifted it to her shoulder, took careful aim, and squeezed off a shot. The explosion tossed her back, a light thing. The owl dropped with a thud onto its pile of prey, bouncing a bit. The children ran back across the weedy yard and rounded the corner of the house, breathless. Cindabilla threw the gun into the room. She heard it miss the clothes pile and bark on the floor. There was another explosion.

"Shit!" she squeaked, and ran away around the corner at the back of the house. There was a pigpen and, beyond, the trash-filled yard with the old pickup. She panted and squeaked with excitement, looking back to see if Daniel followed. He knocked into Cindabilla and they tumbled into muck that Hannah Sessions had raked out of the pigpen that afternoon. Rising, stumbling toward the pasture, Daniel puked. But Cindabilla was laughing, freely cursing as she followed, bumping him. "Fuckin' pig shit!" she squeaked at the end of her cursing.

Over and over she said it, as they ran down past the abandoned '40's pickup, tripping over junk. "Fuckin' pig shit!..." They made it to the pasture and went on towards the woods. Daniel looked back toward the hulking tumble-down barn and sway-backed Cape, thinking he heard something—screaming? But he kept on, Cindabilla's laughter and his own ragged retching diverting him.

On and on they ran until at last the great arms of the woods received them. Daniel knew where he was heading, whether Cindabilla followed or not. He was far ahead of her now, on his way to the stream. All he wanted was to drench himself in the rocky waters. He rolled under the current, careful to avoid the rocks cropped out here and there. He clawed at himself, futilely scraping at the muck on his clothes. He wriggled out of them, flopped over suddenly, looking for Cindabilla.

She stood a little apart, already down to her underpants, dunking her T-shirt up and down in the stream. He saw her thin body, faintly agleam, her breasts like buds. She was giggling, cussing a stream of filthy words, and looking over at him with what seemed a face of pure wicked glee. It wasn't quite light enough in the woods for him to see it clearly. "But we got that owl," she said, breathless, repeating it over and over. "We got that stupid bastid fuckin' cruel owl!"

At sight of her Daniel felt an erection coming on, even here in the cold water. He struggled up, lugging wet clothes under a nearby arched snowmachine bridge. He went further upstream and began again, furiously dunking his clothes.

He heard her call out, "Daniel! What choo doing over theya?!"

"Here's where you ain't. We're not doing anything, Cindabilla!" His voice was cracking and shrill.

"Who said anathin bout doing anathin?" Her voice echoed toward him under the bridge. She was wading after him, her teeth beginning to chatter.

But Daniel did not look toward her. "Stay over there till we get dressed." His voice trembled, the words stuttering out. "W-we're t-too-young t'do anathin'!" He was shivering, his sexual urgency now abating.

Cindabilla giggled, but turned away. She climbed up over the rocks onto the bank. "Good thing water's high this time o'year," she called, wringing out her T-shirt. "We'd nevah get fuckin' pig shit off us." She was squeaky with laughter and kept hearing that explosion inside Ferddy's bedroom, the one he shared with Babette.

Her thin arms and hands worked over the jeans, twisting. Never get the water run out of 'em! "Daniel, I caunt get the water out o'my jeans'n I in't wearing 'em wet. Way too cold!"

After a moment she heard him yell, "Well, put your T-shirt on then." She felt energized, exhilarated. No one ever wanted to do anything with her before. Daniel was surely just about saying he wanted to do something! Glorying, she felt luckier than anything; and glad, too, that nothing was going to happen. It meant that Daniel was to be trusted more than anyone. More, even then Gram or Aunt Nellie. —Neither one knew what to do with her anymore: Cindabilla was too far out of hand. She pulled on her T-shirt and called for him to come over now.

When he came up out of the water and saw her in shirt and underpants, he wanted to protest, but decided not to be bothersome. It would be all right as long as he didn't look at her. He started up the path a little ahead of her in cold clinging jeans. Water trickled down inside and the cuffs dragged in the dirt. "C'mon," he said, trying to jam his hands into the pockets. No good. His teeth chattered fiercely, and he flapped his arms. "N-now what'll we do?"

"You're gont tell me bout Phoenix," she said, a little behind him.

She's so tough, he thought, makes me feel wimpy in comparison. "No," he said. "We got t'get warm! Let's go to Aunt Nellie's. "

"Daow," she said, sounding like Hannah Sessions. "We'll just jump up'n'down and beat the trees with sticks. That'll keep us warm."

He jogged along the path, swinging his arms. All he wanted was warmth, but he said, "Whad y'think happened when the gun went off? Thought I heard someone screaming."

"Let's go back 'n' look in the window."

Jogging through the dark, careful of roots and rocks, they speculated on the uproar that must have been caused by the discharging bird gun. Laughing, Cindabilla spun ideas for escaping retribution. She did not really care. Gram didn't know what to do with her and that meant liberty.

When they reached woods' edge, Daniel grabbed her jeans and wrung them out. "Put 'em on. You won't believe the trouble we'd get in if anyone saw us like this."

So, hopping on one foot then the other, Cindabilla got into her jeans. Coming down through the pasture, they noticed a flashing glow coming from beyond the house. And there was another flashing, blue, coming down the road.

"Police," said Daniel. "We're in trouble now."

She grabbed his arm, pulling him toward the corner when they reached the yard. "Theya won't be trouble fah us if I get in bed 'fore they get here."

She pulled herself over the sill and into her dark room—the room beside Ferddy's. Her pale face glimmering in the opening, she said, "Go back t'Twitchell Cove'n I'll be down tomorrow. Let you know what happened then."

He heard her moving around, probably taking off the wet jeans. Then he watched as she opened the bedroom door, letting light stream in. He heard voices of the police come in with the light, questioning. Cindabilla rubbed her eyes against the brightness, yawning and stretching as she headed toward the kitchen.

Daniel crept away as quickly as the strewn yard would allow. The police might check the area, so he had to get out of sight. He went down past the old barn that loomed like a small mountain over the farmyard, then took its lane to the road. Glancing back, he saw the ambulance, its red lights still flashing, mingling with the blue of the cruiser. He watched as the paramedics loaded an occupied stretcher. Then, in a spray of gravel, it leapt away, took the road and flew down toward the highway. Daniel saw the lights vanish below hill-crest.

Feeling a pang of dread, he stepped into the road. Who was on their way to the hospital? *Don't let it be Gram.* Cinda might as well not have a mother, so little use was she to her daughter. Walking on toward the crest of the hill in the light of the stars, his breathing slowed. He grew thoughtful and calm. What will the cops make of her wet T-shirt? No, better not think about it. Not if you can help it.

But he felt a strange exuberance. Daniel wasn't sure he could help thinking of Cinda and her budding T-shirt.

Gottheim's police officers stood in Sessions' yard, looking at the stiff, staring owl. It seemed to be in shock. Scattered in the bird's agony, the prey pile was strewn at the base of the rugged old maple. But the owl had worked its way out of the shadows, its tufted face and great gleaming eyes staring up at the officers in the light of the stars.

"Those eyes!" The woman said.

"Gawd! In't that th'owl's been terrorizing Gott'im?" said the man.

"I guess. They say it's right out o'Stephen King."

Lifting the flap on his holster, the man said, "Ought put it out of its misery."

"Wait," said the other officer. "What about taking it back t'Mrs. Simon. She's got a permit fah this kind o' thing. Fixed it up before."

"How'd we do that? Look at those talons."

Doubtful, the woman looked around. "D'know. I'd go ask Miz Sessions fah one o'her feed sacks. Stuff it in that with a broom or something. It caunt have no fight left now. I'd say it's half dead anaway." She strode off toward the house.

The other stood staring back at the great malevolent face of the horned owl. Never know what a night might bring, he thought. Guess Babette can relax for a while anyway. He smiled, wondering how it would read in *The Voter.*

Out on the highway Daniel averts his face from oncoming headlights, yet he is vigilant on this stretch, moving off the shoulder when it seems wise. Traffic can be either heavy or sparse this time of night, and the highway is two lanes, dark. But it is wide and smooth with fresh asphalt. Jasper Mountain has seen to it, the owners having friends in the capitol and Blaine House.

Daniel skips over some hunks of stuff gleaming whitely in the black road. What is this stuff? He bends for a piece, examines it. Drywall, coated in plaster. You never know what will let loose on the highway. He walks on a few hundred feet, coming to a couple chunks of wood, some scattered strips of bark. Glad I wasn't here when these things fell. Once, just about here on the approach to the Twitchell Pond turnoff, he stepped on broken bits of concrete, and two blocks of it lay just off the shoulder. That night, recalling Mrs. Thurston's hints, he did not tell Mother about the debris. Because he wanted to justify Mother's faith.

Mrs. Thurston was a sturdy group leader at the middle school, and a good assertive woman, mother had said after the woman's implied censure. She kept silent that night when Mrs. Thurston dropped him off at the campsite after learning he had no ride. Later Mother told him of her faith. She would not check his freedom to walk where he desired, in part because she would not be able to drive him around, as could other mothers with reliable cars.

Daniel is glad of his freedom, enjoying this feel of the rural night about him as he walks along in silence. There are no gang bangers to trouble him in Gott'im. He likes the freedom of his feet, now that they are out of the city. They can bring him anywhere, out of anything, if he is patient.

He comes down into the open beside the pond, looking across starlit waters. The black contour of the surrounding hills, edging the still sky, soothes him. Thanks to his exertion, the wet clothes no longer chill him. His thoughts rise. He is going to tell Mother about Babette. At last he might even broach the subject of battered women. Why did she take it so long from Dad—Petey?

Walking at night is good for thinking. On this road beside the pond the strange new idea surfaces again, as it does whenever he is alone. He has told no one, not even Cindabilla. A new father.

Mother said he has to meet Balder. It's bad enough just knowing the fact. It makes him hoppy as a jumping bean. A new father. The idea jumps around inside ... where everything goes on. The trick is to keep it all in there. It can't show on your face. How can that man at Deep Hole be his father! What he remembers is that creepy look in his eye. Hugely, the world goes on around you ... but inside is where it makes itself known.

He remembers the letter Mother got today. The way she stared at it, held it so long in her hands. How still she went, but how far away. Then suddenly she looked to see if he was watching, and crammed the papers into the envelope again, stood and went into the tent.

Daniel couldn't help but wonder. Does it have something more to do with him? But maybe not. Things are always happening to adults and being hidden from kids. They don't know, but kids can worry more about parents than the reverse. He has always worried about mother.

But things are better for her in Maine.

If he can just get used to it himself.

Dear Chrischana [fifth draft of a letter],

You know me well enough to understand that I would've been right there with you, loving you, caring for our child, all those years ago. Maybe you didn't want to burden me. Maybe you didn't want to subject Daniel to the stigma of Gottheim since it was different here in the '60s. Maybe you didn't want your father hurt by it all. Maybe it was all this. However good these motives, pride was in it somewhere: the belief that it was all on your shoulders and no one else had any help, any say. You acted like, since you were the one pregnant, no one else had a part to play, no one should be permitted to bear the burden with you—not me, not your father, not God whose power ignites life.

Can you, acting alone, conceive, spin out the vast array of chromosomes, the genosphere that lives in the continually dividing cells which form a human being? Was it your plan to sit and knit, to fashion together the intricate eyes and world of sound, the knees that crawl, the tiny hands and innards, the living quivering heart of a human? Did you take any thought about how to construct one? Did you design the interconnected, resilient and generous realm required for its support? If the answer is no, please have the humility to share the upbringing of our child with me.

Please don't think that God is not with you, that God cut you adrift because of our backseat Chevy joy, our mysterious fumbling that led directly to Daniel. Is it anything but our selfishness that makes us separate warmed skin ecstatic sex from the act of conception? The only shameful thing is the way we denigrate it, slight, rob its meaning of importance, say that our sexual union "accidently" created life. In a moment when our desire reached its climax, God was there. The shame is in denying that our sexual expression is an intimate collaboration with God. It's the only way that any of us can come here and together share the realm of life.

For Christ's sake, Chrischana, let me share in Daniel's *past* upbringing. Let me provide some of that support now. I arranged for you to receive child support payments, but there's more I want to do. The man you were married to (or live with?) maybe helped to raise Daniel, so I'd like to return the favor by helping with the other boys, Nathan and Ben (that name right?).

Be reassured. I know from battlefield experience and its aftermath that there's such a thing as retroactive prayer. Prayerful regrets can mitigate the sorrows of the past. Please, please accept the enclosed check for back support. They are expecting you at the courthouse and the bank. I would be proud if you walked into Gottheim Savings and presented the check to start an account for yourself and family. It's a part of my savings, but still not as much as I'd like to give. The rest is needed to help me start building a house, or maybe restore *Simons Ledge*.

I haven't talked to Mother yet, but I will. Then I want Daniel to come here and meet her, spend a little time with us and, if she's OK with it, have Nathan and Ben (?) come sometimes too. I want to be a friend to them, and to you all. Please don't deny me a part. Write back and say I can. Or come visit.

It's true I have a woman friend now, at least I hope so. But you aren't alone. I will always love you, Chrischana,

Balder

At IICE they had shown Theodora her problem: She has always believed there is no help for her in the world. "This seems to be the defining myth of your identity. It can be traced back to that first incident and pattern of your mother's inability to console you." Oh, the clarity of this revelation. After the initial trouble to her soul (some of the simply awful stuff IICE revealed!) ... well! There *is* help for her in the world! Everyone else finds help, and now that she knows what her problem is, she will find it too! I will change my myth, that's all. The world is my store—I *can* take what I need.

Then why is she paralyzed with fright in the gleaming kitchen of her spacious townhouse condominium? Just the sound of that awful chipmunk thrashing around in the cupboard under the sink, angrily chattering—oh God! What can I do?

All the Hepplewhite chairs from the dining room were piled against the cupboard doors, ensuring that there could be no escape into her seasonal home. Why doesn't the thing simply vanish, slipping out the way it had come—on the water pipe...it must've been the water pipe. Why doesn't it just scrape the mousetrap off itself? Is it injured, in shock, unable to think?!

"Why are *you* chattering at *me*?!" screeched Theodora. She kicked the side of the cupboard. "*I'm* the injured party here. You are the stupid animal-witted intruder! Why did you come here in the first place?!" she shuddered. "Ohhhhh! those stupid contractors and their dim-witted carpenters!"

It was a helpless mutter under the breath. Why are *men* put in charge of building houses, anyway? They have no concept of thoughtful design construction. A woman would've known that holes around pipes should be perfectly snug, that foundations should be thoroughly inspected.

She was near tears. Who could she get to come take this thing away? There is no concierge, the groundskeeper was gone, so was housekeeping. Maybe some other Jasper Mountain employee? But it was after hours in the off-season; staff were limited. Besides, she felt embarrassed calling about a chipmunk. She was too harassed to assume a proper demeanor over it.

Hands on hips, she kicked the cupboard again, just to see if the creature was still there. She heard it clinking among the things under the sink. "You awful little beast! Why don't you just die! I would at least be able to carry your little carcass out in the dustpan."

Theodora walked into the living room among the elegant Thomas Moser furnishings, wringing her hands. "I shouldn't talk that way," she whimpered, beginning to cry. "It's one of nature's dim children. I can't just wish it dead." *Think how scared it must be.*

But the animal was chattering again.

The doorbell rang. Theodora froze. Her glance slid to the gilt framed mirror in the entranceway. She was a mess, her auburn hair falling out of its red ribbon, her mascara smudged. Whoever it was would know she was in here.

"It's your neighbor next door, James Fay," came a voice through the door.

With another glance at the mirror she went and peered through the peephole, scrutinizing him as he stepped back to give her a view. Of course she knew of the bespeckled Mr. Fay by reputation.

"Is there something I can do for you? I ... couldn't help but hear. You are in some distress, Ms. Prescott.... Isn't that what neighbors are for?" She wiped hastily at the mascara under her eyes and set her white hand on the deadbolt. In the village she never used the deadbolt, but Theodora did not feel quite safe on the mountain. Too many strangers. Slowly she turned it and slid back the chain. Opening the door she said, "Please come in, Mr. Fay," and turned toward the kitchen area, unable to look him in the eye.

"There appears to be a chipmunk or something in my cupboard. It must've come up the pipes...." Leading him to the sink she saw the ridiculous stack of chairs piled against the cupboard doors—as though seeing it for the first time. Theodora gave an embarrassed little laugh, saying, "I don't think he's escaped, do you?" She looked at him then, flushing deeply. And her fingers flew nervously over her hair, pulling out the loose ribbon.

His smile was brief. "I guess we all have our ways of dealing with crisis." James Fay turned and began removing the chairs one by one.

His tone was brisk, impersonal, encouraging. Theo stood back, somewhat eased of her embarrassment, but still apprehensive over the rodent in the cupboard. She edged against the back door, fearful that the animal would leap out and scurry about the floor. She shivered, picturing a hairy thing rushing among the chair legs. As quietly as possible, she turned the deadbolt on the back door, slid back the chain and set her hand on the doorknob, ready to flee.

James Fay was squatting before the open cupboard, and it was then that she noted his manner of dress. He wore a perfectly pressed three piece suit, and seemed as fresh as though he were starting the day. His dark blond hair was crisply cut, his neck tanned as though he spent all day biking over the slopes of Jasper Mountain instead of wheeling and dealing for Harry and Julius Golding. James Fay was a compact young man on his way. Now he was in her kitchen, answering her distress.

He's a strong person, sure and secure. But I'm humiliated, an imbecilic hand-wringer, scared of a chipmunk. Why can't I be tough and competent like the feminists? I *am* a feminist, she reminded herself. We're not all made of Kevlar. Was he six, five years her junior?

"He's crouched in there by the hot water heater," said Fay, looking up. "It's a squirrel, red squirrel I think you call it."

"You mustn't take it up in your bare hands." Her voice was squeaky and shrill.

He smiled up at her. What a little spook. She's as fragile as a squirrel monkey ... with those smudged eyes. All she needs is a tail. She'd probably run away if I approached her on the street.

"I should've brought leather gloves," he said, still smiling. "Have you got a pair of tongs?"

"Tongs?"

"Kitchen tongs. Like for picking an egg out of boiling water."

Trying to think, she made a move as though to approach a drawer. "Will it?..." But she went bravely ahead, pushing back a chair and beginning to rummage in the drawer.

"Here," She said at last, handing him the tongs. She tried not to look in the cupboard. A sight of the squirrel hunched in there might be too much for her. She had a thousand reasons to protest this method of handling a squirrel, but no words would come. Just let him handle it. He's willing, has the nerve. She took her place by the door.

He approved her stance, saying, "Hold the door open while I bring him out. Then go down to the back door. I'll take him down that way."

Theo's mind was a jumble of objections. Would he take it by the tail? Could it swing up and bite him? What if it wiggled lose, jumping at her throat on the way down? —Another neighbor might come up the walk as they were coming out and disturb the whole process.

Fay reached inside the cupboard and there was nothing for her to do but open the door and go downstairs. At least if it got loose, she would be out of the way. At the bottom of the step she opened the door and peered out. The air had cooled and Jasper was beginning to cast its great shade across the valley. The parking lot was half in shadow. She heard James Fay on the stair and opened the door wide, hardly daring to look over her shoulder. Stepping off the path onto the bordering mulch, she watched him come out. The red squirrel looked plump, larger than she had expected, between the tongs. Its round dark eye was circled with a cream colored eyelet. How still it looked, funny and fat. The little thing must be terrified but at least it was free of the trap.

He set it down in the mulch and stepped back. Looking for it to hurry away, they both backed to the doorway but the squirrel just stood there, at first looking about and considerably slowed from a normal squirrelly pace. Tentatively, it looked this way and that. The man stepped out and nudged it with his foot. It hopped a bit, jerking, but looking up at James Fay.

"Go on," he said to it. "Go do whatever it is squirrels do in the evening."

But the rodent continued gazing up to him.

"Maybe it'll leave if we go inside," suggested Theo.

They stepped back, peering through the screen. The squirrel continued looking at him with what seemed a faint appeal. At last the tiny creature turned and, with a few jerks, started into the shrubbery along the wall.

Oh dear, thought Theodora. What if he comes back?

"I don't think he'll be back for more of that treatment," said Fay as though he had anticipated her.

"Maybe not," She said doubtfully. "But now he thinks you're God and will come back, trying to see you again. Did you see the way he looked at you? And he was so quiet in your hands—tongs!"

James Fay was tickled with her talk. "I don't think so," He laughed, "But you might want to get those holes plugged anyway."

"No, really! He thinks your God!" Now that the ordeal was over, she felt featherlight and a bit reckless. "He'll be like Marco Polo—telling all the other squirrels about this strange dangerous land and its God. These condos'll be crawling in squirrels."

Fay grinned, taking her elbow as she went a little ahead of him up the stairs. At the landing outside her kitchen door they stood lightly talking. She was grateful and he was enjoying her company. "I tell you what," he said, looking at his watch. "Why don't we go get something to eat?"

"Marvelous idea! My treat! You were so helpful, and I owe you *some*thing. Just let me go freshen up and we can walk over to the Gemstone."

"I can't let you do that," he said, embarrassed. "And I thought maybe we could go into town and try that wonderful little Below Street Bistro. I think they're falling on hard times since the end of the season."

She supposed that the cause of this embarrassment was a quaint residual pause at letting the woman pay. But Fay was smarting under the recollection of his treatment by the hostess whenever he took a date to the Gemstone. For some reason Karon kept seating him off by the kitchen when he came in without Harry or Julius. When he was on his own he ignored her choice of seating, but you couldn't very well do that with a date by your side. Could she be jealous of his dating? But she had never seemed to care for him that way before ....

Theodora smiled brightly, adding light to her pale complexion. "Below Street is lovely. I'm sure we can work something out on the question of whose treat. I won't be five minutes. Would you care to come in and wait?"

"Thanks, no. I've got to go next door and let my sister know."

"Oh. " She remembered his sister now: Gloria Fay, the bright young woman who spoke at the meeting to keep IICE from leaving town. Trying to hide her disappointment over the possibility, she yet offered: "Would your sister care to join us?"

"I doubt it. She's been depressed lately. Hides out in her room when she's not working. Probably be glad to have the place to herself tonight." He said this dismissively, but was unable to rid himself of a suggestion of woe. He would be glad to get away from her morbid brooding behind that door. He wished she'd give it up. Was it something to do with that mechanic? He wondered—for the nth time.

"So sorry," said Theo, displaying a long face. Then, hurrying on in her scattershot way: "Maybe she'll snap out of it soon. It happens to me all the time, and then, next thing you know, I'm snapped." Inwardly cringing, she smiled as though it had not been awkwardly put. But the lightness she felt over the squirrel was leaving her. *No doubt I'll make a fool of myself and lose his attentiveness well before the evening is gone. Worse, earn his secret ridicule.*

With a wave she hurried in, shut the door.

What a noodlehead, thought James Fay on his way to the townhouse next door. He had already placed her as the owner—one of the owners?—of Gottheim Chair. The pathetic furniture factory was falling apart at the seams, but it wasn't a bad piece of land there along the highway ... picturesquely situated under Morrill Mountain. He checked himself. Was he doing it again—thinking of people in terms of their property? But you couldn't very well separate people from what they owned before you got to know them. He grimaced, recognizing the pun.

"Gloria!" He went through the dining area. "Gloria, I'm going out!"

He orders the certified Black Angus steak, and she the plank roasted salmon. Together they contemplate a daintily loaded pastry cart nearby, anticipating desert as they await salad. Will it be bittersweet chocolate cheesecake, the peach tart, lemon cherry torte?...

"Gregory works like a demon on these desserts," says James Fay, as the salads arrive.

He set his coffee down to spear a spinach leaf glistening with olive oil. "Because they pay their help one-third more than any restaurant in the area, staff is loyal. Since Christmas Day opening they've had zero turnover. But the business is so seasonal...." His look is dubious. "I don't think they're—and she was an investment counselor who should've known better; runs the financial end, y'know. They've turned this ugly old basement into a cozy atmospheric place. Look at that brick, the polished brass pipes." He shakes his head. "They should have waited a year, maybe two." Listing their difficulties one by one, he emphasizes each with the side of his palm on the gleaming granite tabletop. "They do have their niche, however. The place has virtually absconded with their lives, so they make it by dint of perseverance. IICE will be throwing business their way this summer, of course. Who knows? They may get by. Obviously they love it. They're in their mid thirties but have given up thoughts of a family until this thing flies.... About your age, I'd say." It was an obviously leading statement.

As he looks at her through the glow from hand-dipped candles, Theo thinks, It's the first personal reference he's made. His talk has been of business, at first the Golding's shoreline park and its opponents; then of the recent victory in securing the compromise without eminent domain proceedings on parcels involved. She smiles, not at all unhappy that the conversation has been only his. "That's about right, James." She does not reveal her exact age.

James Fay repays the smile with a grin. The monkey eyes are gone. Theo has changed into something blue, possibly her best color, and tied her auburn hair back in a blue ribbon. The woman is like a bouquet of tiny flowers. Her nose is a tad long and her chin too recessed, but she is elegant ... if aging. Even so, he is having a hard time thinking of her as anything but young. She'll be helpless and young the rest of her life, as trapped in her own nature as an injured squirrel in a cupboard. It's not fashionable anymore for women to be helpless, but if it were, Theodora Prescott would never have to fake it. She will need help as long as she lives.

So will that business of hers. He reminds himself that this is only an observation. So far he has managed to refrain from broaching the subject of Gottheim Chair. How long he can refrain—Well, lately he's not so confident. Just when he begins to congratulate himself on a personal victory, the good air of the accomplishment actually seems to precipitate a fall. And there he is—finding himself hitting moguls on the fragile snow of a new friendship. *Afterward I recognize it.* Karon is puzzling. She's got no business interests, so how did I earn her ire? We've joked since childhood, now suddenly she turns evil. But Theodora is a good girl. Going to like being her neighbor.

The salmon and steak have arrived, odors of the charred and roasted mingling pleasantly. They murmur appreciatively over the dishes.

After a bite, he says, "Funny. I don't remember seeing you all winter—Or ever—at Spruce Grove. Of course we've always rented it out, summers. You didn't just move into that townhouse?"

"On no. I've lived there almost every summer, sometimes only part of a summer. Most people in Gott'im own as an investment, and to have a place to entertain visitors. But you must know. Your folks have had the place practically forever, haven't they? In the winter I rent to skiers, but I like getting away from the village in summer. It can be so peaceful on the mountain." Sheepishly she adds, "I'm not much of a skier, anyway."

Oh, why am I always so apologetic and inferior about the way I live? Or else I'm constantly trying to put a normal face on it. Isn't it perfectly reasonable—normal even—for a person to get out of gossipy insular Gottheim in warm weather?... It *is* only to the other side of the mountain ....

But Fay is saying, "Now that I work with Harry on the project, I want to build my own place. I'm head over heels about the area. So's my sister. Always have been. I think Gloria's a bit wacky over the mountain. Like it has a personality or something. Anthropomorphizes it something awful. Skiing is the thing, though. Actually, business is what really gets me schussing." He takes a turn at feeling sheepish: "Guess you can tell by the way I talk—"

"Or from the pages of *The Voter*." She smiles provocatively. "It's always James Fay this, and James Fay that."

"Yes, well. There's that.... " He does not like what he reads in *The Village Voter*. Except for the parts that provoke or advertise, the little rag bores him numb. He has stopped reading it. There are always others around to crow over its latest spin. Harry enjoys it, of course. If this project were going on in Boston, it wouldn't even make it into print. Small town spite's all it is! In fact, if James Nutting doesn't ease up—once this venture is through ... maybe I'll just get out. That sourball crank editor is nothing but a knee-jerk hypocrite. Like Nutting has no knowledge of the constraints of business success! Even his silly self-important weekly makes its concessions. Has to! —But ... it's nothing to do with little Theo.... He smiles at her.

"Are you teasing me already, Theodora?"

"Oh no!!" She is wide-eyed. "I think it's wonderful!" She ducked her brow, saying, "I'm only glad it's not me! I couldn't *stand* being in the paper all the time."

"Well, now that IICE has made its plans public, maybe the heat will be off me for a while. Give Nutting something else to focus on. He—he's not related to you or anything? I hear that paper has been in his family since the dinosaurs."

"Oh yes, and you can't get him to part with that horrible old machinery. Can you imagine—in this age of electronic production values? He should turn that place into a living museum. Really. If it weren't for its thunder—and the way the whole block shakes when that old press starts up!—people would stand in line to get a look at his shop. I'm surprised he gets anyone to work for him." Drained from the eagerness of her initial response, she sits back. "But people here will do anything, jobs being what they are. Now what was your question?—oh yes. We're not related that I know of."

James Fay is amused. From what he's heard, she might have said the same about herself and decrepit Gottheim Chair. But, likely, Nutting relishes his job as much as he does his attacks: with fierce obsessiveness.

"But, you know," she continues, sitting forward again, "About IICE—I am personally concerned." She sets her napkin delicately aside to pick up her dessert fork as the dish is set down. "We've *got* to do *something* to keep them from leaving! This town *needs* them. You have no idea. IICE gives us our intellectual stature. It's just a *boon* that they've done the courageous thing in announcing their intentions at the beginning instead of the end of the season. They could've waited till then and skipped out of town, gone forever, and free of the heat and tumult that has now assailed them from all corners. Maybe Gloria told you: Our Committee for Community Alternatives to IICE is hard at work composing a response, and, incidentally, is developing an aggressive program of alternatives in case we fail in persuading them to stay. Confidentially, now that you people are increasing facilities at the mountain, and with the proposed upgrading of Gottheim itself, I think their talk about inadequate conference space—Well, it strikes a false note. But it has had its benefits. We've been jolted out of our small town complacency ... into taking a really hard look at ourselves."

Fay is beginning to tire of this talk. His fork slices through layers of clotted cream, currants and chopped pecans. He regretted her indulgence of three cups of cappuccino. The caffeine is not going to let the woman slow down. Secretly, he laughs at the IICE upheaval—while remaining outwardly commiserative with the village. Their desperation is comical. That early warning tactic of the institute's was brilliant. All the commercial interests in town are buzzing like a hive of Africanized bees, galvanized to appease this inclusive bunch of academic witch doctors.

If she could just slow down. There is something he wants to grill her about. "Care to take a little drive in the twilight before heading back, Theodora? Maybe take that high stretch along Uncle Righteous Ridge?"

James Fay's BMW creeps along the backbone of the ridge named for an old settler who had stamina enough to set his farmstead up where frost was not apt to settle. He did not choose it for the views, but Righteous Ridge has romantic views on either side, the best of Gottheim in the area. Spangled in old neglected apple trees, it now bears the scars of burgeoning upper middle-class development. Below, lights of the village prick through the still deep shadows of the June evening. All along the surrounding summits they see the afterglow of sun's departure setting faint rose edging upon the deep blue contours. Looking out, Theo sighs. Here is benediction of day's end upon Gottheim.

Fay does not want to do anything so obvious and loaded as parking along here. He satisfies himself by creeping back and forth along the ridge road. Together they are silent, absorbing and being absolved in the tranquillity of the summer eve's transition from light to dark. They are attentive to the view's call upon the spirit. The flow of caffeine and conversation has ebbed. Earth's radiation into space above has taken off their cares, dissipating them upward, toward that realm without end.

"Nice," is all he can say, quietly. Then, "Nice how when day closes we can look up and see it all open before us. Look at the stars just beginning."

She agrees, dreamily. It is tempting to relax a bit now. Even here in this car, on this ridge, with someone new. Someone Theo wishes she could impress but knows from past experience that it is hopeless. He's so young important intelligent charming. She remembers seeing him here and there with various dates. All young vivacious self-possessed and ski slope rugged. Her dithering temperament cannot possibly interest him beyond this bright moment. Theo is conscious of his arm beside her, the beringed hand resting lightly upon the gear lever. James's masculinity is compact, well knit, and she feels now an acute and pathetic sensitivity to his sexual presence. She sighs. Maybe the squirrel will come back.

Yet James Fay is thinking how lucky he is to be sitting next to someone who doesn't find him overbearing and a bore. In clearer moments, he sees the effect that his overly buoyant self-centered conversation has upon his dates. In the past ten years he has been attracted to the rich skis types, but rarely it goes beyond the first date. He sometimes suspects himself the butt of jealous jokes and, at times, has to credit it to his own pomposity. But attempts at training himself away from it only end up amounting to hiding it. He isn't very good at it, either. Theo *is* quite—a bit ridiculous ... But if anyone can understand that he can.

Back there, in the restaurant, he planned to ask her about that millwright, Simon; the one Gloria.... He works for Gottheim Chair. But now, with evening stealing through the window.... Cannot bring himself to break the peaceful mood. Inject that note of self-interest.

This benediction.... It's not something he experiences often. James Fay smiles, remotely. Neither does he rescue squirrels from a cupboard every day.

Are there darker stretches of highway than those in rural Maine? No streetlamp mitigates the glare of oncoming headlights. With brights on, one drives through a tunnel of trees, attending to road signs with silhouettes of farm machinery or leaping bucks. So dark, the two-lane highways at fifty-five miles per hour are not what James Fay would call safe.

And tonight his vigilance is no different, yet, suddenly charges a hefty horse—! God-a-moose! A young moose, rackless, with monstrous legs just crossing haplessly into his highbeams. Fay's foot jumps to the brake. In his ear comes screaming. Relentless. *Screaming screaming screaming.* Swerving, the animal turns to outrun them, headlong. And Fay's foot is mashing the brake, mashing, mashing. The tires burn pavement, trebling the relentless screaming. Every moose collision story ever heard comes into his mind, boding fatality. Visions of great hooves breaking through the windshield, a massive back—flashing on him, even as he mashes with all his might. The headlamps brighten the gaskins, fetlocks, and straining thews of the animal's rear, approaching even as it runs.

Bumping and thudding, and that screaming as the bumper hits those thick legs. Then, in a lit spray of piss, the moose is gone, flying off the passenger side where Theo is clutching the dash. The scream is clipped off in a relieved whimper. And, accelerating once more, he looks to see her head turned, tracking the sorry beast still yellow in the beams, racing now alongside them off the shoulder.

Anguished, she sees the creature clipping through the thickets. *Baby, helpless child.* Theo feels its desperation, its throttling terror. Innocent discomfited spirit reaches out from it, brushing her own.

She hears the quiet voice of James Fay. "It's all right, Theo ... alright ... it's okay now...." Over and over he says it, gently assuring her.

We made it. The creature is okay. The moose ... us, Theo.... We're going to be all right.

=

Watching through trunks that crowd the downslope, Elda Simon creeps down along the moldering stone wall. In light shooting through, things are plain enough. In shadow the problems lie. Still, she guesses there won't be any trouble spotting Posey's fawn. Why did Sugarloaf have to be born albino? He'll be a doomed deer. Imagine a white buck—or even a fawn—making it through a single season.

Here's a new section of blowdown, a field of light, and she sees that the trail is obliterated. No, not blown down ... the damage is too extensive. These are leavings from logging. National Paper's been through since her visit to this part of the mountain last summer.

Posey, Posey. She wills the deer to appear. The does are off alone somewhere, in seclusion. Each with a new fawn, they will

133

enjoy a quiet isolation. But she can't seem to end her urge to check on them. That white fawn is so dainty and tender. The innocent light of it tugs at her. Every time she catches a shy glimpse of Sugarloaf...it feels like entering fairyland. Posey, Posey, why have you given birth to a storybook creature? When the bearded boys get wind of him, his life goes. Why-oh-why do they want a dead trophy instead of a living glowing animal free to wander the hills?

She tires, having searched all morning over these old hillocks; climbing painfully now over the bleaching bones of hardwoods and the burned brown sprucetops, broken fragments of human industry.

The boys'll be coming soon, a new worry. Entirely different. She has to get down from here to see Daniel. Kinship bewilders Elda. She can scarcely believe she is a grandmother, did not even dimly foresee it.

Almost she could wish to be like Balder's grandmother. Priscilla had a lap wide enough for three children to climb into, a neck strong for them to latch onto. The old woman, her flesh plump and jiggly, was always in smiles. Did an awful lot of baking, or else sat rocking with grandchildren lolling all over her, storybook in hand. Flour was everywhere in her house, children dusted in it, flour sifted onto tables, chairs, the scrubbed wooden floor. Priscilla set them each up with a ball of dough, tiny rolling pins, cookie cutters. While Elda—who lived in the house with one of their sons, Everett, and grandson Balder—was always out with the farm animals: Blue Boy, she recalls especially. There were sheep, pigs, chickens, and geese ... what else?

She dreads this meeting, this collision with a new grandson. What does she know about fourteen-year-olds anymore? You can't play with them, she remembers that much.

Clamoring through the leavings, she has lost the old stone wall, a sure guide in her descent toward *Simons Ledge*. He is from Arizona, think of it! Doesn't know about things like settlers' stone walls. He can't know they hold the earth of Gottheim together. That without them people would forget the salvation of rocks, the old ways. Daow. Can't understand why they aren't marrying, now that he's found her again. Balder always did things his own peculiar way. (Guess I know where he gets it.) Still, she thinks that is no way to handle it, but it's no business of hers. She has her own worries. Going blind is no easy task.

What can she say to a fourteen-year-old boy? You want to bake cookies? Elda doesn't think so. —What really troubles her is his plan to "restore" *Simons Ledge*. So nicely settled now, after all the upheaval of living there with the Simons, of being a virtual stranger, awkward in her task of mothering, having to act like living together was normal. Extended family was all she knew—from childhood!— yet she never got used to it. What a relief, after the grief of dark river partings, to sink crab like into her hole in *Simons Ledge*, free at last to be true to her own nature. Will he really disturb all the foliage-spangled habitat, cut it back, make the yard again, rehabilitate and extend the old garden? And drive all the animals away with those kids!

Three boys coming for visits—if she and Daniel work out. Did he really expect her to said, No, Balder, this won't work after all? That's not how she does things. She does things by just getting along. You don't say, no, I don't want to. When was she ever able to do that? After all these years, she wouldn't want to be that kind of person if she could.

Now, leaving the light of the clearcut, Elda is back in the shadowy woods. Here's the discontinued settlers road, now only a path, to guide her. Soon an overgrown cellar hole will be on the right, an old granite-lined depression bristling with trees, some trees with two-foot diameters. The old Leroy Trowbridge place. People there lived like all those folks whose children now populate Gottheim, working in the woods, keeping the mills running; build the condominiums, operate heavy machinery, clean house, wait on customers. Back then—and not that long ago either—the Tituses cut two hundred cakes of ice down on the pond, kept milking cans on ice covered with sawdust in the ice house, sold cream, fed skim milk to young farm animals, especially pigs. Hogs were raised, dressed, butchered. Salt pork was kept in that cellar, hogshead cheese, smoked hams, pickled bacon, lard that made the lightest crusts and oatcakes. Kept them in good food all winter. Long winter. Lord, she remembers helping in all such preparations. Bringing in the wood! People keep hogs today, too, though. Elda couldn't abide the killing, watching her animals frantic, helpless, aware.

How did Daniel grow up? She doubts his mother kept pigs in Phoenix. The idea tickles her: hogs penned in the desert, next to bright concrete, squat between stuccoed strip malls. Let people remember what food looks like when it walks around: plank-skinned bristly, with glistening snouts. Hoofed, buttocked, curly tailed. Did he see nothing but buildings all day? Find shade beneath cactus?

What will Balder do?—a father! He'll take Daniel fishing, show him a wood mill, and the workings of pickups, how the press operates down't *The Voter*. You don't have to think of what to talk about when you do stuff like that.

The old road merges with the sand and gravel of Fox Hill Road. She calls off her search for Posey and Sugarloaf. Elda passes roadside virgin's-bower. From the corner of her eye, she notes daisy fleabane, hedge mustard and corn speedwell under the eaves of trees and among the rocks. The warmth of late June encourages her. July is on its way. Chrischana will leave her camping place down at the cove. Elda worries about her. Where will they live now? Her and the three kids and no roof. Balder said he took care of it, but how? He never tells her things. It's none of her business. And what meddlesome thing would she do about it anyway?

What a way the world has! A month ago she was middle-aged, now she someone's grammie! Life is crowding up again, has turned itself on its ear, presenting complete strangers in the guise of one's flesh, two generations removed. She's got genes in common with someone named Daniel Twitchell!

The road winds down, down. For a few paces, the ponds open before her, the blue and brown edged in green; limpid waters like a fringed plate. Maybe Daniel will be interested in the great horned owl. Or will he just think her an odd old lady? Will he find it neat to feed an owl? Can he do it without getting hurt? An injured owl. That's some conversation piece!

Daniel Twitchell. A Twitchell, in Gottheim again. What would Asa Bartlett make of it?

"Your mother might've told you: Talking don't spook'em, but noise against the boat'll alert 'em. Knocking oars, dropping things. Gut be careful with the tackle box, the well lid...." Balder and Daniel are sitting among the gray stumps and rocks near the weedy shallows, floating in the green and white wooden boat.

They puttered over the pewter platter of Loon Lake at first light to fish for bass. "A sport'll set out five, six different rods with as many lures, tryin't get bass.... Turn the boat into a reg'la supermarket." He grinned. "...Well, I might change bait, switch buzz bait fah jigs, go to a spinna, try grubs. Depends. You might try practicing with one kind to start, then move t'nother."

Daniel sits in the boat, facing his father over the shiny clutter of an open tackle box, with a beat-up ice chest acting as a live well. They have thermoses and a lunch box with sandwiches, chips, fruit. Orange life preservers are within reach. Daniel is in a T-shirt, having taken off the sweatshirt he had on against the early morning chill. The last of the mist has vanished and sun falls now on his sallow arms. By the time July arrives, his coloring will turn golden brown ... now that he is getting more sun than he has since leaving Arizona. In response to the stream of talk Balder pours on him, he says nothing. Talk about bass fishing: largemouth, smallmouth, tournaments, spawning season, range. He doesn't know what to say, so he sits slumped, just listening, or casting his line. Sometimes it snags, and he rips it back, snarling the line.

"That's all right," Balder says when it happens. "Got expect snags'n a place like this." But he is beginning to run out of talk. Being a father isn't as easy as he imagined. Just three hours into it and already he feels the weight, the perplexity. Actually, he felt it two and a half hours ago. Chrischana warned him to take it easy, not expect anything at first. "He's a quiet kid at home, more so with strangers. You take an engine apart a piece at a time and put it back together the same way, right?" Patience, he thinks. And Balder's native New England reserve with strangers should aid in this spot, but his excitement has crowded his common sense. Maybe this natural running out of steam will help...?

As the darkly bearded man's talk slows, Daniel looks away. He feels sorry for him, but can think of nothing to say. Nothing that won't sound awkward or forced. Even so, except for this strange man sitting opposite, trying too hard to be something to him, Daniel is having a pretty good time ... just sitting in a boat in a lake full of shining water, stubby with stumps in the shallows. He likes casting his line, searching for the feel of it, seeking a strike. But the strangeness of the man's role, the weirdness of being alone with him.... Daniel might have been relaxed and excited in the venture if the man were, say, a church youth leader or scoutmaster. Anything but a new father.

Dad—Petey—was good at this sort of thing; like taking him on his hog into the desert. Once or twice, maybe, he suspected that Petey wasn't his real dad. But it had been impossible to broach the subject with Mother. The fact that he looked like Mother and nothing like Petey, where Benaiah and Nathan looked a lot like Petey, couldn't be relied upon. Lots of families were like that. And Petey never showed a preference, so this allayed his suspicions. It is a relief to know that Petey isn't his father. Maybe it means he won't become like him, and drink and turn mean like him. More and more, now, since Mother told him the news, he thinks of Petey as ... not Dad. It makes him feel strange every time he looks at Benaiah or Nathan. Especially Benaiah. There has always been a ... slight—a distance between them, as if they weren't quite related. Now he knows why. But Nathan is different. He's a little kid and needs someone to keep an eye on him.

They are silent in the water among the stumps. Balder says nothing for several minutes. They sit in the boat, one at each end, casting plastic worms on the surface. They get nothing, and for a moment, each sees the humor in those plastic worms. In silence. After a bit Balder looks at him, saying, "Y's'pose this is what they mean when they say 'dead in the watah'?"

Daniel would shrug, but then he thinks of something, and says, "I always picture coffins bobbing around when someone says that."

Balder grins. "Thought I was the only one with that mental image." He feels his jaw relax, his next cast is leisurely and deft. And here it is—running off with his line. Daniel watches him play it, leaning toward the action. The line closes toward the boat as the flashing of the bass nears. Daniel grabs the net and leans out toward the finny creature. At last a heavy largemouth gasps in his net.

Later, they sit eating baloney sandwiches prepared by Balder before dawn. Munching away, he says, "In Gott'im, people like getting out after working all day'n fish fah togue'n squaretails. You see'em standing alongshore, casting away. You don't get big bass like y'do togue. Winter's too cold. They say it takes bass 20, 25 years t'get near five pounds. That largemouth in the well theya's prob'ly old's you."

"People throw those things back?"

"When they ain't eating 'em." He grins. "Sports y'see on TV are reg'la fanatics about bass, wanting to give 'em a chance. But I like t'bring supper home. It's rare I catch more'n I eat, freeze, or give away."

Daniel looks off toward the low summit of Loon Mountain, its contour jagged with conifers, its sides soft in foliage. Above, clouds have drifted across, white and few. The air, while warm, is mild compared to the glare of Phoenix. By this time it could be 110 degrees, breathless and hot enough to fry your brain if you stayed out in it. He'd be inside reading, watching his brothers and breaking up their fights to the hum of the air conditioner. Maine seems like a painting or photograph to him, one he can live in.

With the corner of his eye he catches movement, across the bright water. There. A long homely face, dark and crowned—an unwieldy crown—emerging from water among weeds. His first moose.

He says so, without moving.

Balder looks toward the shore beneath Loon Mountain. The moose mounts a bit, emerging more, its dark rack festooned in green weeds. Balder glances at Daniel, who can't seem to take his eyes off it.

The boy thinks it's like something from books, fantastic.

His father says, "Have t'see one up close some time. Look into its eyes. Pure dumbness. You'd nevah call a human being stupid again. Creature's eight, nine foot tall. If one's evah close enough'n irritated enough, it just might stomp you t'death."

Daniel looks doubtful. The Moose seems pretty placid to him. After a bit it clambers out of the water to wander along shore. Soon it steps long-legged into the shadows beneath the mountain. "Are there bears around much?" He asks, still trying to catch a glimpse of the moose through the trees.

Balder nods. "What choo waunt is don't surprise 'em. Let them know you're in the woods. Hearing noise, they take off. Bear's faces almost all nose. They smell ya if the wind's right. If you come across one, stay calm, don't run. They bluff pretty hod, though. Scare the crap right out o'ya t'see one charge. Nevah had it happen t'me. Last figure I read was something like twenty thousand bears in Maine, so you're bound t'see one some day."

The calling of a loon comes across the lake. A two-noted call, at once lonesome and solacing. From some distance down the lake comes an answering. Daniel says, "I hear loons on Twitchell Pond. Sometimes at night they sound pretty wild."

"It's defensive. Alerts other loons to theya territory. They go all out t'protect eggs, chicks. They'll dance themselves to pieces, trying to get boats to back off. On predators it works pretty good, but it only encourages humans. The more they dance, the more people move in. A loon goes nuts, running atop the water, wings flapping. Its cries sound like laughter t'people, but it's really disturbed. Summer folks love'em. Once a woman fom away, staying too long like a loon itself sometimes will, about died trying t'get one loose from the ice. She had an ax in her canoe'n was chopping away at that ice—to give it some straightaway and fell in herself. She had tried to walk on ice an inch thick." He grins. "And they say the bird's loony."

"In the desert I saw snakes," says Daniel. "Sidewinders are spooky, moving across the rocks'n sand." He demonstrates the snake's movement with his arm, a swift, lateral looping motion.

"Go out to the desert much?" He takes a swallow from the thermos and blots his mustache with the sleeve of his T-shirt.

Lacking expression, Daniel's dark eyes are like charcoals. He shakes his head. "Once in awhile we rode out. Mother'n Dad both have hogs."

"Harley-Davidson?"

He nods. "She had t'leave hers."

Balder's gaze is solemn in return. His sense is that Daniel is telling him she misses the motorcycle. If so, it's the first personal reference he's made. Balder wants to know more, of course. He wants to know why Chrischana came back. She must not have been married to that other man: All the boys' names are Twitchell.

But he pauses, saying nothing. Then he asks, "Your brothers fish too?"

Daniel hesitates. At last he says, "They try."

Balder grins. "That bad?"

You grin a lot, thinks Daniel. The man is like a monkey.... But he's okay. —*God, this is totally weird.*

It would be a surprise to Daniel to learn that Balder's grin frequently covers a mass of calcified agony. And Balder is thinking, Can't get him to smile. He's not the kind. This kid has been through a war. He seen casualties. He is one.

He looks at his wristwatch, puts a cover on the thermos and starts packing things up. He stops a moment to study Daniel who is crumpling a wax paper bag. "You still okay bout coming to *Simon's Ledge*?"

The boy nods. A new grandmother, too. Will she grin a lot? Will she try to hug me? He looks off toward the trees, tree shadows, wishing the moose would reappear. There are worse things than being hugged. He thinks of Petey on a rampage.

Balder turns away, chokes the engine, and is about to pull the rip cord when he turns back. "You were kind of surprised by my new beard this morning.... I'd like you t'know why I grew it." He pauses, making sure of Daniel's attention. "Theya had t'be a great change ... cause I got a son now."

He uses that word "great" on purpose. He would like to communicate to Daniel how the heavens have changed. That the solar system has rounded a curve, and his view of the universe is new.

But Daniel is thinking, Great, *weird,* change. *Totally weird.*

He had been warned about his new grammie's head gear. Yet, upon his entrance into the gloomy front room, he was taken aback. Elda Simon came out of the kitchen with young birds in her softly spun sandy gray hair. They were four baby birds, and their tiny sharp beaks and round eyes pointed toward the ceiling; giving his grandmother a crowned, jeweled appearance. Her face was flushed, sagging and thin, hollow cheeked. Her dim eyes were the shiest he had ever seen. Creaturely shy, and peering. Somewhat wild, he thought.

"Hello, Daniel," she said, holding out her thin hand. "I'm pleased t'meet choo." The hand in his felt like a thing of bones, fragile and long.

"Did you get choo some bass this morning?"

"No," he said. "Grandmother. Balder caught one, though."

The man went into the kitchen, his gaping fish adangle.

Daniel looked about the room, taking in bookcases under dim windows crowded with dark lilac leaves. He had seen their dried blooms outside. There was an old console television, ratty looking furniture draped in old afghans and quilts. A tuft of dingy stuffing stuck out from the arm of one chair. Even so, the room was neat and clean, everything in place. The worn wood floor was scattered with rugs, once colorful. For all the room's apparent cleanliness, there was a faint animal odor.

"Dahsn't mind my looks just now," Mrs. Simon was saying as she followed Balder into the kitchen. She seemed ill at ease in her own living room. He could tell she wanted to move about, do anything but stand there talking to him. Her voice trailed back, and he moved to follow. "These babies was abandoned—afta theya nest blew down in that storm two days back. I been feeding them. Theya s'weak I had t'pry theya li'l beaks apart."

Daniel entered the kitchen, remembering the night they spent in the Bonneville, thinking of that storm. "Whad you feed 'em?" he asked.

"Milk soaked crumbs. Gaunt graduate 'em to cat food mixed with mashed worms."

The kitchen, like the front room, spanned the house. More light came through its windows, a filtered green light, where vines glimmered at the glass. The counter, or sideboard as Cindabilla would've called it, was gleaming wood. Tins, brassy and colored, lined it along the back. Balder stood at the sink, water running. He was filleting fish, attentive, but saying nothing.

Mrs. Simon walked over to him and peered at the fish. "That's a good bass, Balda," she said.

He grunted, looking over his shoulder at Daniel. "You can sit at the table, if y'waunt."

"That's okay. I sat all morning."

"Yuht," said Balder, grinning, thinking maybe he should bring up the moose sighting again.

But Daniel is startled suddenly by scrabbling across the floor. Two chipmunks, tails straight up in the air, come out of nowhere.

They are on the gleaming countertop. One has pried open a tin. Now, their bushy backs bent, their hind quarters twitching, they grab for tidbits. Peanuts, he sees. Turning them rapidly in their tiny paws, they send specks flying.

Balder grins at the look of astonishment on Daniel's face. "That's Dip'n Chale. Forgot to tell you about them. They come in through holes in the stone foundation. Holes behind cupboards, too."

The scampering sent the birds from grandmother's head flittering about the room. Daniel's eyes widen, watching them flurry in circles, crisscrossing below the ceiling. Slowly, he shakes his head. Nathan and Benaiah are not going to believe this.

Balder is grinning again. "More's in the barn. What choo got out theya now, Mother?"

"Not much just now. A rabbit, couple rabbits. Fox from an illegal trap. Birds. Young moose with damaged tendons in his hind leg. He'll be all right; just keeping'em quiet so he don't go lame. Oh—an owl. Quite a story, that owl. Keeps getting shot."

The owl! thinks Daniel. Got to see that owl. The one that sent Uncle Ferddy to the hospital ... and stopped him beating on Babette! This place is better than a—a book! It's *being* in a book. He's beginning to wonder if it's worth all the weirdness, the babysitting and comfortless camping with little brothers and hordes of biting insects. It's almost worth the hazing he got in middle school (not quite).

"C'mon," grandmother is saying as she crosses toward the back door. "I'll show you."

Daniel follows, looking back once at Balder. The older Mainer grins, his teeth flashing in the dark foliage of his face. His cap of hair gleams whitely, vivid in contrast. Daniel smiles back. He turns and steps out onto the granite stoop.

He's on the path among the green overgrowth, smiling all the way to the barn.

The Gott'im Epistles

Dear Miguel [fragment of a letter from a resident of Quaker Plantation],

Howz it do? Thanks for your last.

[...]You remember my blather that most of my ancestors were Welsh coal miners, but probably don't know how it was for them. As children they carried 50, 60 pounds three hundred feet to the surface, in order (ultimately) to make profit for wealthy mine owners. Virtual slaves, denied education, forced to pay a perpetual bill to the mine owners for bare necessities. With their breaking bodies they brought up the fuel that warmed all England and blackened the skies of London. I haven't forgotten this, so I'm on your side. I admire your forthrightness, and your feelings, and especially your paintings of people in their place. But here's where I differ. You wrote, "They don't love art," of MFA students who failed to repress visceral reactions to your paintings. You even suspected them of racism for this reason.

Sweetie, you know what a reverse snob is. What's a reverse reactionary?

You write me that "People want nice, sensical romantic images instead of the tortured realism of these fragmented souls." Yes, many do. But does your love of art condemn those with an affinity for whole images? Should the classical or romantically inclined be pushed out of the gallery because your full-hearted gritty realism doesn't nourish them? Can everyone enjoy the same dish? Should people who can't eat broccoli quiche starve? How can people sit at the table when their food is taken away by peer pressure? Or by the authority of teachers like yourself?

You said something good about the arrogance of painters whose sole object is themselves, as opposed to the breadth and interconnection found in community: "Finally it's the cause and the impact of work that counts, not the painter." Wow!! Maybe you'll consider reading one of the portrayers of rural Maine. Carolyn Chute has just caused a ruckus here with the *Beans of Egypt Maine*. These earthy writings tell some of the stories of this place. It might work toward establishing a rapport between wasp and chicano. The coldness and ego of Mainers in a certain socio-economic slot might have more in common with your arid village counterparts than do those middle-class mindset suburbanite Latinos you tangled with.

(oops—my reaction is showing.)

Later, El

Dear Editor,

Now that snow cover no longer hides the mess, I'm writing to express our indignation over the unsightly places one finds in Gottheim's lovely countryside. We're skiers who've moved up here weekends in order to enjoy the beauty of these mountains. Some of our neighbors in this rural neighborhood don't seem to care *what* the place looks like. Junk vehicles, parts, assortments of trash, rags tied on trees as *decorations*!, refrigerators, bedsteads—an old dental chair set out for passersby to admire?! I'm tempted to call some authority to make abutters clean up. But we want to give neighbors a chance to do right on their own. Have mercy on your neighbors who have put a lot into their homes and lawns, and appreciate the overall aesthetic framework.

Joe and Mrs. Sixpack, you know who you are. Please get to work on this right away.
Jamie and Frederick Sludlinger,
Quaker Plantation

Dear Chrischana,

I figured Gottheim was small enough, if I sent this letter to the post office you'd get it somehow. I was surprised as hell to find you and the boys gone, but on second thoughts wasn't. Can't really blame you. Last night I dreamed a gorilla was beating the shit out of me. Drinking did it, like it did to you. You had a hard time.

You know it's not easy for me to write this, but I miss you so damn much. I love you dammit Christy. Never realized how much till I came home from school and found you gone. Before I always promised to mend my ways, and you always gave me a chance. Guess I ran out of chances after that last binge.

No more binges, period. I need you so much, Christy. I recall every inch of your body. All your loving ways, how you put up with so much, so long. Remember the Sunday mornings in bed? Remember the funny papers on the floor with the little guys, or that last long desert ride? I miss the little bikers so much.

Christy, I'm human, flawed. I know it. Have mercy. God, if you could just exercise that famous sweet mercy one last time. This time I'd get counseling—like you always said. I'm ready for it now. Just write and say you're coming. I'll go into counseling the day I get your letter, even join AA. You know how good I can be when the devil's not around. Together we'll keep him away for good.

Think of the boys. They can't be doing well. You've got no money, family (I remember that much). Please take my week's pay, here in the envelope, and get what you need. Write and I'll send more, the expenses to return you all, if it means having to drop out of MMI. Hell, I'd hock my tools to get you back. My life back. Please bring back my life, Christy.

Peter

Dear Editor [three drafts],

Some of you may have heard of the grants from the Maine Humanities Council, being offered for the purpose of studying and making known town history. This could include studies on the following: genealogy, antiques, back issues of *The Voter*, letters and records of every description, oral history, architecture, songs, poems, literature, and just about anything else you'd care to name.

Some of you in the primary grades, middle and high school, churches, adult education, fraternal orders, the Grange and what have you, might be interested in applying. What are your separate histories? For our part, we here in the Gottheim Historical Society are hoping to present a series of discussions on these topics and more. We're interested in questions such as, what has small-town life contributed to the formation of American culture, what do we contribute now, and is there a future contribution to be made?

We're also interested in how great Aunt Fanny braided rugs and did she use peppers when canning corn? And what date, precisely, did the peavey make an appearance in the woods around

Gottheim, supplanting the cant hook? Can anyone shed more light on our clock's origination? With the post office commenced on a search for new quarters, might now be a good time to search out the history of the mail service in town?

Methods of dissemination might include plays, short stories and songs, a theme parade, art projects and puppet shows, or displays: botanical, artifacts, and old-time craft.

Some of you understand how interesting and absorbing this all can be, and how it to might elevate the children hereabouts beyond a mass culture purveyed through your televisions each night.

Don't forget your local stories of the supernatural. We got tales of hauntings in Gottheim and towns roundabout to yield a small body of folklore. How about forming story groups designed to scare history into the ignorant?

Asa Bartlett

Dear Editor,

We the undersigned are looking for a new meeting place for early morning coffee. This is the unofficial Gottheim selectmen's critics and old gossips' coffee club, meeting in Decatur's every morning. We'll be needing a dite o'donuts, bacon and eggs, flapjacks, coffee, what have you. To begin after Jasper Mary Day. We have a little more to do than a man on the town, but not so much as to prevent unofficial meetings absolutely essential to maintaining town business. Send suggestions to *Entrepreneur de bois*, P.O. Box 47.

On behalf of Decatur, we are some exercised but, owing to financial consideration, won't mention at who.

Etc.

Dear Editor,

The Committee of Community Alternatives has assigned me to oversee the compilation of studies designed to find direction for Gottheim's future cultural and economic stabilization in the wake of IICE's previously announced departure. Negotiations are, of course, ongoing, and, after our hard work, there is no reason to hope that the Institute may continue to return each summer. My first step is to initiate study circles designed to bring the diverse minds of the community together for discussion. Area businesses, art, theater, and church groups, and school organizations will want to choose representatives to attend these directional sessions. The initial meeting, to be held in the multipurpose room of Hazel Newell High-School, will be announced when all parties have chosen their representatives. Write to the committee care of me at P.O. Box 1070, Gottheim.

We on the committee have high hopes of a bright future for our town, and are looking forward to your input before the end of the month, if not sooner. Remember, this is *your* community. *Your* commitment is vital to our effort. There are exciting times ahead in Gottheim.

Gloria Fay

Balder,

I'm sorry to take so long getting back to you on your "proposal," so convincingly (and charmingly) put in Decatur's Diner a few weeks ago. You really threw me. I'm sure you know this.

I want to be thoughtful and complete in my answer. In fact, a *lot* of thought goes into it. Your ideas have forced me to focus on the big picture, to quit drifting along in my childish joy at just being in

Gottheim at last. I'm astonished over your being a father. But it's helped me focus, as I'm sure it has you. You are on a new path, one (I see now) you hoped for all along. We are very different people in our pursuits. No matter the psychic and physical attraction between us, the determining factor must be the direction of our individual hopes and dreams. They clash. Hopelessly.

For instance, I strongly believe that the ideal size for a family in our present era is two, a family of spouses. Humans must consider the strain upon our planet's resources, and act accordingly. Naturally, I'm realistic enough to see that others aren't going to fall in line with this. I have no fear that we as a species will die out through lack of breeding! But there are just too many people in the world today, and I've got to do what little I can to keep competition for resources down. And a responsible thing to do in the face of *Malthus's Dismal Theorem* is refrain from bringing more people into the world. In the case of your son, of course, it's too late. (Yes, I see the irony: In the case of my own presence, it's too late as well.)

And I am honest enough to admit that the argument of competition for resources has a personal taint. My own life would be drained by a family of children. Even one child requires an enormous amount of energy and expense. One sees women shriveled up by the demands of family. Worn out, yet unfulfilled. I wouldn't have a child and then deprive it of the things it wants. Take sneakers. Currently one spends as much as sixty dollars for a decent pair. Multiply this by all the child's other desires and expectations. In another age, an agrarian age, children were an asset. They worked to keep the family going. But today, in our consumer oriented society, they're a liability, a drain on family resources. Also, the real work of being there for all the details, the logistics of family life, falls to the woman. Currently men require prodding to fulfil their obligations in regard to sensitive caring, or plain household chores. Such prodding, such work is never-ending and there's no vacation from it.

You speak of building a house. I can visualize the kind of house you want. One full of kids—kids hanging out windows, and giggling under the covers, whooping out of control. A place where they can safely get into trouble, and grumble while being made to do chores. You don't want a house with TVs, computers, VCRs, white drapery, a dishwasher. But the kids themselves would not want to be without these things. You want a house that can stand up to dogs, cats, flying parakeets, or goldfish wriggling on the floor in a puddle, a house with gooey fingerprints on the furniture. I can tell you, Balder, that is not what I want. Perhaps one day I will indulge in such a daydream. I can't rule out the possibility, or the urge to romanticize over it. But I hope to God that's all I allow myself. Life is so much more than this squalor would permit.

Looking back over the course of our relationship, I now see hints as to the kind of man you are in regard to lovemaking as well as housekeeping. We differ here as well. At first it perplexed me that we never made love. Now in light of your fatherhood I'm more perplexed. All I can think is that you've changed since Chrischana's child was conceived. Coupled with our abstinence, little things you said lead me to think you now believe dating should be an activity for selecting a mate. In other words, sex is to be a serious matter, robbed of its spontaneity. And no longer a playful encounter. I remember your crack about people seeing it on the level of skateboarding. You disparaged it as a diversion like table tennis. These remarks may be a cover for phobia. By confining sexuality to marriage and procreation, you stunt it, closing off the great field of freedom it deserves. You've managed to turn the joy of human sexuality into a form of drudgery. This is repressive and a bit sick.

Making an effort at honesty, I'll admit to an occasional emptiness in my pursuit, but remain convinced that this has more to do with an inappropriate choice of partner than to the lack of marital union. But Balder, I had to overcome quite a bit to achieve my liberation (I was raised Baptist), so I'm not about to revert to traditional morality.

Please don't be offended. I'm trying to be as honest as possible. I wouldn't want to be false either to you or myself. I avoid self deception. Isn't it only right?

Finally, we come to the most profound part. Love. Our love must not be lost in all this, but it's what I fear most. Looking back over this letter, I see I'm no closer to solving the dilemma love poses. We love each other. But for how long? And under what stresses will our love fail? Will the present conflict signal the beginning of love's failure? I don't know. And I don't know where we go from here.

I do love you.
Gloria

Dear Olive,

Please accept my condolences on the death of Horace. I won't trouble you trying to express sympathy. Please, if there's anything I can do? Maybe we could go fishing as we did in the old days when it was you and Horace, and Griselda and me. You just got to get some rest. I keep thinking of the strain you been under, straightout. Couldn't we just do something to remember him by? Talk of the good times, or something, as a memorial to him? Oh Lord, when it all ends, Olive. I still miss her.

I'll be by, of course. And see you at the wake.

Asa

Dear Editor,

Many people know that Horace passed away last week, and have sent their condolences. Such an outpouring of food and help at home, and, well, just plain—their presence, you know. I appreciate it ever so much. As one put it, it's hard when it all ends. But you folks, you folks have made it so much more bearable.

I won't be doing my news for a while. Please send your neighborhood items to Greta Blake. She'll see they get put in the paper.

Olive Lovejoy

Dear Editor,

Won't someone explain to us at Hazel Newell why German has been cut? Don't people realize the place language has in our college prep? This doesn't even mention the other cuts made. Don't people in this place care whether kids here get a decent education? Recently you eliminated half a million dollars from our budget because of higher property values. Why? If, as everyone says, property values have tripled in one year, why are taxes being cut? Shouldn't it be the other way around, taxes raised?

Gottheim Academy recently received a donation from an alumnus for five million dollars. This person graduated from there at a time when town kids, not just preppies, were also educated there, tuition free. If Hazel Newell had been built then, wouldn't that alumnus have attended and left us the money instead?

I heard one of our neighbors say that we ("kids today") need to learn to do without. The same neighbors just bought an eighteen thousand dollar car. Is this how you do without in the 1980's?

Jenn Trowbridge

Dear Editor,

The little girl who wrote last week about Spanish or German being cut just doesn't understand the burden these taxes put on folks. *Wages* haven't gone up to cover taxes. *That's* what we pay them with. We got to get some relief or people will start losing their property. What are they teaching in school, anyway? And what good does a college education do around here? You have to leave to use it.

Minnie Virgin

Chrischana,

I guess you know what would be happening to you if I had you here right now. Seeing my check returned without cashing—no explanation, no nothing, not even asking how I am—made me mad enough to choke you skinny. Good thing your in Goddam. I felt like killing you. I don't care if they lock me up till I stink.

In fact, I'm coming to get you. This note, I just decided, is a little something to get you thinking. Don't go believing I'll change my mind when this binge goes. I'm for the mailbox now.

Petey

P.S. Thanks for returning the check. Now I know for sure you're in Godham.

Dear Editor,

Just a reminder about the upcoming Jasper Mary Day. We need more, albeit last minute, entrants for the parade. Kids in costume, animals, theme floats, baton twirlers, anything. We have enough veterans on motor scooters, but if that's all you have, you're welcome.

There will be booths on the common, the Franco Fiddlers, used books for sale on the sidewalk in front of the library, the quilt drawing, art displays, refreshments and the ever popular logging competition. Can Alvin Robichaud hang on to the golden axe one more year? Don't forget the dueling guitars and the pie contest. Cast your vote for this year's Jasper Mary at Pardner's drug, the Foodliner, or Cross's Hardware. There will be fireworks as usual on the Academy lawn at 10:00 p.m.

The Jasper Mary Day Committee

Dear Chrischana,

Please forgive and ignore if you can the last letter I might have sent you. I think I wrote you when I was drunk and am sorry if I did. I would never harm you if I could help it. I want only to love and treat you with the respect you deserve. You put up with a lot because of me. But I love you and the boys.

Please, can't we talk? I really want to come there and see you all again. With counseling we can work it out. We've got to. I just can't give myself up for lost. Or us either.

I'd ask you to call me, but can't blame you if you don't. I'll pack up everything—my tools—as soon as this season at MMI ends, and drive to Gotheim. I don't expect to stay with you, but just want to be close, know you and Ben, Daniel and Nathan are near.

Love, Peter

Dear Dad, how are you? I am fine. Here is my pitcher from last year in case you lost yours. Don't forgit what I look like OK? Send me your's. Bald door is nice. I love you.

Nathan [letter was not sent.]

Jasper Mary

Back...back... remote in fleeting mists about the Meguntic
Mountains.... Long ago there nestled a scattering of cabins high above
the foggy ponds of a wooded vale. The people there were hardy,
early astir, lighting fires and milking the family cow. They looked
out from hardly won dooryards upon a world misted over, the smoke
of their stone chimneys sinking to mingle with the clouds of the New
England pond valley. Below, in those vapors in summer, lived
remnants of the Arossagunticook Natives who then populated
mountains along the river of the same name. The hardy pioneers of
Farmingham Royal, as they first named the town, looked down upon
the natives both literally and figuratively—deeming them shiftless,
childlike and slothful in comparison to their own rigorous, high-
minded and provident Yankee and Puritan descent.

    Away through Mountains wound the Arossagunticook River,
toward the distant sea. The river was checked and channeled by the
dark bulks, which had once been sharp and high but were now ground
down and low, rounded by monstrous implacable ice that hunkered
mile-high over this part of the continent. An age had passed. Debris-
laden tongues of ice had melted out of the valleys, leaving the
Arossagunticook and its tributaries flowing seaward; some of them
scattered with specks of gold, all of them paved in part with smooth
cobble, a legacy of glacier's patient exercise upon the sharp heights.

    Downstream from the pioneer community of Farmingham
Royal the river fell, great and creamy, over rocks where salmon
leaped in season, ardently searching for the exact streambed where

they were spawned two or three years before; before the epic journey of life that brought them full-circle to the pure and home-scented place where they began.

Here, above these falls the Natives called *Roccomeeco*, a woman was born to be great among her people by being the servant of all. Jasper Mary. She was a full-blooded Roccomeeco Native, satin-skinned, dark eyed and solemn-seeming, yet full of the lore of her people; able to convey, with a deft story or incident, a world of truth to her hearers. Along with her knowledge of herbs, root, and flower, and a detailed understanding of skies, Jasper Mary kept the lore of her adopted faith, the Catholicism so dreaded and feared by early Puritans, and belittled by their settler descent. The natives had been taught by voyaging Jesuits, their Catholicism assimilated and flourishing transmuted among the natives of the Meguntic Mountains.

Jasper Mary grew to be an itinerant herbal healer, traveling the river's valley from its obscure sources in the northern mountains to its mighty meeting with other such rivers in a bay near the sea. Jasper Mary learned the river's creatures and their ways, its shoreline features and flora, its legends and historics and hauntings. I knew where the white heron nested, where leaves were good for fever, how to glean from carrion the stuff to make boxes and pouches and poultices. My quill boxes and purses were sought after, the pioneers bartering for things from their store. And Jasper Mary knew each settler along the great tortuous length of her river, watching of their comings and goings, their uprisings and downfallings. In telling herself their stories, Jasper Mary came to understand their strange ways.

All the world of the Arossagunticook was hers to observe, hers to catalogue, hers to watch over in prayer. The settlers' knew this. Yet, by those of Farmingham Royal and other settlements roundabout, Jasper Mary was most known for her treasure. For, although every household had been touched in some way by her medicine, and though many heard her familiar throaty voice weaving stories, or chanting to the Virgin and her holy Son as she paddled down river, the thing most spoken of in every home was Jasper Mary's treasure. It was thought that Jasper Mary knew where tourmaline was hidden. She knew how to find beryl, jasper and gold. She knew where crystals grew in white clay, "as though raisins for the plucking from plum pudding."

The stories she told were those of her travels along the river, of her adventures among the wildlife, of odd backwoods characters from her forays into deep wilderness. She liked also to tell the tales of her hero Culuscap, a mythic Dawnlander who had some characteristics in common with her Lord. The English and their Yankee descendants said that Culuscap was just another Indian and that he possessed no greater qualities than those found in any Indian chanced upon along the river. But, to the Abenaki, Penobscot, or Passamaquoddy, Culuscap was the human embodiment of heaven and earth. He was, if not actually born of his grandmother, then raised by her. He had a mischievous or evil brother, was always ready to accept and meet challenges, responsible for creatures, and helpful in forming the surface of the earth. The mythic Dawnlander, while full of a sinewy temperament, was also capable of being temporarily deceived.

The end of Culuscap, as Jasper Mary told, was death at the hands of his brother. Yet there was a persistent, lingering belief among the Natives that Culuscap would return once more to help restore all things. The English scoffed at this, saying Culuscap was just another dead Indian, and asking when his dust would rebuild itself into skin and muscle and bone; when would it grow eyes and see again?

Many of the Indians stopped telling the stories of Culuscap. They told stories of a hapless character named Jack, instead. The many asinine adventures of Jack—a derivative of the English Jack-and-the-beanstalk—kept them entertained. This Jack was also a Native, not very bright, but who nonetheless managed to scrape by with the help of kindly fortune. Jasper Mary still told the Culuscap stories to Natives, and also to the children of settlers. Oddly, once grown, the children forgot the stories, although some would listen raptly if one of their little ones chanced to repeat what was heard of him from the healer. Others would simply shake their heads and laugh.

She was buried near a tributary where gold was known to wash down out of the north. Today, nearly two hundred years after the mists closed over her grave, Jasper Mary is most remembered for her famous curse. She is less remembered for her murder by thieves bent on unearthing her treasure.

As the tale goes, one of them later bragged about the deed while on a binge. But the other kept to himself afterward, relating the story only once, to his sister when he was ill. He told of Jasper Mary's calm facing of death; how she had said she was old and, like the salmon, ready to return to her source-stream. And that she had always wondered what the face of Culuscap looked like; that she believed it was as the sun burning mist off a pond, reflecting out of the water in morning. The hard thief did not believe her, suspecting a bluff to disarm them. He ended as a hermit in the woods. Or maybe he hanged himself. A corpse of nibbled bones was found scattered beneath a weathered noose not far from Jasper Mary's grave. But the other thief knew that her treasure lay elsewhere.

Though her death was written in local history, it is the curse of Jasper Mary that lives on in the collective mind of Gottheim today. Two towns to the east, on a tributary called Sabbath, the healer was once turned away in a snowstorm by folk unfamiliar with her.

They had come up from Massachusetts intent on settling a goodly piece of land in the District of Maine. One raging night, they were startled to see a strange Indian calling at their isolated cabin.

"Shelter me!" I, Jasper Mary, cried as the wind tore.

"Nay, but we know you not!" hollered the householder through a crack in the latched door.

"All you know is I perish!"

Yet they would not be entreated. Thus, Jasper Mary uttered her curse, and went away through obscuring snow. Her voice fell, half absorbed by the snow, saying, "Curséd the earth of this place. Endeavors not prosper here!"

Two hundred years after, the people of Gottheim and Quaker and Copenhagen remember the curse. Today's descendants of the old settlers still watch along the rapids of Sabbath River to see what prospers. They notice the thick beds of poison ivy growing rank and dark and laden with noxious white berries. They see that the streambed holds no fish, having absorbed toxic tailings from a hundred years' old abandoned mine upstream. They point it out when a business fails on the ground of my curse.

They shake their heads ominously. But they do not laugh.

It was the cool of morning when Chrischana climbed through the ravine between old hills to reach an overgrown lane leading to Twitchell Farm. The old place is high on a knob of Blackwell Mountain called Buck Hill, so far from the highway that traffic is scarcely heard. Both the knob and rounded off double summit of the mountain are clearly visible from sections of two roads that also parallel the curving river. The mountain is of the same batholith but much lower than nearby Jasper Mountain.

Morning's early coolness has now withered away, and the exertions of her climb dampen Chrischana. She takes a few swallows of water, caps her recycled juice bottle and rounds the last leafy bend. The house is still lost in the leaves, and she approaches slowly, partly for the tender associations, partly in sorrow for the house's neglect. Olive Lovejoy has warned that during the years of Chrischana's absence Twitchell Farm was continually vandalized.

As a girl her feelings were ambivalent, sometimes appreciative, sometimes irritated over its isolation. But more often she was glad she had to look far to see another dwelling, though her girlfriends sometimes wondered over this. "Don't choo get lonely up theya y'self?" Babette Roebuck would ask her again and again. The hill had been named for one Philo Buck, who went mad because water could be hard to come by during the dry season. In those years he lost a crop seemed nearly every August. But on this side of the hill water from springs could be found. Sometimes the hill would almost burst with water.

She comes to a rusted gate, locked shut by Enan Pale who bought the old place at tax auction during her absence. She is on top of the hill, the mountain slope above her now visible, and clearcut across its flanks. Maybe 550 acres in soft green. Had she seen the cut last year, she would've been saddened by the ugly brown wounds slashed across the slopes. Daniel Albert Twitchell supplemented his income setting traps there, and his daughter learned from him. She knew how to skin the animal, scrape, stretch and cure pelts; check traps early and late to avoid unnecessary suffering. She justified her trapping as a way to keep disease down in fur-bearing populations. Back then. Not now. Now she feels the helplessness and fear of the trapped.

She slides under the gate. The thickets thin, and Chrischana sees the house, darkened by the beloved crowd of old maples in the dooryard. The roof of its porch is fallen at one end, the floor rotten, a pillar askew. Debris spills out one window, littering the porch: shattered glass, tattered curtains, stuffing filthy with mildew. Coming around the side of the house she walks on pieces of asphalt shingle, splintered wood, the foxed backs of old and familiar books. She looks to see that the inset structure of the early Greek revival doorway is still intact, but the door itself is gone; the walls on either side agape. As she peers in, the smell of must and decay assaults her. Chrischana recognizes the old bedsprings tossed willy-nilly, the upended bookcase, the slashed-to-ribbons couch where her father sometimes snoozed. Just beyond the door frame, the tiny crooked stair winds toward the second floor, its treads showing worn where once she carefully placed her young feet, dreaming of previous inhabitants of the Twitchell line. Someone must have worked hard, getting that bedsprings around the stairwell's corner. She steps back. Belowstairs, and under the gaping separation of floor and foundation, a black cellar hole lurks. The massive slab granite foundation stones have been jerked from their moorings. In disbelief she stares at them, puzzling. How could such heavy big things be moved? Was it but frost causing them to fall inward?

Still wondering and staring into the bleak dark below, Chrischana is aware of salt taste in the corners of her mouth. She licks her lips, the salt blending with saliva. Till now she had been unaware.... Chrischana has been silently weeping.

Chrischana takes the old settler's road, the twitch trail down toward the Lower Intervale Road which travels alongside the Arossagunticook River. The intervale is good bottom farmland, hidden in spots from either the river or the highway. She is hiking to Gottheim, on her way to celebrate her first Jasper Mary Day since her return to this place from which she sprang. In the village she will meet her children and Balder, and together they plan to watch the parade.

It's still a long walk, on top of the early morning's climb, but it will give her time for reflection. They can't take this camping much longer, Daniel especially so. So much falls on him. She now knows what she will do with the money Balder has given her. A down payment is all it will take to secure part of the old property. She has heard that Enan Pale is thinking of putting it on the market. An article in *The Voter* tells of funds available through Maine State Housing Authority, loans for first-time low-income buyers. Balder's money—Daniel's money really—is enough to secure one of those loans. But sadly, the old house is beyond repair. Will that nix the loan? *Look into it, that's all. Just have to check.*

A view across the river opens out as Chrischana walks along. Tiny in the distance she sees that burned-out building on the highway beneath Morrill Mountain. Odd—this view of a blackened cross-timber jutting above the fallen roof. Ithiel Whitman's building, isn't it? From here that cross-timber looks like a crucifix.

She passes the Franklin P. Mills farm, a connected dwelling with smaller attached house, stout ell, and unpainted patinaed barn; the main house with those austere Federalist lines. Already the yard is choked with bales in wagons, spilling over, ready for the conveyor to the open loft. No one in sight to load it with the hay. As she passes, its green fragrance fills her nostrils. The family may be in the village, joining the gathering townsfolk for the parade.

Sweating, breathing hard, she picks up her pace. Lonely this last piece of the walk. For a moment she almost wishes Peter was here, walking alongside. There had been good times, too; and companionship. Peter could be entertaining, funny, loving even ....

Chrischana can't wait to meet the others outside the Bond Block. Should she really try to get something going up on Buck's Hill? Oh for a house to hold, shelter, comfort them. A safe place. She must, they all must live in the Town of Gottheim with her people. No harm will come to them here. *Forget about Petey. Don't think of him again.*

Tucked into foliage pricked by white steeples, the village of Gottheim lay in a gleaming valley of waters. From a distance it was a dream of New England, settled by descendants of East Anglians, steeped in peace. Looking down from above, was there anything of evil to be seen? Could the high view show nothing sordid or cynical to recommend it to contemporary literary interest? Maybe the stream of soot that occasionally shot skyward from a village mill currently working the bugs out of its new generating system? Even this process was performed according to strict federal regulations, so that, if the smoke was dense and particle-filled it was intermittent. And didn't it lend a kind of pungency to the scene? That little touch of dark and soot which kept it from becoming unreal?

Watching from above, the dark Angel descended down past the summit of Jasper Mountain each year to watch Gottheim's annual parade in her honor. For many years, in the early decades perhaps, she likely found clean mountain air. This year she traversed low level ozone, sent northward from the vehicle-infested eastern corridor. Now the Angel crossed over the opaque, smelly Arossagunticook, silent witness to the river's corruption by a paper mill farther upstream. Even so, the scene below the spirit was, on the whole, fair; like a garden dotted with white, and wild with rugged plutonic beauty. Even the tiny charred cross-timber, cocked at an angle, jutting above Ithiel Whitman's small white burned-out building by the river, did not mar the garden's beauty when seen from above. Did the people of Gottheim deserve the beauty because they were scattered and few? Did they deserve because of their ancestors' struggle to make and keep the Town habitable? Or did they deserve this beauty?

The dark Angel—austere, agéd, composed—drifted down each year to the far end of the village above the Greek revival rooftops of brick-built Gottheim Academy. She peered down through green leaves at the colorful assemblage of parade participants on the wide central lawn below. Already the band music was lifting, its drums beginning. Small children picked up their tiny streamered bicycles. Floats lurched into place behind tractors, four-wheelers, or on the decked beds of pickups; each with its theme of historic, recreational or occupational significance—anything to show the value of life as it was lived and felt in the community: logging, farming, and teaching. There were tableaux of sport fishermen, of wildlife, homecraft and quilting; of hunting, dogsledders, of skiers crouching and descending a hill of painted wood and cotton batting.

Slowly, the high school band leading, this living line made its way off the wide sloping lawn, filing down School Street. Approaching toward Front Street and the Common, it passed the vanguard of sidewalk watchers. Along one side of the common stood the churches. Below their large, four-square steepled whiteness, stood happy white people of every age and description ... with, in these mid-1980s, a very few alien dark faces from India, Asia, Africa, or the Middle East: These offshore representatives of the International Institute for Coordinated Experiments, dotted the white crowd assembled beneath the dark Angel's gaze. Without their lush complexions, flashing smiles and vivid eyes, the crowd would be hopelessly pasty and bland. The Angel understood: For these people of color, such whiteness in the town's streets was like a wall, an impasse, never to be penetrated by intimacy in their brief sojourn in New England Gottheim.

Under the Angel, and merging with Front Street, snaked the line of music makers, marchers, horse-mounted participants. Floats and vets on motor scooters, the gleaming humpbacks of old model cars, all followed by silent red or yellow fire engines from every community roundabout Gottheim. The Angel drifted, searching the crowd with her quiet American Indian eyes. Her solemn gaze intent, penetrated every joyful heart or sorry hidden thought of each one below her gaze. She was also deeply aware of the collective spirit expressed. And, invisible to the people, imps—naked and ridiculous—scurried among them, cavorting before her eyes. These raced from one cluster to another, mocking and grinning, laughing, winking, playing pranks.

Through chinks between storefronts came the gleam of Hutchins Pond, reflecting sunlight among the marchers and watchers who were otherwise shaded here and there by large old trees, standing at intervals along the main street of Gottheim.

Moving majestically above the parade, the dark Angel matched her pace with that of this year's Jasper Mary, the Angel's namesake riding below. The girl sat restive, astride a dancing brown pony, its halter trimmed in the dark feathers of ravens. Like some of her predecessors, she was part Indian, a fourteen-year-old whose great great great great great grandfather had once posted tokens at portages between lakes to the north. But this knowledge was now lost to the girl who rode tensely, trying to keep her ahistorical mount without a loss of dignity; but finally slithering in agitation to the pavement before Cross's Hardware. She loosed the reins, determined now to walk flat-footed to parade's end in her moccasins.

Now the dark Angel above felt an added weight of glory descending behind. She glanced quietly back at lucent clouds approaching, a great multitude of witnesses descending toward the crowd. This vast throng, full of faces, pressed above her, watching with the same austere attentiveness of Jasper Mary herself. Pressing gently upon the hometown scene, the great cloud of watchers shed a quality of fullness upon its descendants below.

The true Jasper Mary, who descends from Jasper Mountain each year to see her parade, now lowered toward the dismounted girl, speaking some quiet words in an Algonquin tongue. Immediately the girl reached out and took the pony's reins again, throwing herself upon its back. She sat straight, tangling her fingers in the pony's black mane. The aura of the crowd on either side swelled with applause and whistles. The little pony and its rider went dancing along Front Street, the ancestors of all looking on from above.

Daniel, Balder, Nathan, Benaiah, and Chrischana stood together outside the brick block where *The Voter* was weekly published, watching the parade pass along Front Street. In Balder's hands was a grease-spotted bagful of chocolate chip cookies, and, as fast as the boys could dig for one, they dipped chocolatey hands for another. Chrischana had arrived at last, just in time to see this year's Jasper Mary slither to the pavement. The woman watched the girl continue several paces, her hand still futilely grasping after the pony's halter. Chrischana smiled. "Same thing pretty much happened to me the year I was Jasper Mary." Bending to Nathan and Benaiah, she said, "Watch'n see if she climbs up again."

Nathan, all hyper movement with skinny limbs, leaning out into the street, watched the Indian girl in buckskin and fringes lunge for the pony and take to it again. He shouted with the crowd, tugging on his mother's wrist and gesturing. "Did you get back up on the pony, too?"

"Yes'n it wasn't easy. I was deeply embarrassed."

"Deeply, Mother?" said Benaiah, mocking. The sun had brought out his brown freckles, leaving the rest of his skin as fair as ever. "You'n Daniel always put things so funny. Why don't cha say 'really', like everybody else?"

Balder said, "If I know your mother, Ben, I'd say she's not like evah body else." Then he grinned at her. "Good thing!"

Chrischana smiled, her white teeth crisp in her glowing native features. She looked over at Daniel, who returned her smile. His own sallow skin had taken on its accustomed summer glow. She was glad of that smile. Daniel was a happier boy than he had been. They had all benefited from Balder's influence.

"So, did everybody vote for you to be Jasper Mary?" asked Nathan. He moved constantly, alternately hanging on her or pulling away and waving his arms at nothing in particular.

"Not everybody. Of course not. But enough to get me on the pony. Once you're up there y'wonder why y'wanted it s'bad. Everyone gaping at you, watchin' if you'll flub up. I'd never want t'be Jasper Mary again."

"You were one of the best damned Jasper Marys this town ever had," said a quiet voice behind her. "I remember that from my summer trips home."

She turned to find the keen stern green-visored face of James Nutting gazing at her. The editor had come out of the newspaper office to watch the parade. He had been standing behind them, quietly, ever since Chrischana made her way through the crowd. Nutting had what, to some, was the disconcerting custom of quiet. He could be a surprisingly invisible observer. Some called it the ability to eavesdrop undetected.

Chrischana chuckled. "Like being unable to ride a pony is an asset."

"Most of 'em can't ride," he said dryly.

Now, from the end of the parade came the whooping of fire engines. James Nutting said, "This is where I get out." Then, looking at Balder, but taking in the rest of them with a gesture, he said, "Come see me after the parade. I might have a job for someone." Then he was gone, threading his way back to the wood and plateglass office door.

"Wow!" said Nathan, pretending to kickbox Benaiah. "Did y'see his hands? They were purple!"

"I'm gonna make you purple," said Benaiah, fiercely yanking his brother's upraised leg. Nathan lost his balance, tumbling into Daniel. Chrischana put her hand on the middle brother's arm. He jerked away. "He's always provokin' me. I don't haf'ta put up with it!"

"You hev t'learn self control like th'rest o'us. You too!" She said sharply, wheeling on Nathan who was sending faces. "You both—of all people—know how important that is."

The gaze of Balder was upon them, watching this family episode unfold. Huffy, Benaiah turned away. Nathan was sober for a moment or two. Then, blaring, the gleam of firetrucks approached, drowning every other sound.

Where Front Street turned back toward the highway, the parade was disbanding in Decatur's parking lot. Above them, the Angel Jasper Mary began ascending toward the mountain. Likewise, the forebears of townspeople, both Yankee and Native, ascended too. Like so many cottony seeds on the winddrift, they dispersed, drifting toward the four directions. Into the blue they went, and beyond, toward black reaches where starlight struck through thinning atmosphere.

But one seed, one ancestor, stayed behind. Ruddy and robust, this ancestor descended, going down through the roof of the diner. He stopped by the grill at Decatur's elbow. The bald bespeckled man, aproned, sweating, stood frying burgers in anticipation of lunch. Already, participants of Jasper Mary's parade were pouring in for—as they supposed —the last lunch ever in the decrepit diner. The ghost of Dewey Decatur could remember the day this diner was lifted from the old Atlantic and St. Lawrence Railroad to this spot near the loop to the highway. Earlier, in the middle of the last century, the railroad had elevated Gottheim beyond its prospects just when the village was looking as though it might fade. Neighboring Copenhagen, for a while more prosperous, was bypassed and sent into decline instead. Dewey, the ghostly former proprietor, watched his son work the grill.

True to its habit in trouble, Jeffy Decatur's mind was working over this, that, and the other thing. He wondered if he had strength to stay on his feet, worried that the pie and Jell-O salad were enough. Would Melvinia, Linda, and Annie get the orders out on time? Already these were overflowing at the window. An ungodly amount of burgers and bacon and steak were growing beneath an exhaust fan seemingly unable to budge the breathless heat in the kitchen. But the roar out front covered his burbling agitation. Whimpering, he muttered about it all. Decatur wrestled with his great grief at having to end it all today. Today! The day his life took one final nasty turn.

"I'm glad you're not heah t'see it, Fatha," He said. "What would you do t'see Decatur's Dinah coming to the end this way?"

Putting his ghostly arm about Decatur's round sweaty shoulders, the ruddy angel smiled. "Don't matta a jot, Jeffy," he said. "They's lots to do in life. No end of things to do, now, and afta."

Jeffy said, "It's all I'm useda, this dinah. All I evah wanted to do. All I evah did."

"Daow," said the angel. "You forget the potridge huntin' we done in season. 'Memba all them bids we got those Wednesdays? Taken Wednesdays off to go get some woodcock?"

But Decatur muttered, "You was always heah, standing on this spot, grillin' 'way...."

"Nope. I'd take Wednesdays off. 'Memba them stupid spruce grouse? Dumbest bids y'evah did see. Won't beat way proper—like potridge. Just stand theya so's to get its fool head blowed off. Why, I never let you shoot 'em, 'twas so unsportin'."

"Waunt the air s'good in season?" reminisced Jeffy with a murmur. "The way the sun looked, turning the woods gold in evening, goin'home? Then it'd sink behind the mountain'n all'd be back in shadow, like when y'stotted."

"Yuht, Jeffy boy. Just like that, all sunk t'shadows. Life was like that in Gott'im. Course, it always bust up again, mornin', but we f'get that—feelin' low, like. Just wait, Jeffy. It always comes back gold again."

His son said, "I could retire, s'pose. I can still walk'n get around good's evah. A bit slow, with these pains'n all."

" 'N you got friends, all retired, in't they—'bout? Always hangin'round heah. Can spend moah time with them. Let someone else stot coffee, mornings, somewayas other. You just set theya drinkin'it!"

Decatur slapped cheese on four burgers, reached over to lift a basket of fries from hot oil, give it a knock.

Dewey Decatur continued comforting his son. "It's not s'hod—dyin'. Now now don't go getting all worried again! I know it looked bad ... way I went, cancer'n all. But then I saw 'twaunt nothin'.

169

Only seemed bad at th'time. But, I tell the truth, Jeffy. It's nothing compared t'afta. You believe me, now."

Decatur was agitated again, appearing not to notice, shovelling burgers, dumping fries.

His father chuckled. "Y'know, them spruce grouse in't s'dumb. It all tuns into somethin' else. 'Memba how that potridge tasted? Just lightly grilled, a li'l onion, diced bell pepper ... keep's a body in repair." The ghostly arm continued around Jeffy's shoulders. "It's like that with us. We all go fah somethin'. Got to nourish the ground, put somethin'back we been takin'way. We all get our turn. It goes down, comes back up again'n we feed young'uns, comin'up behind. Dyin's deep, no doubt! Deep to see what happens. All s'many stories fah God to fill his book with. Retire. Set'n watch stories unfold in th'town. You got your story, I got mine, Melviny's got hers'n they all come together like Sad'y night suppah, all dished out. God eats theya too. He's got a kind'o fondness fah this diner, y'know. "

Decatur smiled, wiping his sweat prickly cheek and forehead on his soiled and salty shoulder. "I can do it," he muttered. "I can do it."

"Knew you could," said the ghost. He turned away, going into the wall. He walked through Melvinia just as she grabbed a pot of coffee to service the counter—where plates and elbows crowded, punctuated with greasy salt and pepper shakers, napkins, and sugar in tall glass dispensers. He sat above the countertop floating next to Asa Bartlett's head, his leg crossed over his knee. Asa was leaning back against the counter as usual, propped on his elbows, surveying the crowd. The ruddy angel said to him, "Glad you could make it t'the closin', Asa. 'Memba times when your fatha brung you in fah doughnuts'n milk, mornings? Steam'd be on the windows, it still cold'n dock outside?"

Asa Bartlett lifted his glass, cooling his forehead with it. He smoothed his brick red hair down. Came a smile on his face with a far off look. Those crispy fried doughnuts ... not like them delivered in the truck, mornings now. Crispy, yet soft ... fresh, hot ....

—

The office of *The Village Voter*, which they now entered, occupied the ground floor of the Bond Block. Daniel took immediate note of its large press, a small job press, proof stone, and tall glass type cases: all filling the room to the back of the building, where the door opened on a closet-sized office.

In front stood the counter where advertisers, town officials and the various Town correspondents conducted business with the editor, whose cluttered desk sat behind. The counter faced large, gold-lettered plate glass windows looking onto Front Street.

Approaching with his family, toward the counter where Mr. Nutting stood, Daniel saw that the interior was far from clean. It smelled of gasoline, grease, dust and printer's ink. The nutbrown floor needed sweeping. Loosely knit dust balls had collected in grimy corners. Beyond the counter Daniel noticed a heap of slashed paper beneath a giant cutter. On the ink-stained floor around the Miehle press were scattered bits of broken metal. Now the great press itself filled his gaze. Around him, Balder and Mother talked with Mr. Nutting, while, chirping over everything he saw, Nathan hopped about like a cricket. But Benaiah, too, stood fascinated by the silent behemoth standing like a presence, filling the room. It must have weighed several tons, and appeared to be powered by a gasoline engine—if it could in fact be animated.

"How's the ol'blue babe behaving, Jim?" Balder was asking. "In't been that long since we commiserated over the ol'thing has it?"

"That's what I want to talk to you about, Simon." Nutting's long leathery face beneath the visor had a greenish tinge. His brown eyes were intent but opaque as a couple of pebbles. "It's about time for that overhaul we talked about. How soon can you do it?"

Balder ran a hand down the back of his head, considering. "D'know. Might stot Monday night, s'pose. If it takes a while, go nights during the week and hope I don't get stuck at the mill."

"Well, don't worry if you get hung up. We're all set t'go down at Farmington Press till the job's done." Nutting looked at Chrischana across the counter then. "This place is filthy," He said.

She smiled. Nathan, standing behind her and smoothing her long brown braid with his fingers, said, "We haven't seen anything like it since the dry cleaners in Phoenix!"

"Nathan!" exclaimed Chrischana. She looked at the editor, flushing. "Are you offering me a job?" She could not keep the hopefulness out of her voice.

But the editor said, "I'm offering one to Daniel."

Daniel glanced at Mr. Nutting and saw that he was looking intently back. "Young man, I need someone to clean up around here, run errands. Maybe even learn to set type. Would you be interested?"

"Sure," he said. It was something he did not need to consider. He wanted the job. But —me? he wondered. They had not met till now.

The editor must have noted that something quizzical in his eyes, for he said, "There something you want to ask me?"

Daniel nodded, returning the brown gaze with one of his own. "Why me?"

A slow smile worked its way through Nutting's gaunt green features. Then it was gone. "The English teacher, Mrs. Melville, recommended you." He might have added some of her praise, but James Nutting didn't believe in such attempts to instill self-esteem. He thought self-esteem came subtly, slowly, through working well. Curmudgeonly Nutting refused to pat young people on the head.

Wonderful, thought Chrischana. Quietly glowing, she turned to Daniel.

Benaiah wriggled his way between Mother and the counter. "I want to sweep, too," he said.

"I only need one."

The boy pulled away and went to the door to stare out.

"I need you Mondays, half a day, and Wednesdays. It might work into more. Have any trouble getting to work?" Daniel looked to Chrischana.

She said, "I think we can work it out."

"His day to take it easy in the office," said Balder when they were out on the sidewalk again. "He does births'n obituaries on Sad'days."

"O-*what*-you-airys?" asked Nathan.

The parade watchers had disappeared, leaving Front Street to those on errands. Most people had drifted over to the common for more festivities and concessions. Balder looked down at Nathan. "Obituaries. They go in the paper, saying who died. Births'n obituaries tell who's gettin' started and who's gettin' done."

"Anybody we know?"

"Not so far's I know." He grinned, stepping back as a woman in jeans came brushing past to get into Nutting's office. "What's a rush, Elvegy? Big sale at th'greenhouse next week?"

"Oh, Balder." She recognizes him, gasping, clearly distracted. "Didn't see you with that beard."

"You'd be s'prised the numba people saying that lately." He looks strong in her face, seeing that she is too upset to notice her old classmate, even now failing to acknowledge Chrischana after an absence of fifteen years. But Chrischana recognizes Elvegy Bisbee, a former high school field hockey star. Her twin, Albinia, was once Chrischana's rival for certain boys.

Her hand on the doorknob, Elvegy stays. "I couldn't take it anamore, Balda! I finally got the court'n state police to find Albinia. My twin's murderer is being exposed!"

His mind suddenly putting it all together, he stares at her. They all stare, transfixed. The woman is electric with purpose, and looking ravaged by exhaustion or grief. No one seeing her now would be able to say how she looks ordinarily when composed and working in her garden, or tending plants with subdued concentration in the greenhouse at Blanchard's Fields. Elvegy Bisbee Blanchard is bent out of her customary calm, has largely been so since the disappearance of Albinia. Frantic, scarcely glancing at them, she says, "C'mon. Come with me into th'Vota'n you can heah all'bout it. Ithiel's gont'pay!"

Held by intrigue, they follow, Chrischana wondering vaguely if she shouldn't be taking the children away.

Beyond the point of mere curiosity, Ben and Nathan's small faces are blanched, gripped. Even Daniel is rapt over this revelation. It is as though Elvegy's devastating story, told there among the fibers, muscles, nerve cells of her being, has gone into their deeply impressionable souls.

Chrischana glances quickly at Benaiah, his pique over rejection gone, a thrall to this fierce unfolding. What has happened to Albinia Bisbee? Is it Ithiel Whitman, the class personality? How can it be? It must be someone from away. People I know aren't murderers, least of all Ithiel. I dated him before Balder. Chrischana is sucked headlong into the mystery, into the storm of Elvegy's spirit, helpless to heed the hesitation she feels for the children.

But Balder Simon is more familiar with the story of Ithiel and the twins. And, hearing Elvegy, he recalls that look of fear on Chrischana's face which he saw at Deep Hole. And he glimpsed the significance of her return to Gott'im. So now, ushering them all into the office, he gives her a keen look, saying nothing in response to her torn unspokenness. The consternation in her grave Indian features ....Jee-zuz, he says to himself. Do you know what you're doing, Balda boy?

Kinetic Elvegy is calling the editor away from his typing. "Mr. Nutting! The day I told you'bout is heah! They'll have to try Ithiel fah murder now! I come t'give you my quote. Put it in your next edition!"

He rolls back his squawking desk chair and grabs his note pad, comes to the counter. Chrischana, Balder and the boys hang back, but Elvegy waves them close, saying, "These good people— Godfrey! it's Chrischana Twitchell! You're just in time t'see what an evil maniac our class voted Mr. Congeniality. Ithiel Whitman is—" her eyes grow large and shiny. She gestures toward the window. "She's being " An agonized groan tears up from within. Helpless, she bends to the countertop worn smooth by the elbows of Gottheim's generations: weeping with violence, the whole of her psyche pouring forth.

Gaping but mute the witnesses look on.

From somewhere James Nutting produces an old box of Kleenex, and, discarding the first two as dusty, he begins feeding her clean tissues, one by one. The crumpled human takes them in on curled fingers, crushing them against her weeping eyes and wet nose. For long moments she gulps and hiccups. Then, subsiding, still clinging to the countertop, she gulps back her grief. She quiets.

Out of profound silence, Elvegy stands upright, again gesturing toward the window. In a low voice she mutters, "They ah breaking up the concrete he poured over her four years ago."

So it happens that the monumental treasure of Albinia Bisbee Whitman's body is extracted from the basement floor of the Pine Hill condominium. Right where Elvegy Bisbee Blanchard said it would be.

It was no small feat of studied deduction which led her, after many months of turmoil, to pinpoint its resting place. But to convince the authorities—years. Years: There lay the crushed remains, the wretched human leavings; while those in charge dreaded the sight of Elvegy Blanchard coming. For years Ithiel made people laugh, played with their sympathies, put up a brave front. Ebullient, likable, embraced by the community, but so arrogant and deceitful that he boasted to himself that his savagery and irreverence would never be exposed. Who could believe that warm jovial Ithiel Whitman would harm anyone, let alone his wife, whose disappearance and apparent desertion he mourned?

Oh, it was all right, he told himself: She had it coming. She always had it coming. And finally it came to her. But it wasn't going to ruin his life—a pile of skin and bones and hair. Put on this earth to provoke him, he guessed. God, how he hated to see her twin coming—so like her. Having to smile at Elvegy, try to soothe, reassure. Having to watch her run around with that pieced-out plaguéd story of murder. Why didn't that goddamn Blanchard do something about her?

———

James Nutting steps to the gate in the counter separating the pressroom from customer service. He walks to the door, holding it open for Balder and company. "I know you folks will want to get over to the common or something," he says, leaving them no choice but to be on their way. And, spent now, staring at the floor, Elvegy makes no further claim on their attention nor any attempt to say goodbye. As they exit, Nutting gives Balder a dry look, thinking, *You've got a lot to learn about fatherhood. You don't subject children to this.*

James Nutting was once the father of children. The husband of an academic, too. Once upon a time, and in Toronto. Children suffer the most in divorce. Some things are too intense for children to endure. The revelation of murder, for one.

He was a newspaperman in that city. Any city would do for a dream nurtured since childhood, in this very office; his father's office and his grandfather's before. A hope nurtured right here at the proof stone on the other side of the counter. He had to get out of this stifling village. So he left the proof stone and Gottheim Academy in the early '50s, stretching to the task of establishing a reputation in journalism. Thoughts of a career at *The Village Voter* numbed him. He was fearful of Sinclair Lewis's "village virus." The idea off settling into the complacent, self-satisfied status quo—the Town columns concerned with who ate where last week, headlines bleak with purchased property or the petty minutia of selectman's meetings, school board wrangles, continual tension over property taxes, endless rounds of school sports coverage—it was more than he could tolerate. That was before Boston College, before his stints at Midwestern newspapers and the big break in Toronto in the '60s and early '70s, where he was, at first, exhilarated but ultimately enervated by reportage on university demonstrations, sit-ins, riots, bomb threats, arrests. Toward the end, he could not shake the creeping conviction that he was merely pandering. His thoughts began returning to Gottheim, to his father's concentrated face beneath the ancient visor he himself now wore. And, to his bemusement, he began to yearn for the village and the din of the old flatbed cylinder press.

For a while he fought it, like an immune system recognizing invading antigens. But, in his reading, he came across Ruth Moore's *The Walk Down Main Street*, reminding him of the rich interplay between townspeople in small town Maine. Gladys' Hasty Carroll's *As the Earth Turns* surprised him with its sure language, calm spirit and lament over the decline of small family farms. These and other Maine authors had the good sense to portray with fidelity an idea with growing appeal to him: Small-town mores, so often transmitted with pettiness, could actively work to preserve cultural identity. He had to smile, finding that this was no longer a negative virtue to him. He was freed in believing that this ancient mechanism for keeping people from doing damage to themselves and others need not always be viewed with a cynical eye. Gossip and censure could be tolerated with humor when the offshoot was a positive model. Living and working to preserve a good name was not, in itself, an evil preoccupation, as once he supposed. It might save an individual, a family, an institution much needless pain.

He's been here ever since, preserving even the old press ways against the pressures of progress. And sometimes he smiles inwardly at the realization that he is now the troglodyte he once abhored. Even so, the nature of James Nutting is essentially unchanged: He was always a rebel.

Closing the old wood and glass door behind Simon and the Twitchells, he turns back toward the sagging Elvegy. "Will you have some tea while we talk, Ms. Blanchard? It won't take long to heat the kettle."

Out on the sweltering street, the five walk slowly toward the Common, blinking in the light of day, trying to process this charged encounter.

Passing beneath the shade of an old maple, Benaiah breathes, "Someone got murdered—and buried in cement ...." His arms and freckled features begin loosening. His face takes on a look of awe. But Nathan's pinched little face looks up at his Mother. He is silent, blanched. I'm scared, his large eyes seem to say to her. She draws him near. Clinging together, as one, they walk on. Benaiah catches her arm, she lets him hold her hand. Walking slowly behind, Balder and Daniel look on, matching their pace to that of the trio ahead.

No one says anything. Each mind is busy with its own thought, the children especially haunted by pictures. A cement truck backs up to a prone body. Dead, or alive? Wet heavy stuff flows out, battering, crushing a human face, a human body, a woman. Bony contours harden in concrete. The face in the truck cab is savagely grinning. The drunken face of Dad.

Quietly, Nathan begins crying, wiping at his tears with hands filthy from chocolate and the dust of the window ledge at *The Voter*. Chrischana holds him harder. Her grip on Benaiah's fingers is so painful that he prys at it with his thumb.

Maybe Daniel'd kick me in the butt, Balder is thinking, *do me a favor.* The look he recollects from Nutting could not have been more dead on. But even now, some small corner of his mind holds to the thought that what he has done in exposing them to Elvegy's agony is not misplaced. But the cost is high. These kids will probably not be able to sleep for nights to come. But maybe they are clear now of whatever danger there was in Phoenix ....

Chrischana's thoughts are increasingly more disturbed. Withdrawing into herself as she walks, attention to the pain of her children fades. Whelming memories, evil memories, wrap her in a blistering haze. She thinks of Petey's notes and grows dry. The heat of Phoenix has come back on her, searing. Sealing her in slow paralysis. From somewhere outside this burning, she recollects her mind upon arriving in Gottheim, how it sustained her over the months, and even after Petey's disturbing note: the people of Gottheim, her people, would not tolerate spousal abuse in their midst.... She had forgotten much about life here, especially that of families other than her own. But now this about Albinia and Ithiel, about Elvegy's grueling quest, and the helplessness of Babette Roebuck under Ferddy Sessions. It would take more than being voted Jasper Mary, more than a parade or being elected to wear buckskin, fringes and feathers.

There comes an unconscious check in her dazed gait, slowing the entire group. It's as a revelation, coming to her: *Jasper Mary was murdered for her treasure.* Petey will surely come here and try to take the treasure of Gott'im away.

Behind her, Daniel was also thinking of Petey ... and Petey's face hovering over wet concrete. The man will be coming after her, he is sure. He saw the postmarks on a couple of letters. Now he imagines Petey coming out of the Post Office. Petey, walking along Front Street ....

Daniel jerks his head up suddenly, looking at Balder. Balder is drawn from his own thought, finding the gaze of his son. Terror is flashing out of those eyes.

No, Daniel! It won't happen. *We won't let it happen to Mother.*

If only there were some way to assure him of this.

But, at last, Balder is certain. Chrischana has come back to Gottheim for the saving of her life.

The Common

News of doings at the Pine Hill condominiums went through Decatur's Diner when Gilbert Tuttle drove down from Jasper Mountain, purportedly for lunch. Pudgy, with a slight waddle and fluffy hair sticking out from his ball cap, Gilbert had been mowing grass outside Pine Hill when State Police arrived with the warrant, Elvegy's lawyer, and a jackhammer operator in tow. The site was cordoned off at the door but, out back, Gilbert lay between clumps of arborvitae, peering into a basement window. He saw a woman and two kids routed from the morning's laundry, and in no time the place was full of officers and others, working to unearth the remains of Elvegy Blanchard's twin sister. When the place filled with cement dust and noise, an officer opened the window, ending Gilbert Tuttle's career as outside witness to the proceedings. His new role, of tattler, commenced. He made it safely down mountain, streaked over the highway toward the last good lunch in Gottheim, burst into Decatur's, red-faced and important, to spread the news about the body breakout.

Huffing, he finished, "Elvegy Blanchard finally gut someone t'listen to hah," and plunked down next to Asa Bartlett, trying to appear nonchalant. But the big news had agitated him out of any dry demeanor he now tried to achieve. Next moment, breaking through the resultant roar of conversation, Tuttle stood, loudly proclaiming, "Guess I'd betta head ovah t'*The Votah*'n and tell old Nutting. He'll be wanting a quote fom an eyewitness."

Bespeckled Asa said, "Can't imagine what Albiny'd look like after all this time under concrete. But choo know, people won't believe he done it even if her poor bones prove it. Ithiel Whitman's too popular fah folks to stand any monkeying if Elvegy is wrong. Shouldn't you have waited before coming down here to spill the beans? S'pose it in't true? S'pose nothing's there?"

Flushing, Gilbert Tuttle saw the flaw in his dance as town informant. He huffed back to his pickup and pulled out, narrowly missed by an eighteen-wheeler rounding the curve and over the limit. He was in a rush to get back to the ski resort, but he needn't have bothered. Even as the event unfolded, a multitude of scanners were tuned to it. News of the investigation buzzed through the festive community and onto the Common, spilling over to stir the little crowd around the secondhand book table outside the library. Patrons at art displays, concessions and craft booths were set humming. Participants of the ax and chainsaw competitions were thrust from the limelight, then distracted, by the news. A few of the town's teens swarmed to vehicles to go up and test the gruesome rumor for themselves. A carnival caravan of rust buckets and pickups rattled and roared out to the highway, heading for the mountain.

Subdued and expressionless, Daniel Twitchell was wandering the Common with his friend Cindabilla when her cousin Albertine rushed over to offer them a ride. She gave him a dirty look and he turned back toward the street. Cindabilla, in overalls and a T-shirt with her toenails painted a rich purple, chewed on the ends of her long honey-red ponytail, a habit of hers in nerve wracking situations. "Assholes!" she exclaimed, her light eyes narrowing. "Why'd they waunt go look at Albiny?! It's like a big party t'them!"

Daniel shook his head slowly. He kept walking, his hands jammed into his pockets, gaze on the dried beaten grass of the Common. He was unaware that this bit of land had been deeded to the Town by its founding father, his ancestor Mahalalel Twitchell, to be used as its green for all time. Daniel scarcely noticed the empty cotton candy cones, hot dog wrappers, styrofoam cups and shiny gum wrappers scattered against the stalls. He had been looking forward to this day, to his first Jasper Mary parade, now that he and his mother and brothers were in Gottheim.... But the whole thing had soured....

Frowning, he glanced into the white sky, wondering why the sun yet shined.

Babette Roebuck and Chrischana Twitchell stood before an exhibit of woodland watercolors, quietly talking about the discovery of Albinia's body. Like last time, when Babette carefully avoided mention of her own brutal boyfriend, Ferdinand Sessions, they spoke once again about spousal abuse. Ferddy was still laid up from when Cindabilla filled his buttocks with buckshot. Of course, Cindabilla had steadfastly denied all accusations. He was healing some, and Babette had not been attacked since. But the owl was a lot on her boyfriend's mind.

"Heah's the card of that place I was telling you bout, Babette," said Chrischana. She held out a purple business card. "Remember, we got a place to go f'help in time of need."

Babette hesitated, then reached for the card. She was a thin woman with bottle black hair, partial to wearing pastel halter tops with jeans and gold braided sandals. She loved the sleek new Mustang she drove everywhere, bought with her dowel mill wages. Babette had lost a child in the womb because of one of Ferddy's drunken blows. Now it looked like she would never be able to conceive again. Her once smooth skin and blue eyes had made a baby-doll face irresistible, but now, at thirty-four, confidence was gone, her good looks seamed and scarred. She read Chrischana's card. *Abused woman's advocacy project.* The words shamed her, but she thanked Christy in a low voice, adding, "And thanks fah telling me bout what happened in Phoenix."

Briefly touching the other's shoulder, Chrischana nodded. Admitting her suffering and humiliation at the hands of Petey Prince had been difficult, but there had been a small gift of relief in that telling, even in the sharing out loud of that grief.

There was nothing more to say. The two women turned away, ostensibly studying the exhibit before them.

Seeing them there, a tall ungraceful woman threaded through the crowd toward them. She wore outsized glasses and a blond ponytail, and the members of her body moved as though imperfectly acquainted with one another. Hers was the red secondhand Subaru with hand-painted bumper stickers, one of which read, *If you object to logging, wash your butt instead of buying toilet paper*. Wearing paint speckled corduroy overalls and T-shirt, the self-styled sometime neopagan came up to them, grinning. "Babette! You're interested in one of my paintings!" She laughed like a horse from a face that might've belonged to one.

"Uhm ..." stuttered Babette, smiling, looking away.

"Just admiring the lady slippers," interposed Chrischana. "You can really sense theya delicacy in the paintings." The other was still shyly silent, so Chrischana introduced herself as an old friend of Babette.

"Eloise Patadoe," said the other. "(Now you know, Babs, I have to kid.) No really," she whinnied. "It's my name! Tell her, Babs. We used to work side-by-side, planing dowel rods at Blodgett's. Thanks for the compliment," she said to Chrischana. Indicating her portraits of the wild woodland orchids, she said, "These things are icons. The academics and humanists broke all the Christian icons but then discovered they still needed icons. 'We need icons,' they said, and that made it okay again."

Chrischana smiled. Babette looked bewildered. There being no other reaction, Eloise said, "So, you were born in Maine?"

Chrischana nodded. "Grew up heah."

"In the village?"

"Up on Blackwell Mountain. The old Twitchell farm."

Smiling toothily, Eloise said, "I've been in that beautiful old wreck, painting its angles. Teen-agers go up there, have a high old time—both senses of the word! How much longer you think it'll stand?"

"D'know. Was up theya speculating early today. I'd like t'see that painting sometime—not in the market now, just." She added hastily.

"Come out to the studio in Quaker town. Watch those rocks on the Quarry Dog Road, though. You might bottom out. Can't miss my goat yard. Mine is the only other place without a dental chair in the dooryard. Ya see that awful letter in *The Voter* a couple weeks ago? Woman wants to turn the mountains into suburbia. She must think property values are the sun. Hasn't got a clue what it takes to— where else can you store things when the shed overflows? Someone should tell her—maybe I will!—that the place she complained about is owned by descendants of the very first settlers in Quaker town. Besides, the chair looks dandy!"

Babette was looking again at the advocacy card. Chrischana smiled seeing her slip it into the pocket of her jeans. Eloise paused, and Chrischana asked how long she had been in the area, painting and, "raising goats, is it?"

"Oh, I washed up in Quaker on the back-to-the-land movement spawned here in Maine by the Nearings, maybe a decade or more ago. "I've got the goats, a garden, and painting (can't make money on that!)."

"She can too, Christy," said Babette. "I saw an exhibit of hers down't Naples. Wouldn't believe the people buying 'em theya."

"They don't buy 'em here," Eloise whinnied. She gestured to show how people stayed away. "They can't stand my personality, my clothes, the smell of goat, my uppitiness, or whatever. They cast their eyes up or down or sideways when they see me coming. Wear this pointed little glare or frown. Anything to avoid acknowledging my existence. –Or they'll just stare at you daring you to speak. I display the watercolors here to remind them that *I* at least acknowledge my existence." She said the last with a shout directed at the Common in general.

Chrischana laughed her throaty laugh.

Encouraged, Eloise continued. "It's the famed New England reserve, taciturnity, whatever, which is really just a throwback to English snootiness. Cold, very cold. (present company excepted, no offense meant, girls.) Maybe they can't stand me because my descent is verbose Catholic Celtic, and darned if those Angles don't just hate us for it, if they did invade the place we had first, namely the British Isles. People think the British part is the snooty part, but it's the other way around. Practically the only thing to crack that reserve is a stint away—among strangers. Because then they know what it is to be a stranger in a strange land. The friendly ones are those who went in the service or college someplace. They come back here either chastened or broadened by a taste of life with people they aren't related to."

Ponytail swinging, Patadoe shook her head. "One thing you didn't want to do on moving here is offer suggestions. Big mistake. Nothing so uppity as someone from away with an idea of how to do—

anything! People've been run out of here for that! They couldn't take it anymore—having a brain and not being allowed to use it. But things are changing. Folks from away, office people, begin outnumbering locals. The fact that Goldings and their skiers have money makes a big difference. You can't win a peeing contest with someone who has forty million bucks!"

Babette and Chrischana looked at each other, smiling, embarrassed, shaking their heads. The trampled space around the art exhibit got wider and wider, emptying as people veered past the foghorn of Eloise Patadoe's voice. Trying to cut through the mist of indignation surrounding her, she continued. "And gossip! The men are the worst! The sweetest people—nice li'l old ladies or teenage boys'll shred you like a pack of mangy coyotes. Can't wait to see some of 'em hung out to dry on that judgment day of their ancestors. They think they're good because they don't smoke, drink, cheat or say fuck."

As, lips flapping, Eloise blared on about the evils of Gottheim's gossip, Chrischana looked out over the old Common, stretching away in movement and color beneath scattered shade trees. The bawling of chainsaws came to her ears from a knot of people near one end of the green. Amid the buzz of static and screeching feedback, the Franco Fiddlers ended a set at the other end of the Common, up on the old gazebo. Her gaze wandered toward the fire station across the street. The engines had returned to their bays since the parade. She glanced back at Eloise.

"My problem is in being bereft of the 'propa humil'ty.' D'you know they wouldn't even tell me about town meeting?—what it was about, where it was held, *when*? I'd ask about it and get this evasion. If it weren't for *The Village Voter*, new people wouldn't know *what* was going on. Not that I appreciated the village rag back then. Bored me cross-eyed. Those town columns! I mean, can you really care that the Goosepimples came up from Lewiston to dine at the Frecklefaces on Sunday? That Bert and Gertie Petunia went shopping in Waterville and came home with two hamsters, one black and one brown? Or how about those help-wanted ads? 'Models for TV and national magazines, no experience necessary, for details call this toll number.' The community bulletin board's handy, though. And Nutting, the editor, isn't bad, either. He can really think when there's something to think about besides sign ordinances. Maybe it was even his editorials that gradually drew me in, or the letters to the editor. Anyway, now I can't wait to read his ol'bellyache each week. It's like following the endless story of Gott'im."

Suddenly, cutting through the cacophony of the Common, the deep-throated town siren blew. From all over the green, men came running toward their vehicles. Many ran to the fire station to hop aboard the gleaming machines and rumble way. Even as the trio watched, the bright engines flashed and screamed out of sight around the corner onto Front Street. An old car approached along the street near the exhibit, slowing to where Chrischana, Babette and Eloise stood. Daniel leaned out the window of the crowded backseat, where Cindabilla was also visible, calling to his mother. "We're going up Blackwell Mountain! Someone said the Twitchell Fahm's on fire! Meetcha back at camp latah, okay?"

But Chrischana stood abashed and unresponding. Before she could gather herself to answer, the car listed away. The Twitchell Farm! The farmhouse had stood there only this morning, lonesome and memory-haunted. Can it really be burning?

She heard Eloise mourning, "There goes poetry!"

And Babette had taken hold of her arm, murmuring. "Ah you all right, Christy?"

No, she thought, and felt a prickling sensation starting behind her eyes. As a force of emotion welling, the morning's tide of grief surged again. It heaved up fully loaded with sadness and anguish and fear. Chrischana fled.

She had to get some place and hide. Flooded, her gaze sought the row of buildings beyond the Common's crowded edge. There was the open doorway of the library, gaping and dark within. Swiftly she made for it, weaving through the throng. Snatches of conversation, about concrete and a body and fire, pelted her as she went. She swerved past piles of picked over books and hurried up the granite steps. Momently, the library's darkness cooled her, and the privacy of the cramped stacks beckoned. Tucking herself away behind the dim loaded shelves, she sank gratefully to the wood floor. But the tears did not flow, nor the sobs she thought she had desired.

She sat back, lolling idly against an old shelf of biography. She let her face lean on the bindings that held printed pages of people's lives. Lives that were worn out, sorrowful, depleted ... like her own. She sighed, thinking of them. Lives lived out, done. Dedicated, challenged, achieving. Withered or splintered; depressed or uplifted by temperament and circumstance. Again she sighed. What is this strange experience we hold in common? So commonly we go on, day by day, task by task. What keeps it all together, fitted out with atoms, molecules and cells ... charged with the current of life? Does it go anywhere, mean anything, like I was taught? But others had also taught that we are just mishmash, happening together during an aberrant break in the chaos.

Another sigh. She turned on her hip, ran a fingernail idly down the spine of a volume, wondering about the life within: did C.S. Lewis know, the author of the Chronicles of Narnia? She had read them to her children. He understood life, didn't he? An Oxford don, rational; yet with a blazing imaginative streak sure to have originated in another world.... And now returned again back to it, whole?

She thought of Daniel as a mewing babe, emerging out of bloody earth, smeared life with an innocent gaze. Her first. His life, like in these books, concretely freighted with the elements of a story. That's the way Daniel would think of it. He told her not long ago that life was a ... a story in a body. Is that it? Is God merely after a good story? Does he only require interesting reading?

The tears of this morning, moments spent walking on fragments of her life, the lives of mother and father, and father's mother and father: The people were story and life. They held her in their blood, every one of them. She had learned this in her reading, that she was carried in their DNA, down through generations, as surely as if they'd passed her in a handbasket. A vast intelligence inhabited the replication of her genes, precise in its myriad chromosomal thoughtfulness.

Maybe I haven't studied biology for nothing after all ... still time for that nursing career, right? She lay limply, smiling, grateful to forget fear, wishing she could sit here quietly musing forever.

But the hardness of the floor stirred her to movement, and she decided that the comfort of this place was strictly spiritual. Better go look for Balder and the kids, scare up some lunch. She rose wearily, shaking with hunger from the morning's hike. She bent to brush the dust from her knees.

Did Daniel sound like a Mainer just now?

What mockery would Petey make of that? No. Don't think about it.

—

Afternoon on the Common, thought Gloria. My First Jasper Mary Day. She enjoyed the culture of New England Gottheim. The place has artists, a theater group, an academy, IICE—skiing! It's a cultured resort community coupled with the more rowdy blue-collar element. She rejoiced in its being much more than the constricted little hamlet of cliched small-town America. You could breathe here, influence things, give of your training, your talent and imagination. And you can *see* the results of your efforts in this place. Here you can experience significance.

She was out of the condo, out of her room for good. Ready, eager even, to see Balder. She had hoped to see him here, planned to just bump into him. But she had said it all in the letter, given him something to think about. She had nothing more to say, but there was a bit of worry ... that he had not responded yet. She had been liberatingly honest ... and now it was just the waiting—to see what came of it.... *Do you know how often I think of you, your humor, that grin?* Miss you, even those whiskers and that awful scarring on your arms. She stood in the shadow of the gazebo, scanning the crowd.

But people kept stopping to talk. She must've seen every committee member, Chamber of Commerce associate, or IICE delegate she knew. Where is that old New England reserve when you need it? —Well!—Many of these people aren't Mainers, but visitors or transplants like me. No wonder there is kinship, warmth in them.

Since that day of disillusion in Decatur's Diner she found more comfort in the newcomers. But it was not what she had expected, hoped for. The dour old Mainers would never let her forget that she wasn't one of them. Do they practice that stone face in the mirror each morning? There are a few, certainly, who aren't suited to it. They really work at stemming expression. In Boston we gave it up before I was born.... Conversely, does Balder have work allowing himself the luxury of that grin?

Would it kill them to yield up a smile now and then? Wait— there's a blond head at the hotdog stand. A frown puckered. *No,* she thought, *not broad enough in the shoulders.* Behind her the Franco Fiddlers trooped onto the bandstand, began opening instrument cases, fussing with amplifiers, joking. She smiled as one cracked a dumb-Yankee joke. Well, turnabout's fair play! A frontal on all the Frenchman jokes endured over the generations. Some were now even opting for reverse assimilation, rejecting what their parents had strained for. Here's insight, she thought: This is where the more voluble expression in locals will come from. That warm French temperament can come out of hiding now.

Is that him in that group way down by the logging competition? A white-blond head and tall athletic frame. Gloria began moving that way, checked twice by friendly acquaintances. She moved on, smiley polite, but firm. Oh no—he had Chrischana's boys with him, two of them it looked like. At least the woman herself isn't with them. Her worst worry had been that they'd come to Jasper Mary Day as a unit. (Don't even think the word family.) *Relax. Balder, you will not get to me.* I am what I am. I will not change for you. I must not be dishonest. Cannot pretend to be thrilled with your ideals.

The chainsaws—two of them in a heat to sever logs—were deafening as she approached, lightly set her hand on his shoulder. He turned. *Oh those ice-blue eyes.*

"Glory be t'Gloria!" He ducked to say it low, into her ear. "Can we talk sometime?"

She smiled. His ear was still bent to her and, low, she pleaded into it. "Now?"

He straightened to grin down on her, and she noticed how thick and dark his beard had grown. He shook his head, raising his voice. "Caunt! Bonding!" He stood back a bit, with the boys.

Brightly she hid her letdown, irritation. "Of course! Bonding!"

"How about tonight? Honest-t'-God date! The movies in Farmington, Fiddlehead Restaurant—The works!"

"Ooo, that's it!... The '55 Chevy or the Caprice?"

"I can afford t'be wishy-washy on this!" The saws stopped suddenly and he grinned over his loud pronouncement.

She sparkled with laughter. "Well ... okay, I'll drive then! Can't give up an ounce of control, can I? *Simons Ledge* is up that road above the second pond?"

"Yuht. Betta make it 5, 5:30—theya's the drive down."

"Of course." Suddenly self-conscious, she looked at the boys. The younger looked like he could do with a wash. The other was tousled and taller. "Are you enjoying the competition?" she asked them. No response. Gaily, "Have you ever seen competing chainsaws before?"

After the perverse manner of children, Nathan had suddenly reverted to a strange-adult-abashed silence. Ordinarily, she supposed, Benaiah probably wouldn't have responded anyway. The two simply stood there, staring at her. And Balder made no attempt to intercede. In the past he had been so sweet at soothing the little rudenesses and rejection of Mainers. But—these aren't little Mainers ... are they? Suddenly she was abashed.

Now (desperately bright), "I always worry: The saw'll kick back, a log will rebound, something.... A sliced chest wouldn't go over very good...." Words were failing her.

She raised her hand abruptly, grinning the glistening middle-class grin that meant nothing. "See ya!"

Gloria turned and fled.

"Something tells me weah too late," said Balder, driving, his hands on the wheel, one elbow at rest outside the Chevy window. Already, down the highway, they saw the diner's parking lot emptied out, one straggler pulling away. Looking on from the passenger seat, Chrischana murmured agreement. Slowing, Balder downshifted.

"I'm hungry!" wailed Nathan from the back seat where he was tussling with Benaiah. The younger had started it with a few injudicious pokes, and his brother escalated with jabs and punches. Grunts and thumps issued out of the back seat.

Chrischana turned, hissing. "If you don't stop, I'll make you get out'n walk! Balder, pull ovah, now!" Gravel growling under the tires, the car scraped onto the shoulder. The woman glared at the thunder-faces looking up at her. The boys lay tangled together, locked in arrested battle. She swatted at him, saying, "Nathan, get on the other side of the car!" With one final pinch of his brother's arm,

Nathan rolled to the far end of the seat. Ben gave a quick slap in return.

"Is it necessary to embarrass yourselves'n me in front of Balder?!" (Pause.) "Well is it?! Answer me!"

Nathan's lip quivered. Ben looked sullen. Chrischana's gaze grew sharper.

"He started it!" (In unison.)

"Answer!!"

Benaiah shifted his look past Balder's blond head, which had not turned to look at them. "I'm sorry," he grumbled.

"Me, too." Nathan's voice was more positive, but thin and subdued.

"S'right," answered the man. He pulled back onto the road and coasted down toward Decatur's. Chrischana continued glaring at the boys. "Don't cross ovah the drive-train," she warned Nathan.

"Is that what that big bump is called?" he wondered aloud.

"The same," answered Balder. "Sometime I'll show y'how one works."

"Great!" said the boy, fully revived.

"You too, Ben."

No answer. Then, "Okay. " (Still cloudy and low.)

They pulled up to the glass door, where a sign shouted, *CLOSED*, in big red letters.

"That's the end o'that!" said Balder. But he did not pull away. They sat there, the aqua decades-old Chevy idling before the dining car from the old *Atlantic and St. Lawrence Railroad*.

People around here, even sometimes people from away, knew this history. The minor iron god, the railroad, was once worshipped here, along with the other gods of progress and profit. Yes, even by the thrifty people of Western Maine. Beginning in the nineteenth century, when the steam whistle and steely rumble were first heard in these old hills, pious parishioners would sit in Gottheim's pews, listening for the whistle, while droning hymns but thinking hard about some future destination, whether near or far.

... This is all as Eloise Patadoe would have it: Droning, they sat and thought how many board feet, or how many bushels of potatoes or apples they'd get to the markets in Portland, Boston— heck, Brazil! They heard the morning's text, thinking of bonnets, newfangled sewing machines, books, periodicals, gadgets for peeling apples (just stick one on the prongs and turn the handle!); stuff chugging its way to them in the mountains. The Meguntics, which their ancestors brought them to, wouldn't be so isolated any more— *Hallelujah!* A second sacred hymn, and the droning acquired some vigor and a lilt. They were singing for real now, ready to hear a sermon about loving one's neighbors and welcoming a stranger. It will be a lot easier with that new piano for the parlor is on its way.

But this is all cynicism, sour grapes. A failure to show the proper humility before the great gods of science industry progress. "Genius" and "perspiration" changed our common culture: the way we want to spend our days, or cultivate our nights. To suggest a better use of genius would be uppity. There's no matching the way we get things done now, save lives, transport lives, counsel lives. Heck, we're on the verge of creating life!

These are the things Eloise Patadoe says when she can get anyone to listen. But they don't. She's too mouthy, too awkward, a slob. Avert your eyes! Give that woman a wide berth!

"Now whad we do?!" Nathan popped up from the back seat, stood on the drive-train, his gaze on Balder's in the rearview.

Balder gave the sign a last look, peering past Chrischana at the streaked windows, the dull metal and maroon of the diner's exterior. Place is older than I am, he thought. *Everything passes, just so.*

"Well," he looked into the rearview again. "What say we go up t'the house fah taco salad, something."

"Yeah!" yelled Nathan.

Balder pulled the Chevy slowly along, grinning at Chrischana. She had turned in her seat and was looking back at him, leaning against the door. He thought about the day she had, its many losses. The T-shirt she wore was lettered, dark green with a line drawing of a raised fist clenching a set of pliers. *Defend God's Wilderness.*

Balder looked away. He shone his self-mocking grin out the windshield, easing the Chevy past the classic, but now abandoned, piece of Americana.

He said, "We'll just go up ovah home."

Like this? Try the entire cycle.

THE GOD'S CYCLE